Praise for *Frozen*

"A relentless chiller that leaves you guessing and gasping again and again."
    —**David Morrell**, *New York Times* bestselling author of *The Brotherhood of the Rose*

"A thrilling, beautifully paced skyrocket of a novel."
    —**Peter Straub**, *New York Times* bestselling author of *In the Night Room*

"A captivating novel of cold and meticulous suspense, Bonansinga's *Frozen* rings a bell that defines eternal evil in all its manifestations, in fact spanning six thousand years of the entity we call evil. This thriller is like no other serial killer novel. It has everything—a unique setting, a compelling lead character, a new twist on forensics, and the latent evil of mankind."
    —**Robert W. Walker**, author of *Absolute Instinct* and *Final Edge*

"*Frozen* will send chills down your spine."
    —**Barbara D'Amato**, award-winning author of the Cat Marsala mystery series; former president of the Mystery Writers of America; former president of Sisters of Crime International

SHATTERED

JAY BONANSINGA

PINNACLE BOOKS
Kensington Publishing Corp.
www.kensingtonbooks.com

PINNACLE BOOKS are published by

Kensington Publishing Corp.
850 Third Avenue
New York, NY 10022

All Kensington titles, imprints, and distributed lines are available at special quantity discounts for bulk purchases for sales promotions, premiums, fund-raising, educational, or institutional use. Special book excerpts or customized printings can also be created to fit specific needs. For details, write or phone the office of the Kensington special sales manager: Kensington Publishing Corp., 850 Third Avenue, New York, NY 10022, attn: Special Sales Department; phone 1-800-221-2647.

ISBN-13: 978-0-7860-1877-2
ISBN-10: 0-7860-1877-1

First printing: December 2007

10 9 8 7 6 5 4 3 2 1

Printed in the United States of America

In loving memory of
Junior Parrick (1926–2007)

ACKNOWLEDGMENTS

Special thanks to Michaela Hamilton for teaching me the dark arts; Peter Miller for ruling the shark tank; Tina Jens for tender loving care; Lance Catania for painting the nightmare with light; Robert Oxnam for his indispensible first-person account of mental illness, *A Fractured Mind*; and Jeanne Bonansinga for remaining my number-one reason for living.

"Who will pity a snake charmer bitten by a serpent, or any who go near wild beasts?"

—*Apocrypha*, Ecclesiasticus 12:13

PART I
The Mississippi Ripper

ONE

Gullibility killed the cat. This silent refrain had been echoing through Dina Dudley's thoughts on a regular basis since she was a teenager and had swallowed Robbie Pettigrue's story about being a test subject for a male contraceptive pill. Time and time again, Dina had found that it wasn't curiosity that did the feline in. On the contrary, it was a person not being curious *enough* that did the damage. It was a girl not bothering to question her mother's blind insistence that her husband—i.e., Dina's dad—had gotten his drinking under control. Or it was a girl— i.e., Dina—not investigating the background of a dreamy stockbroker boyfriend who turned out to be a coke dealer. In fact, it almost seemed as though Dina Dudley was getting more gullible with age. Her closest friends claimed it was simply a side effect of her being so bighearted. And it was true that Dina had a thing for shaggy dogs, hard cases, losers. But there's a point in every gullible person's life when trust turns to recklessness.

As a matter of fact, tonight, as she lay bound and gagged on the cold, corrugated iron floor of a battered van's cargo hold, she was silently cursing herself for letting her gullibility finally do her in. If only she had been one iota of a degree more alert. If only she had been a single, infinitesimal scintilla more suspicious . . . she probably wouldn't have stopped to help the little milquetoast in the hunting cap wrestling with his flat tire. But that's not who Dina Dudley was. Dina Dudley was a sweetheart. Dina Dudley was gullible. And now it looked as though Dina Dudley was a dead woman.

Bone thin and sinewy—in recent months her cokehead boyfriend had taken to calling her Skinny Minny—she tried to move in the darkness, but her arms ached, her wrists bound so tightly behind her back they felt numb, the plastic shackles digging into her tendons. Her denim jacket was torn, her jeans cold and wet where she had peed herself. Her matted copper-colored hair dangled in her face. Duct tape covered her mouth, smelling of chemicals and grime. Fear constricted her throat.

Dina tried to see through the unrelenting shadows. Her best friend, Jenny Quinn, lay against the opposite wall, whimpering, also bound and trussed like a piece of meat. Raw, watering eyes, hot with horror, stared back at Dina. That was the worst part, seeing her friend Jenny like that, her old pal from Belleville High, always so bubbly, always the first to go on the roller-coaster or play spin the bottle, now reduced to a mewling little caged bird. All because Dina had to go on this idiotic wilderness camping trip. Two girls from the suburbs of St. Louis. Making like they were Lewis and Clark.

Meanwhile the van vibrated and rattled, grinding through its lower gears as it climbed a steep grade. Where in God's name was this sicko taking them?

Breathing through her nose, sniffing the rancid air of the van, Dina tried to think. *It's not too late,* she urged herself, *maybe you can still get out of this, Jenny's a wreck, she's no help now, but you can stay calm, wait for an opening, maybe surprise this guy.*

The van made a tight turn suddenly, pressing Dina against the wall.

Then the vehicle squeaked to a stop. Dina's heart started thudding in her chest. Her mouth went dry. She could hear footsteps now, crunching in gravel, coming around the side of the van. Icy terror spread through her veins like cold poison, searing her nerve endings, making everything feel numb and sluggish.

Not now, she scolded herself, *don't freeze up now!*

The rear doors clicked, then slowly creaked open on rusty hinges. The odors of pine and fish rot and river mud flooded the van.

The dark figure stood there in the moonlight, calmly looking in at his captives. Everything about him was average, ordinary, nondescript—from his duck-billed hunting cap down to his dirty khaki pants. "Hello again," he said in a convivial tone. "Sorry about the bumpy ride."

Dina tried to latch on to some detail about him, some mark or scar that she might remember later for the cops, but it was difficult in the darkness. His face remained in shadow, his head haloed by moonlight. In fact, from the moment he had attacked them on the side of the road a few hours ago, Dina had caught only fleeting glimpses of the man. All she could tell for sure was that he was middle aged, probably white, very strong, and spoke with a flat Midwestern accent. Modulated and genial. Like a TV game-show host.

"Don't you worry your pretty heads now, ladies," he murmured as he went for Jenny first, grabbing her by the ankles, eliciting an anguished moan out of her. Then he started pulling her from the cargo bay as though he were removing a canvas bag full of dirty laundry. Then he said something else that sent an electric bolt of panic down Dina's spine.

"It'll all be over soon."

That was when Dina realized that this polite psychopath was going to kill them both; maybe rape them or torture them, and then kill them. Something buried deep inside Dina awakened then, and she decided—right at that moment—she was going to fight. She was going to go down swinging.

She flexed her bound hands in preparation for . . . *something*. She wasn't sure what.

The moments seemed to stretch interminably as the madman lifted Jenny Quinn out of the van, then carried the trembling girl off into the shadows of the forest. He was gone for only about fifteen seconds but it seemed like hours as the adrenaline sluiced through Dina's skull, making her ears ring and her scalp crawl. She smacked her dry lips on a sour metallic taste as if she were sucking coins.

Then she made one last critical discovery: her legs, although bound at the ankles, were loose. They were *loose*! She could still kick, and she could still jump. It only took seconds to make the decision.

His footsteps were returning. *Crunch-crunch-crunch!* Dina cocked both legs back like springs. The man's shadow fell across the open rear doors. Dina held her breath. The killer was talking as he came into view: "I promise this will only take a few more—"

She kicked out at him with both feet as hard and suddenly as she could.

"Whoa!" The man jerked backward instinctively, just far enough to avoid getting brained by the bottoms of Dina's size-eight Naturalizer boots. The kidnapper stumbled backward, tripping on a pothole, then sprawling to the pavement and landing on his ass with a grunt, giving Dina just enough time to shimmy frantically toward the opening.

She leaped off the edge of the van, then furiously hopped, sack-race style, across the gravel shoulder toward the darkness of the woods.

It would have been hilarious in any other context—this feisty suburbanite doing the bunny hop across a deserted road in the dead of night—but not now. Not with the keening moans of Jenny Quinn a few yards away. And the mucusy growling of the man who was no longer polite. He was rising to his feet behind her, grumbling something obscene.

She reached the threshold of the forest and misjudged the angle of the slope.

The ground seemed to cave in beneath her, and before she knew what was happening she was falling, falling through darkness. For several breathless moments she careened wildly, head-over-heels, seeing stars, falling, falling, the world somersaulting like a crazy black carousel.

She landed on the banks of the river, in the weeds, the impact like a Roman candle going off in her head.

                    *   *   *

She had no idea how long she lay there, alone in the dark. The pain gripped her like a vise, pressing her against the rocks. Her back, twisted in the fall, sang out in agony, and her legs, still bound at the ankles, were jackknifed underneath her. She could not breathe normally. Probably one of her lungs had been punctured. But none of that mattered anymore because the worst was yet to come.

She could hear twigs snapping, the nimble footsteps coming down the slope in the darkness, the lunatic moving with catlike grace for a man his age. His shadow swept over her like a shroud. She closed her eyes.

The terror had boiled out of her now. She felt no fear. Nor did she feel any of the sorrow or regret that she would expect to feel at such a time as this. Her life didn't pass before her eyes. She only felt a vague sense of disappointment in herself, a sense of loss.

To die in such a tawdry, messy fashion, at the hands of a mild-mannered psychopath, felt like pure anathema to Dina Dudley. She had spent a lifetime grooming herself to be frugal, orderly, neat, and prudent. For the last nine years she had worked her way up the corporate ladder at Haglett and Myers to become one of the most efficient estate planners in the Midwest. The brutal hours had cost her a marriage, and now—*now*—she was going to go out like a common roadside hooker, strangled in the weeds with her own nylon stocking, and the world would count among its population one less gullible knucklehead.

The figure loomed over her, breathing hard, searching for words. "You just *had* to . . . *had* to do it the *hard* way," he said between gasping breaths.

As though he were a headmaster addressing an insubordinate student.

Dina felt her spirit shrinking inside her, a balloon with the air squeaking out of it.

Something snagged her hair then, an iron grip tightening around a hank of her meticulously colored burnt-chromium-red locks. Her head was jerked back with enough force to dislocate a cervical vertebra. The duct tape slipped off her lips, dangling from her chin.

Fresh pain screamed in her neck, choking her, stealing her air. She braced herself for the cool touch of a razor across her neck. She closed her eyes. She prayed it would be quick. *This is it, Dina,* she lamented in some far corner of her brain, *the last hurrah . . .*

Except the razor never materialized. Death never came. At least not in the way she had expected.

She felt herself being dragged—backward, headfirst, her legs completely paralyzed—back across the cool hardpack, through the weeds and the brambles. The nutcase was dragging her by the shoulders, like a sack of lawn clippings, back up the side of the hill. She couldn't see her captor, couldn't move. She wondered if the fall had broken her back?

She tried to focus, tried to make sense of what was happening.

It was obvious he was dragging her back up to the road, his labored breathing coming out in ragged puffs. She could smell him. He had too much aftershave on. If there was one thing that turned Dina Dudley's stomach it was a man who drenched himself in too much aftershave. She had to say something. She knew she was going to die. What difference did it make?

"You dunk yourself in the Aqua Velva tonight?" she uttered through clenched teeth at the faceless figure hauling her up the hill.

"Beg your pardon?" His breathless voice still had that creepy courtesy.

"Let Jenny go. Please. You can do whatever you want to me, I'll suck you off."

"Oh, I'm sorry," he said, the tone of his voice like a government bureaucrat politely denying a permit. "I'm afraid I can't do that."

"Do what?" she said. "Get a blow job or let her go? Come on, please, she's just a kid . . ."

"I'm really very sorry."

They had reached the crest of the hill, and Dina could smell the piney exhaust fumes of the road. Headlights blurred in her eyes. It had begun to rain— a thin mist coming down—and Dina couldn't see very well. She felt herself being propped against a tree.

Now she could hear the faint mewling cries of her best friend, maybe twenty or thirty feet away, still muffled by the duct tape.

The lunatic had gone back to his van and was fiddling with something just inside the rear doors. It looked like a toolbox. Dina wanted to chew off his testicles. "C'mon, let her go, you got me, you can do whatever!" she called out to him. "Why do you need two of us?"

The man paused. He turned around and looked at Dina. He was smiling.

The grin turned Dina's heart to ash.

His reply was soft and courteous. "Because it only works with two."

TWO

In the predawn gloom, over the soft hissing of the baby monitor, Ulysses Grove heard the chirping noises first.

He stirred awake next to Maura, rolled over, and blindly muted the beeping cell phone. At this hour, on *this* phone, the call could only mean one thing. Section Chief Tom Geisel—or possibly his trusty assistant Shirley Milch—was on the blower from Quantico with another pair of Mississippi Ripper victims. Grove snatched the phone out of its charger and levered himself into a sitting position on the edge of the bed.

A rangy, chiseled African American with a marathon runner's physique and dark almond-shaped eyes, Grove wore his customary Michigan Wolverines boxer shorts and sleeveless T-shirt. He hadn't been sleeping well in recent weeks, and it showed in his stooped shoulders and somnambulant stare. Part of the problem stemmed from his bad eye.

Injured in hot pursuit outside a New Orleans

cemetery, Grove had nearly lost his left eye during an altercation with a psychopath named Michael Doerr. The cornea had sustained severe ocular contusions and subconjuctival hemorrhages, mostly from Doerr's knife work, and later Grove worried that he would spend the rest of his life the butt of Sammy Davis jokes. Over the last twelve months Grove had undergone three separate operations to save the eye but, unfortunately, the surgeons at Johns Hopkins were only able to avoid the need for a prosthetic. The eye that remained in Grove's skull was virtually blind. Grove had happily accepted the prognosis. He wore the scars of past cases he had closed like war medals.

And other than slight adjustments in his driving, reading, and writing habits, the only drawback to the partial blindness was the dreaming.

Grove had started having nightmares in which he saw things—prophetic things, apocalyptic scenarios, troubling visions—through his blind left eye, and *only* through that eye. His good eye never worked in these dreams, always blurred or flickered out like a TV tube with bad reception. But the *blind* eye saw everything, inexplicable things, road signs spattered with blood, shadowy figures lurking in the woods, ghostly horsemen riding over the bones of battle casualties. One night he dreamt he could see the future through his blind eye, and he woke up in a sheath of sweat after seeing his own family lying murdered in their beds. His psychotherapist referred to all this as "understandable" and "even healthy" considering the sights Grove had seen over the last few years.

But it wasn't merely angst over his blind eye that

was currently keeping Ulysses Grove up at night. Nor was it workload. Nor was it the emotional obstacle course of his young marriage or the stress of juggling his professional life as the FBI's top criminal profiler with his role as a loving father. The thing that was disturbing Grove's sleep these days was *anticipation.* He was very close to identifying the Mississippi Ripper. Over the course of twelve months and eight victims, Grove had amassed a hundred-plus-page profile.

It was only a matter of time.

Which was precisely why Grove snapped the flip-phone open with such vigor this morning. He glanced at the display. It was a Virginia prefix, the number registering in Grove's sleepy brain like tumblers clicking in a lock. This could be it. The crime scene Grove had been anticipating. The final puzzle piece that closes the Ripper down. Gooseflesh crawled on Grove's arms as he rose, cupping his hand around the phone, answering in a hushed tone. "Grove here."

"Morning, Sunshine," said the familiar voice on the other end. Tom Geisel had been section chief in the Bureau's Behavioral Science Division for nearly a decade and had trained Grove, and now the low, gruff, whiskey-cured voice had an almost soothing effect on Grove's ear. "Sorry about the hour, Slick, you know how it is."

Grove's scalp prickled as he slipped out of the bedroom and into the dark carpeted hallway. The baby was asleep across the hall, the nursery door slightly ajar. "Dirtbags never sleep, huh?" Grove whispered into the phone.

"True enough."

"Mississippi again?"

"Two white females, looks like the same sig, same MO, everything lines up."

"The dump is where?"

"Sixteen miles south of Quincy, Illinois, right on the river this time."

"Okay. That's what office? St. Louis?"

The voice said, "Yep . . . Bill Menner from Central Midwest is heading up there as we speak. Your ticket's already booked, waiting at Reagan. Flight numbers, departure times, map to the scene—it's all on your e-mail."

"Great, great," Grove said with a little nod and glanced at baby Aaron's door. A flannel sculpture of Winnie-the-Pooh hung from a hook, the words Mommy's Little Helper in fuzzy yarn-script across the top. A tiny, sharp frisson of guilt twinged in Grove's gut: It was a Sunday, and he had planned on spending the entire day relaxing with his wife and baby. Now all that would have to wait. Grove thought about it for a moment. "How's the scene this time?"

A slight pause. "What do you mean?"

Grove shrugged. "Good security? Good first-on-the-scene coverage?"

Another pause. "Um . . . fair."

"Fair?"

Geisel's voice dropped an octave. "Some yahoo at Pike County HQ called in the media wagons. The place is already crawling with hacks."

Grove licked his lips, visualizing the circus of tungsten lights and microphones milling about the edges of the yellow tape. He had seen it before, and it could be an enormous distraction. But now the vague guilt stirring in Grove's belly turned into something else entirely. *Bring them on*, he thought for a brief instant, way down in his tangled subconscious. *Let them see it, let them see the process.*

The feeling had been brewing in Grove's midbrain for months now, ever since that first pair of victims had been discovered in a vacant lot behind a riverboat casino in Davenport, Iowa. The first in a meticulous series: always a pair of victims, posed postmortem, exactly twenty feet apart, facing each other, one killed an hour or so before the other— increased levels of serotonin and free histamine in the wound sites indicating struggle, probably torture. A banquet of physical evidence had been retrieved over the months from murder scenes snaking along the Mississippi River valley from Rock Island to Memphis: size-eleven triple-E shoe prints, DNA from secretions, clothing fibers, carpet residue, and latent prints galore. No positive matches yet, nothing in the index.

Yet.

But the most important part, the part that kept Grove tossing and turning at night, was the repeating pattern of dual victims, the precision with which the victims were posed, and the staggered times of death. The purpose had not yet announced itself to Grove but the revelation was imminent. Grove could smell it in the air, a trace of something acrid at the scenes. In his restless dreams it lurked along the periphery of his blind eye, something coalescing behind the shadows: *the meaning of the act.* Once Grove knew the meaning, he would find the perp. It was only a matter of time. Grove knew it. His colleagues knew it. Perhaps even the killer knew it.

Maybe that was why Grove secretly craved the cameras. He was a celebrity now, his recent cases thrusting him onto the public radar screen.

Grove was the man who had hunted down the demon-haunted Richard Ackerman in the famous Sun City case. He was the guy who caught a ritualistic killer in the eye of Hurricane Fiona. And of course, there were the private battles nobody knew about: the bouts of depression, the spiritual crises, and the push-pull of Grove's African ancestry. Perhaps most important of all, though, was Grove's fabled yet grudging relationship with the paranormal. After years of experiencing what can only be described as eerie intuition, he was tired of denying it. "You are who you are, Ulysses," his shrink had kept repeating only months before Grove had taken the plunge into marriage and fatherhood. And now Grove had taken the advice to heart. He was through fighting his true nature. His métier. His calling.

Let them watch.

"Okay," he finally said into the phone. "I'll call you from the scene, let you know how it's going."

"Good. Let's put the lid on this one before this prick kills again."

Grove said good-bye, snapped the phone shut, and went looking for his travel clothes.

Maura rolled over and gazed through sleep-crusted eyes at her husband of exactly eleven months as he primped at the mirror. Even in her groggy, half-conscious state she had to smile. "You know, if I didn't know better," she murmured in a hoarse voice, still thick with sleep, "I'd say you were dressing up for some secret booty call."

He wheeled around with a start, dropping one of his cuff links on the carpet. "Oh . . . sorry . . . I woke you up, didn't I? I'm sorry."

"It's okay, the milk fairy just dropped by again." She gestured down at her swollen, heavy breasts, which felt like two inflatable life preservers lying on the mattress next to her. In the six months since she had given birth to Aaron she felt as though her narrow-hipped body had been taken over by aliens. She had gone from a B-cup to a double-D in a matter of weeks, which had delighted Ulysses to no end, but had given Maura about as much sexual pleasure as an anvil strapped to her ass. Now her nipples tingled sorely as she struggled into a sitting position against the headboard. "I like the polka-dot one better with that shirt," she said with a quick nod toward the closet.

"You think?" He gave her a quick grin, turning toward his elaborate tie rack. He had at least fifty silk ties of every conceivable pattern and hue meticulously strung along the burnished chrome conveyor.

"And I'd go with the Florsheims instead of the Bill Blass," she added, rubbing her tender breasts, feeling like a water balloon about ready to pop. She watched with a wry sort of amusement as Grove fiddled with his motorized tie rack.

Ulysses was a fussy dresser, immaculate and finicky about things such as silk shirts and French cuffs and Windsor knots and high-polished Italian loafers. It was something that Maura County had suspected about the man from time she had met him—after all, how could she *not* notice all the Armani socks and cashmere scarves—but now that they were married, she was witnessing the whole range of this quirky behavior on a daily basis. Even at the wedding last summer, Grove had agonized over the tiniest minutiae such as the color of the groomsmen's ascots and the shape of the napkin holders. The Bureau guys had teased him unmercifully about it—joking that he should just come out of the closet and be done with it—but it made Maura love him more than ever. Somehow all the fastidiousness seemed to Maura like a defense mechanism—a way to compensate for the gruesome messiness of his work. But lately Maura was beginning to wonder if there wasn't a darker vein beneath Grove's behavior. Perhaps an early stage to some obsessive-compulsive disorder? It was silly to worry about such things, of course, but over the last couple of years, Maura had become a worrier.

She wasn't sure exactly how or when she had acquired this trait. As a journalist, she had encountered many terrifying and traumatic things while keeping her intellectual distance. She had written about abominations of nature with little personal risk or involvement. But after meeting Ulysses Grove, this emotional distance seemed to close. She started getting personally involved in her stories—a little *too* involved, in fact—which had led to a series of near-death encounters. But that was all ancient history now. She was retired. She was a wife and a mother, and she was happy to watch from the sidelines. Just so her husband stayed out of harm's way . . . as he had promised her the night before their wedding.

"You don't have to look so happy about it," she finally wisecracked as he finished snuggling the prescribed polka-dot tie against his Adam's apple.

"About what?" He gave her a look as he slipped into his pin-striped suit. "What are you talking about?"

"I assume the call was from Tom Geisel?"

Grove didn't say anything, just stared at her like a boy anxiously waiting to run onto the playing field.

She let out a sigh. "Most people would consider this sort of news kinda *bad.*"

He looked deflated, and finally told her where and when the new murders had occurred.

"How long will you be gone?"

He told her he didn't know for sure but he promised he would call her from the hotel after his initial look at the scene. He said this while hastily running a lint roller over the perfect creases and double-stitched seams of his tailored suit. Next he pulled on his Burberry overcoat, shot the sleeves, and took one last glance at himself in the mirror.

Then he came over and gave Maura a tender kiss on the lips. His breath smelled of Listerine. "I'll call you tonight," he murmured in her ear.

"Just remember to take your folic acid pills," Maura said with an exasperated sigh.

"I will, Mom." He gave her a grin, turned, and strode out the doorway.

"And wear your galoshes!" she called after him.

"Yes, Mom!"

His footsteps receded down the hallway, then down the stairs. A shuffling pause at the front door for a moment. The sound of his keys jangling, and then the door opening and closing.

The abrupt silence that followed made Maura's ears ring. The tidy little two-story seemed to hang there in suspended animation like a dollhouse, perfectly set in its little picket-fenced lot in its little picture-postcard Virginia suburb. Utterly still and silent except for the muffled hiss of the baby monitor, and the first cooing noises of Aaron coming awake. Maura took a deep breath, then hauled her bloated self out of bed.

She wriggled into her robe and slippers, then padded across the hall to Aaron's room.

In the dim, perfumed world of the nursery the baby was stretching and rooting in his crib. Maura went over and hovered there for a moment, gazing down at her precious little man. The baby made a few mewling noises, then blinked awake, his miraculous little eyes fixing their gaze on Maura.

It never failed to delight her, making eye contact with her baby like this. From the moment of his birth—a Caesarean delivery due to complications with Maura's narrow uterus—the baby's little almond eyes seemed to focus preternaturally well on their surroundings. Maura had always laughed off the clichés about some babies being "old souls" (a New Agey expression that she had always detested), but now, with the advent of the ethereal, caramel-skinned Aaron, she had begun to wonder if there wasn't something to the hackneyed phrase. The baby seemed to possess some kind of strange alertness.

"Look who's up," Maura said softly, opening her robe, and urging a nipple out of her nursing bra. The baby let out a tiny squeal and smacked its lips at her. Maura grinned. "The dairy bar's open for business."

She lifted the baby from its swaddle, then carried it over to the corner rocking chair. It took a few moments for the baby to latch on. A moment of pain before the delicious warm current began spreading through Maura, accompanied by the delicate little sucking sounds.

Maura had never been this happy. She closed her eyes and said a silent prayer of thanks.

Then she added a few thoughts for the families of victims number nine and ten.

The bodies had been found—like all the others, within twenty feet of each other—in a thick stand of weeds and cattails along the Mississippi. The remains were on the Illinois side of the river, which meant the investigation would fall under the jurisdiction of the IBI. But when word began to spread that these were victims of the Mississippi Ripper, the state Bureau called in the St. Louis FBI field office because of its superior CSI facilities. Word had also spread to both print and electronic media. Local affiliates from as far north as Chicago and as far south as Memphis had dispatched news vans. The *St. Louis Post* arrived early, followed by crime beat reporters from WGEM Quincy, the *Peoria Journal Star*, the Bloomington *Pantagraph*, and the Chicago *Sun-Times*. By midmorning the area was teeming with vehicles and personnel.

Adams County is an 800-mile slice of floodplain crisscrossed by winding blacktops and dotted with hardscrabble little river towns. To the east, the landscape rises up and buckles and rolls over limestone bluffs. It's a rugged, disheveled corner of the state, with much of the working class eking out meager livings on factory farms or at the calcium carbonate processing plant south of Quincy. Plus the Big River has a kind of solemn weightiness to it, tugging at the land like a gray pall. Especially on rainy days like this one. Especially at scenes of human misery. Like this one.

By midmorning uniformed officers had set up a cordon of yellow tape around the perimeter, midway between the edge of the river and the adjacent access road, in order to keep the onlookers and media folks at a safe distance. Plainclothes investigators huddled down by the bodies, which had been covered with white sheets (now soaked through by the drizzle). By the time Ulysses Grove arrived at the scene, around eleven o'clock, the crime lab people had burned through six "megs" of digital photos. Hundreds of little numbered flags had been staked into the moist ground along the bank, labeling key pieces of physical evidence such as shreds of cloth, footprints, and blood streaks.

Grove arrived with all the pomp and circumstance of an incognito rock star. They chauffeured him through the snarl of traffic and throngs of reporters in an unmarked FBI minivan with tinted windows and headlamps flashing hypnotically. It had begun to drizzle, the sky turning so dark it looked like black-lung disease. The unpaved road had deteriorated to muck, and it took forever to get Grove down to the scene. En route, he sat quietly in the rear of the van with his digital camera in his lap, waiting patiently, oblivious to the cacophony of lights and voices piercing the mist.

When he finally reached the general vicinity of the scene, Grove asked his escort—a genial, portly field agent from St. Louis named William Menner ("Big Bill" to his friends)—if he could be let out at the top of the slope, behind the crowd, far away from the body dump. For the briefest instant, Menner seemed nonplussed by the request, but then graciously obliged without comment. He told the driver to pull over behind the medical examiner's van.

The driver did as he was told.

Grove thanked the men and got out, then carried his camera up a muddy rise and into a thicket of loblollies. He stood there, gazing through the curtain of branches down at the scene like a lone surveyor preparing to measure a plot of ground for some obscure building project. Through his functional eye he saw the peripheral buzz of police cars and eager reporters like a radiant corona of glowing light. He saw the inner ring of yellow tape fluttering in the misty breeze. He saw the tiny numbered flags dotting the weeds, leading downward, closer and closer to the clutch of grim-faced investigators and morgue attendants in their ghostly white hazmat suits. Finally his gaze took in the forlorn nucleus of all this activity: the ragged pale lumps, buried in the weeds near the water's edge.

What he was doing was starting the *spiral.*

The "spiral" was a technique that Grove had developed years ago as a first-year investigator. Designed to take in the *whole* of a scene, and to move from objective to *subjective* space, it began with Grove physically stepping back as far as possible from the victim while keeping the victim in view. With his bad eye he had gotten into the habit of turning his head at severe angles so he could scan the scene with his right eye like a periscope. With each scan he moved slowly toward the victim in an ever-tightening spiral pattern, sweeping the place with his good eye, taking pictures from each vantage point. (Looking through a viewfinder had actually gotten easier with his bad eye; he didn't have to squint or close one eye to orient the other eye to the lens.) Throughout the process he made sure he looked at the ground and foliage, as well as the trees and the sky, for any clues that might have been missed. But the search for *physical* evidence was only part of it.

What he was *really* doing was getting the subjective feel of the environment, the killer's point of view, the way the perp *saw* the act.

But on this gray, drizzly morning, down by that great muddy river, Grove had gotten halfway to the bodies before he noticed something strange was happening around the periphery of the spiral, something that *never* happened at sensational crime scenes such as this one. He had been so busy taking photos of the twisted poplars and the weed-whiskered road, moving around *behind* the crowd, keeping his focus on those sheet-covered victims, that he hadn't noticed the sudden quiet. And the faint, muffled noise underneath it. Behind him. Beside him. All around him.

Grove paused.

It sounded like leaves rustling, the hushed yet

expectant whispers rippling through the crowd. Grove looked up and realized that all eyes were on *him*. The reporters, the onlookers, the morgue attendants, the uniformed officers—even the other plainclothes investigators—all of them watching him now. Watching and waiting for the great and mysterious Special Agent Ulysses Grove to do something brilliant. The whispering faded away. The ensuing silence was so eerie and incongruous it made Grove's flesh crawl.

Of course they knew who he was. For years he had been a regular fixture in the tabloids: the "monster hunter" from the FBI with his "mystical methods." Even his budding romance with science journalist Maura County had gotten all kinds of ink. And his looks had only made matters worse – not long ago he was featured in *Ebony* magazine's Fifty Most Beautiful People of Color in America, and later that year he appeared on national TV as a guest on *The Tavis Smiley Show*, discussing the recent increases in black-on-black violence with his rakish eye patch still in place from his recent surgery.

But now, this morning, Grove realized he had been wrong about letting the media watch him work. This was a bad idea. This was a huge problem, and he had to do something immediately. He turned to Agent Menner, who had been discreetly following along, and Grove started to say something like "Let's move these people further back"... or "Let's put up some privacy curtains so we can work in peace" . . . but he abruptly stopped himself.

A spark—a revelation actually—flashed in Grove's mind, so powerful and unexpected it practically took his breath away. He looked up at the hundreds of people gathered in the drizzle like an audience at some macabre play. Camera lenses were trained on him, microphones aimed at him, pens poised to capture his every gesture. It was almost sensual, the power it conjured in him. Like a blast of hormones. Then he looked back down at the sad little bundles of human remains in the weeds twenty-five feet away, facing each other, their rain-spattered shrouds marbled with bloodstains.

The realization nearly peeled off the top of his head. "Agent Menner," Grove murmured, unable to tear his good eye away from the victims.

"Yes, sir." The stocky field agent now stood beside him, waiting, his arms crossed against his barrel chest.

"I'm going to need you to do me a favor." Grove started walking toward the victims.

"Anything you need," Menner said, trundling along in the muck.

Grove approached the first victim. He had to step over a low strand of yellow tape connecting a pair of evidence flags; then he sidestepped an ambu-gurney left in the weeds by the medical examiner's assistant.

Finally he reached the closest white-shrouded bundle of human remains. It lay at the base of a leprous elm tree. "I'm going to need you to get a specialist down here, Agent Menner." Grove pulled out his rubber gloves and knelt down by the victim. "Immediately if possible."

Menner produced a small spiral-bound notebook from his pocket and prepared to write.

Grove's pulse quickened as he peeled the sheet away from the thirty-five-year-old female Caucasian lying in the fetal position. As Grove would later learn, her name was Dina Louise Dudley, and the ligature marks around her neck suggested that she had been strangled to death well before her evisceration. Like all the other Ripper victims, she would show a marked increase in free histamine and serotonin levels in her blood, indicating torture. But the method and motive for the torture—up until now—had remained elusive.

Grove looked at the other sheet-covered lump lying in the cattails twenty feet away. The ME would place *that* victim's time of death at one to two hours earlier than Miss Dudley. Like all the other scenes. Two dead women, offset times of death, a perfect matching set.

"Okay . . . what kind of specialist are we talking about?" Menner finally asked, his voice sound faint and distant to Grove's throbbing, ringing ears.

Grove didn't answer. He reached down to the blood-speckled face of Dina Dudley and touched the wet, dark tracks on her cheeks. Then he brought his fingertip back up to his tongue and tasted it. The salty, alkaline tang of tears was shot through with a telltale bitter flavor.

"How the hell did I miss it?" Grove was muttering more to himself than anybody else.

"Excuse me? Agent Grove? You say something?"

Grove stood. Swallowed hard. Put his gloves away. Then looked at Big Bill Menner. "I'm going to need an ophthalmologist down here on the double."

The burly investigator wasn't sure he had heard him correctly. "Pardon?"

Grove didn't blink. "An eye surgeon. I know a doc in Washington who can refer us to somebody around here."

THREE

In the hour and fifteen minutes it took Special Agent William Menner to go and find the only qualified ophthalmologist in the Quincy/Hannibal area, very few onlookers left the scene. If anything, more reporters arrived. More remote trucks, more talking heads, and more bystanders dressed in yellow parkas and hooded sweatshirts. They pressed up against the fluttering cordon tape, while the CSI people waited in the mist down by the bodies, drinking cold coffee from paper cups and grumbling about the delay.

For most of that time Ulysses Grove sat in the back of a squad car, scribbling in his notebook, reviewing photos and diagrams of the Ripper's earlier victims stored in his camera—always in pairs, always facing each other, always with the offset times of death. Grove hadn't told the other investigators anything of substance yet, and he hadn't made any calls to Quantico. He had to be sure his theory was correct, and the only way he was going to be sure was to have the eye surgeon confirm his suspicions. But it all seemed like a forgone conclusion now. He knew he was right.

Grove knew he was right because he felt the same delicious mixture of exhilaration and relief that he had felt so many times before when a case had cracked wide open—the soothing rush of a thorn pulled from his side. He had felt it while hunting the Hurricane Killer, when he stared into that thermograph of a deadly storm bearing down on New Orleans. He felt it a couple of years ago when he gazed upon the Mount Cairn mummy posed in precisely the same postmortem position as the Sun City victims. He felt it when he was hunting Keith Jesperson and saw that happy-face sticker in that squalid restroom in that South Dakota truck stop. This was the part that Grove never told anybody: it was like a drug. It was the only moment in his life when he truly felt alive—when he finally turned over the correct stone and saw evil clearly, saw it in the light.

Was this the mysterious part of him that people talked about behind his back? Was it the part of him his mother called "his birthright"? Old Vida Grove, the eccentric Kenyan woman whom the neighborhood kids back in Chicago had called the voodoo lady, had always thought her son Ulysses was born to be a shaman, a visionary. And who was *he* to question his gift? Who was *he* to resist his own destiny?

Let them watch.

A sudden muffled thud pierced Grove's thoughts, and he turned with a start, just in time to see Agent Menner standing outside the squad car, rapping his knuckles on Grove's window. Grove rolled it down.

"I got a Dr. Samuel Habbib here from Quincy's Blessing Hospital." The beefy FBI agent jerked his thumb at the gentleman standing behind him in the overcast light.

"Good, excellent, thanks a lot." Grove opened the door and climbed out.

The rain had lifted, and now the gray sky hung low over the pewter-colored waters of the Mississippi. A chill breeze was blowing in off the Missouri side, and the air smelled of fish reek and ancient boat oil. Grove lifted his collar, then extended his hand to the surgeon standing behind Menner. "Appreciate you coming down, Doc, especially on such short notice." Grove gave him a perfunctory smile. "I'm Agent Grove. Ulysses. Surgeon out of D.C. did some work on me last year, Stanholm at Johns Hopkins, gave us your name."

"John Stanholm and I went to medical school together at Oxford," the little man marveled, shaking Grove's hand with a nervous tic of a smile twitching in his face. He was a diminutive Pakistani man with a narrow, pointed face and a receding hairline. He wore a North Face windbreaker that looked a little anachronistic over his hospital tunic. "I'm guessing you had an open-globe injury to the left eye?"

"I'm impressed, Doc."

"I wish I knew what this was about." Habbib seemed unnerved by all the spinning light and forensic minutiae around him. He glanced over his shoulder. "I've got a LASIK procedure scheduled at two o'clock."

"This should just take a minute. C'mon." Grove gave Menner a nod, then ushered the surgeon under the tape, down the slope, and across the rain-slick weeds.

The doctor was visibly jittery. "I heard something about a double murder?"

"How's your stomach, Doc?" Grove asked as they approached Dina Dudley's corpse. Grove reached down and peeled back the shroud.

"I'm still not clear as to what you gentlemen want me to——"

The doctor's gaze fell on the brutalized corpse of Dina Dudley, and his voice stalled. He cocked his head as he took in the grisly details, the blood-stippled features of her face, the ligature marks around her neck like dark purplish worms, and the abrasions around her eyes. It looked as though somebody had scourged her eyelids and forehead and scalp with barbed wire. "Oh, dear," Habbib muttered under his breath, aghast, staring and staring.

"I'd like to draw your attention to the wound patterns on the woman's eyelids and forehead." Grove pointed a rubber-gloved index finger at the blackened, coagulated cuts and puncture marks across Dina Dudley's forehead. "I'm curious to see if you draw the same conclusions I have."

"Oh . . . boy . . . oh, boy . . . oh, boy . . ." The doctor kept staring and then, all at once, his posture changed, as though he were seeing something new in the tragic remains. "Wait a minute. Yes. I see. I see what you mean." The doctor pursed his lips judiciously like a man pondering a formula, then looked up at Grove. "You're thinking these wounds are from a speculum or some kind of retractor."

Grove gave him a mild smile. "You're the expert, Doc. You tell me."

* * *

They all wanted to know what was going on. Everybody within a five-hundred-yard radius of the scene. They all could feel it—from the lead investigators down to the lowliest morgue wagon attendant—the buzz of revelation. They could smell it. They could see it in the way Grove had rounded up all the St. Louis field agents, the medical examiner, Special Agent Menner, the Adams County sheriff, and the surgeon from Blessing Hospital. The group had been ushered over to a quiet corner of dry land between the paramedic trucks and the road, safely inside the cordons, far enough from the crowd to be out of earshot.

Now the group was huddling with the intensity of a Super Bowl team in the final minutes of the game. Onlookers were craning their necks to get a glimpse of what was happening inside that huddle. A few rogue cameramen had wandered over to the edge of the gravel shoulder, right up against the yellow tape, aiming their lenses and boom microphones at the strange powwow fifty feet away, trying to glean a word, a phrase, a gesture, *anything* that would hint at what was being said. But the river winds and rustling trees drowned most of the voices.

Grove and the Pakistani doctor knelt, side by side, inside the circle of investigators, scraping a crude diagram in the mud with sticks. It looked like a human face with one eye wide open. With the tip of his branch the doctor traced a hook above the upper eyelid, tugging the lid up. "You see, a speculum works like *this*." He spoke to the group with the patience of a kindergarten teacher showing flash cards. "It's designed to dilate the opening of a body cavity."

Grove chimed in then: "In past victims we just wrote off the abrasions as part of the torture . . . even the meticulous placement of duct tape adhesive across the forehead. We just figured it was part of the bondage and torture component."

The doctor nodded and went on: "In ophthalmic surgery, the speculum retracts the eyelid for the duration of a procedure, allowing access to the sclera or pupil."

"Plus there's the eyedrops," Grove added. "We won't know for sure until we get the lab results back but I'm betting there's artificial tears on the victim's face."

"Artificial tears?" This was Menner. "You lost me there."

"If a retractor was used to keep the eyelids open," the doctor explained in a soft, accented voice, "it's highly likely there was Perfluoron or some kind of saline compound dropped into the eye at regular intervals."

One of the lead investigators from St. Louis spoke up then, a slender, gray-at-the-temples man. "I think I see where this is going."

Grove nodded deferentially at the man. "Go ahead . . . Agent Watkins, is it?"

"That's right. Joe Watkins. Belleville field office. This is about watching, isn't it?"

The group got very still.

Grove gave a grim little nod. "It's about the second victim being forced to watch, yeah."

A long pause.

In the far distance the sky rattled with thunder.

Menner thrust his hands in his pockets and mumbled under his breath, "God, I hate the sadists."

Grove looked at the big man. "Right again. This is definitely a sadist we're after here, a pure sociopath, but he's the trickiest kind because he's probably a highly organized personality."

Menner looked at Grove. "Meaning he's good at it? Cunning? Smart?"

Grove told him that was exactly right.

The sheriff jumped in then. "Okay, so what are we looking for here?" He was rubbing his thick neck as he spoke. "Somebody with medical training? An eye surgeon?"

"I don't think so," Grove said, then shot a glance at Dr. Habbib.

The surgeon was nodding: "I have a colleague in Cincinnati, he goes to third world countries and shows them how to make eyelid clamps out of paperclips."

"And the eyedrops you can find at any Walgreens," Grove added. "There's also a battlefield crudeness to the way he tapes the victims' heads to trees or whatever . . . lampposts."

"So where does that leave us?" Agent Watkins wanted to know. "We can't canvass every drugstore in the Midwest."

Grove looked over at the two shrouds in the weeds. "We look for somebody who fits the profile . . . and who's all about *watching*."

Another moment of tense silence as the group mulled that over.

"And a control freak," Grove added. "That's really important, the control part . . . and the watching part."

* * *

Less than fifty feet away, standing in the chilled river breezes, the killer watched. He watched the scene with fervid intensity through the lens of a TV camera. In fact, he watched with something close to awe as the handsome black FBI agent enlightened the team of investigators.

The killer wore a nylon WJID-TV ST. LOUIS windbreaker, hip-wader boots, and a heavy battery belt connected via electric umbilical cord to his video camera's yoke. It was the standard uniform for a remote news cameraman at the NBC affiliate, at which he had been an employee for nearly ten years. But he wouldn't be able to work there much longer if this brilliant profiler from the FBI found out about his compulsion.

On one level, the cameraman greatly admired this dapper African American criminologist. He had read several articles about him, and had seen him in the flesh on two other occasions: last year at the scene of the Davenport killings, the two nurses from Augustana College, and a month later, in Memphis, those two fry cooks, strangled and gutted in the alley behind the Popeyes Chicken place.

On each occasion, it was an added bonus to watch the great Special Agent Ulysses Grove inspect the cameraman's handiwork (while the cameraman taped it all for the world to see). In Memphis, for instance, the experience was so exciting it gave the cameraman a temporary erection, and he had to leave under the false pretenses of food poisoning.

But now it was quickly becoming apparent that the investigation was progressing faster than the cameraman had hoped. This prodigious profiler was going to eventually track the cameraman down . . . and ultimately learn about the warehouse. That much seemed certain.

Right then the cameraman froze.

Through the lens, in the distance, amid the huddle of FBI agents and sheriff's deputies, a gap had formed between two beefy investigators, and all at once, Ulysses Grove became visible in all his Burberry and pinstriped glory—and he was glancing *this way,* as though he were gazing through the cameraman's own lens!

Like a drill penetrating the bone of the cameraman's skull and burrowing into his brain!

The cameraman lowered his camera, turned away, and trundled back toward his four-wheeler. He had to get out of there. He could not take it anymore. He couldn't breathe. He climbed into his truck, slid the camera across the passenger seat, then fired up the engine.

The SUV lurched, and he almost ran over one of the reporters as he roared back toward the two-lane. He didn't even look back. He was shaking as he sped away into the overcast afternoon. Something had to be done. Something had to be done about this genius from the FBI.

Something drastic.

FOUR

Henry Splet, ace cameraman and father of four, drove through the gated entrance of Pinehurst Meadows with an ash pit of worry smoldering in his stomach. He drove past the flower beds and flagstone ramparts, with his windows rolled down, despite the rain. He couldn't breathe with the windows shut. He needed the cold, wet air on his face in order to think.

A thin, stooped man with a translucent pale complexion, Henry was one of those types who always looked like his clothes were too big, his skinny neck swimming in his collar. Today was no exception. He looked so wan and fragile in his WJID windbreaker that he appeared almost spectral, ghostly. It wasn't just his advanced age—which, at fifty-seven, was ancient for a news camera operator—it was also his demeanor, the way he carried himself, his expression. In the rearview mirror, he saw his sunken, haunted, gray eyes, his emaciated cheeks. He looked like death.

He steered the SUV onto Elderberry Court, and

headed for the last driveway on the right. Home sweet home. Time to put on his good-Christian-husband-and-father mask. Henry wore many masks, but this one was his favorite. It almost made him forget his secret compulsion. He grinned as he turned in to the driveway of the tidy little split-level ranch house.

He parked and turned off the SUV as the rain drummed against the vehicle's roof. Through the windshield, which was quickly beading with raindrops, he could see his cozy little domicile: its gabled roof pitches and pale blue siding accented by lushly planted flower boxes. The flower boxes were Helen's handiwork. Helen Splet insisted on a cheerful, herbaceous home. She grew up in the Pennsylvania hinterland, the daughter of an Amish dairy farmer, and she still clung to many of the old ways, despite her conversion to evangelical Baptism in her early adulthood. From the butter churn on the porch, to the Early American antiques throughout the house, Helen wore her country roots on her sleeve.

"Daddeeeeee!"

Henry was getting out of the SUV when his youngest came toddling across the porch, the screen door slamming. The three-year-old was named Ethan, and he was a carrottop with perpetual tracks of green snot under his little pug nose. "Daddeeee—Daddeeee—I make poopoo in the toi-wet."

"Attaboy!" Henry scooped the redhead off the steps and hugged him. "I knew you could do it!"

The little boy jabbered about getting a sucker for his good work as Henry carried the child through the front door and in to the fragrant living room. The air smelled of pot roast and lemon wax. Helen

Splet, her dishwater blond hair pulled back in a severe bun, her once-luminous blue eyes now getting a little creased around the edges, came striding in from the kitchen, wiping her hands on a towel. "Daddy's home," she called up the stairs.

An immediate rumble of footsteps issued from the second floor. Helen smiled as she approached her husband, kissing his cheek. "Long day?"

Henry put the child down. "How did you know?"

"You look tired."

"You don't know the half of it," Henry said and put his battery belt down on the little deacon's bench by the fireplace. With mild surprise he noticed a ruby fleck of blood under one of his fingernails from the murders he had committed the previous night in the woods along the Mississippi. "Three breaking stories in one day."

He went into the bathroom and washed his hands, paying close attention to his nails. Then he stared at himself in the mirror for an inordinately long moment as his fingertips dripped. Finally he emerged and went into the den where his daily martini was waiting for him (dry, two olives). Helen had already laid out his nightly pre-dinner ritual on a TV tray next to his Barcalounger: an ashtray with his pipe, a fresh pouch of cherry brandy tobacco, the day's *St. Louis Post-Dispatch*, and the mail.

A whirlwind of children blew into the den as Henry went through his mail and sipped his martini. Caleb, his oldest, wanted to talk about the chess club. Rachel, his ten-year-old, wanted Henry to know it was high time she got that pony he had been promising her. And little Mary just wanted to sit on Daddy's lap while he perused his mail and his newspaper. Henry took it all in with good humor and fatherly patience . . . right up until the moment he saw the little banner headline across the top of that week's *Time* magazine.

A twinge of alarm pinched at Henry's gut.

"Dinner's ready, everybody!"

The sound of his wife's voice snapped Henry out of his daze. "Be there in a sec!"

Henry quickly thumbed through the magazine until he got to the *Current Affairs* section and saw the subheading at the top of the right-hand page: "Superstar Profiler Zeroes in on Latest Quarry." Henry's hands trembled as he skimmed the article written by the Midwestern bureau chief, the gist of the story laid out in the opening paragraph:

St. Louis, MO; Famed FBI criminologist, Special Agent Ulysses Grove (Issue #44:15), claims he is about to nab another killer. In an unprecedented buildup of evidence—both circumstantial and physical—Grove now believes that positive identification of the suspect known as the Mississippi Ripper is imminent. "We now know so many things about this person," the profiler explained from his Virginia office Friday. "We are fairly certain he is white, middle class, probably the head of a large family. Very likely a tradesman or artisan in some technical field." Grove went on to explain that due to DNA results from recent double homicides in Davenport and Memphis, the Bureau is literally days away from finding a match. "It's only a matter of time now," Grove went on. "And chances are he will turn out to be the guy next door."

"Sweetheart?"

Henry looked up from the magazine like a man coming out of a dream. "Huh?"

Helen was standing in the archway leading into the dining room, drying her hands in a dish towel, a strand of hair dangling in her eyes. Behind her, the kids were taking their seats at the table. "Are you all right?"

Henry smiled with a twitch. "You bet . . . just a little bushed. Man-oh-man, that smells good. Let's dig in."

He went into the living room and took his place at the head of the table. A steaming bowl of mashed potatoes sat magisterially in front of him, puddled in the center with melting butter. An array of comfort food spanned the center of the table: brisket, gravy, green bean casserole, and buttermilk biscuits. The air was sultry with caramelized odors.

"Caleb, please, pipe down now with the Gene Krupa," Henry said to his son, who was drumming his silverware on his plate, while Rachel and Mary sat like good little girls with their hands folded for grace, and Ethan scratched invisible pictures on his highchair tray. Helen took her seat, and Henry tried to concentrate on the dinner prayer. "Thank you, Father, for these Thy gifts which we are about to receive, from Thy bounty, through Christ our Lord, amen."

Everybody parroted his amen, and then the bowls were passed, and meat was sliced, and food was spooned onto plates, and Henry tried to act nonchalant, smiling at his little girls, winking at his wife, grinning at his sons, while somewhere way back in the beehive of his psyche, he was plotting, scheming, trying to figure out what to do about this annoying, nosy agent from the FBI, this handsome black pest.

By the time dessert was served—Henry's favorite: sponge cake with Hershey's chocolate sauce—he knew exactly what he was going to do about Grove.

That night, Grove took the red-eye back to Virginia. It was a blustery spring evening across the Eastern seaboard, and the flight was delayed for a little over an hour due to lightning storms over the Smoky Mountains.

Grove took advantage of the downtime on the tarmac at St. Louis International to text-message the Ripper task force. He told the key people back at Quantico about the breakthrough with the eye surgeon, and he lit a fire under the lab people to put a priority rush on the DNA samples from the Adams County scene. This was the final act before apprehension. Grove could sense it like the whiff of sulfur before a match head ignites: He was going to catch this son of a bitch. Very soon.

Hopefully before the bastard had a chance to kill again.

Grove's plane finally got airborne around 7:30, and hammered up through the turbulent atmosphere with Grove holding on to his armrests and loose file folders for dear life. He had grown so accustomed to flying that he rarely even buckled his seat belt, but tonight was different.

Tonight he buzzed with nervous tension, and was hyperaware of the flickering slipstream of icy rain outside the hermetically sealed fuselage. He tightened his belt and loosened the collar of his crisp blue oxford-cloth shirt. He still wore his Armani jacket with the orchid silk hankie tucked into the breast pocket, and the sterling cuff links fastened tight. He still looked neat, and orderly, and professional—like a successful black attorney or a renowned African American captain of industry—all of which helped him think and stay organized.

In fact, for most of that short, bumpy flight back to Reagan International, he made lists in his notebook, in his tight, obsessive ballpoint scrawl: people to brief on the latest developments in the Ripper case, calls to make the next day, tactical assignments to make once the Ripper was identified. The two-hour journey passed in a flash, and before Grove even realized it, the plane was on its descent into Reagan.

The airliner landed in a flurry of noise and flashing silver light.

Ten minutes later, Grove was inside the terminal.

"I'm also going to need you to run a check of all the major medical schools in the Mississippi River Valley region," he barked into his cell phone as he strode through the glass tunnels of Reagan International Airport. He had his raincoat slung over his shoulder now. He had only been on the ground for a few minutes but already had a team of four people on a conference call. On the line were a couple of data specialists at Quantico, Agent Menner in St. Louis, and Dr. Wendal Booth, the head of the School of Ophthalmic Surgery at Iowa City Medical Center.

"May I ask what you're looking for?" Doctor Booth's tobacco-cured voice broke in.

Grove told him he was looking for anything out of the ordinary, any record of failed ophthalmology students, dropouts, disciplinary problems.

"That's a wide net," the doctor said with a wry chuckle.

Another voice piped in: "What are we matching them with?"

Grove recognized the voice of Petra Bartoni, a young whiz kid working her way up the ranks of the FBI's byzantine headquarters staff. Grove told her to match them up with anybody in the same region with a criminal jacket or a history of mental illness.

"Got it."

Another voice: "Been a lot of press on this one, a lot of flight opportunity."

Grove let out a sigh. He knew the sound of skepticism in Big Bill Menner's voice, and he knew there was a distinct possibility that the killer could *indeed* be halfway around the world by now. But something bone deep inside Grove told him that the killer was within his grasp. A clock ticked in his brain now—the same clock that always began incessantly ticking as he closed in on a subject.

"I think he's savoring all the ink," Grove finally said as he descended the escalator into the baggage claim area. Ahead of him, the giant glass doors loomed, streaked with rain, leading out into the parking complex. "We can talk more about this tomorrow . . . right now I'm going to have to sign off. We can reconnect tomorrow with the lab people."

Everybody said their farewells, which was followed by a series of clicks.

Grove snapped his phone shut, then shrugged on his raincoat, grabbed his suitcase, and headed for the exit . . . completely oblivious to the complex dance that had already started.

FIVE

By the time Grove got home it was close to midnight. The rain had stopped hours earlier, and now the stars had come out over the Shenandoahs. Grove's little neighborhood lay glistening in a hushed tableau, the air perfumed with pine and wet tar. Only the crickets and the dripping gutters were audible as Grove pulled his sedan into his garage.

The house was as silent as a church. Upstairs Maura and the baby were both sound asleep.

Grove went into the kitchen and found a note Maura had left for him on the butcher block island welcoming him home and telling him about the leftover pork chop in the fridge and Aaron's new bottom front tooth and the basement toilet getting clogged by a stray baby wipe. Grove stood there in his damp raincoat, savoring every word of the note.

All this banal domestic minutia was a salve on Grove's burning, restless soul. He was still plagued by visions of dark men and dark acts, still driven by a blood heritage he could not fully understand. But just as he was born to hunt monsters, he was also born to be a husband and a father.

He was making himself a nightcap—a single malt with a splash of water—when he heard Aaron stirring and cooing anxiously behind the door at the top of the steps. Grove put down his drink, then hurried up the carpeted stairs, careful not to wake Maura.

Aaron's room was sultry with powdery baby smells and humidified air. A night-light burned in the corner—an orange plastic Tigger head. As Grove entered he could see the silhouette of his firstborn son busily flapping his arms inside the bars of his crib.

Little Aaron Grove was a big, brown, doughy baby with huge eyelashes and close-cropped nappy black hair. His looks were a pleasing mixture of his light-skinned black father and WASPy mother, though his personality was all his own. He was simultaneously cheerful, noisy, and sickly. He always seemed to have some sort of discharge going, either a leech trail of snot from his little turned-up nose or a crust of gummy mucus in the corner of each gigantic doe eye. But whenever he grinned his snaggletoothed grin at Grove, he was just about the most beautiful creature ever to cross Grove's path.

"C'mere, Slick," Grove muttered genially under his breath as he scooped the baby out of the crib.

"Puh!"

The word—if you could call it that—came out of the little duffer on a half belch, and the sound of it made Grove's eyes water with glee. It wasn't exactly a perfect enunciation of the word "Papa," but it was close enough. Grove hugged the baby to his cheek and breathed in the talcum and cream aroma of the child's latte-colored skin.

"You been a good boy for Mommy?" Grove looked at Aaron's mouth, saw the little white Chiclet peaking out of his drool-soaked lower gum. "All the teething keeping you up?"

"Puh!"

"That's right—Puh's here!"

Grove hugged the baby once more for good measure, then turned, carried the child out of the room, and descended the stairs.

Maura had left a bottle of breast milk in the fridge alongside the pork chop, and Grove made himself and the boy a midnight snack. Grove sliced the chop thin, toasted a kaiser roll, and heated the bottle in the microwave. Then the twosome retired to the screened-in porch jutting off the rear of the house to dine in the dark silence and watch the distant storm retreat over the northwest range of the Shenendoahs. They snuggled into an Adirondack chair, the baby in Grove's lap, chewing contentedly on the bottle's nipple, Grove munching on his sandwich. The cool air smelled of ozone and pine. In the far distance the heat lightning snapped across the granite peaks like tinsel.

Grove could not get the the Mississippi Ripper out of the rear chambers of his mind.

It was something that he avoided whenever possible—thinking about this stuff around his family—but sometimes it was just plain irresistible. And tonight he could not shake the sensation that he was on the cusp of another takedown. All he had to do was collate the latest breakthroughs with the lab, and get Brian Dunham at Quantico to do his magic with the Violent Criminal Apprehension Program data, and close the net.

Aaron tossed the empty bottle across the porch, and then fidgeted in Grove's lap.

"Okay, okay already," Grove murmured and rose and gently put the baby down on the Astroturf floor where a pile of Fisher-Price plastic beads and blocks lay strewn. Aaron immediately started cooing and batting at the toys.

Grove started pacing, thinking about something he forgot. He pulled his cell phone out of his pocket and placed a call to Los Angeles. It was 10:00 P.M. on the west coast and still early enough to catch Cedric Gliane, the world's foremost DNA expert, before he faded away for the night.

"Gliane here," the voice crackled in Grove's ear.

"Cedric, it's Grove."

"Ulysses—"

"Sorry to call at this hour—we're redlining on the Mississippi Ripper. Is this a bad time?"

There was a pause, a sigh, and a series of rustling sounds on the other end.

"I can call back in the morning," Grove said, pacing across the porch, keeping Aaron in his peripheral vision, the sound of the wind rattling something in the backyard.

"Naw, it's okay, I'm just wading through a sea of junk e-mails," the voice said.

"You're gonna get a new series tomorrow, Cedric, and I'm wondering if you can put a rush on it."

"From the St. Louis scene?"

"Yep, got a whole boatload of material off the vics this time, both secretions and tissues."

Another pause.

Grove listened to the banging sound echoing across the darkness of deserted lawns, blending with the low intermittent rumble of thunder. What he *didn't* notice was that Aaron had crawled all the way over to the opposite corner of the porch, and the banging sound was coming from the screen door, which had blown free of its latch, and now Aaron was crawling through the open doorway.

The voice in Grove's ear said, "You airlifting it?"

"Yes, sir, Hollister's got his Tactical guys on it, they're flying it out to you as we speak."

"Okay, I'll clear my desk in the morning and have the rapid-test back to you before 5:00 your time."

Grove did not notice his baby boy vanishing into the darkness of the rain swept backyard. The child was barely visible now, just a ghostly outline through the porch screen, trundling awkwardly over rain-damp grass toward the shadows beyond the bird-bath.

"You are the man, Cedric," Grove said with a satisfied nod, planning out the next day's activities.

"Just do me a favor," the voice said.

"Name it."

"Just catch this guy already."

"I will do my—"

Grove looked up then and saw many things at once: the empty porch, the banging screen door, the pale shadow of something moving out in the backyard. He dropped the phone. He leaped across the porch toward the open door. His heart raced as he stumbled outside.

He froze.

The child was maybe twenty-five feet away—maybe thirty feet—it was hard to tell in this light. But what made Grove abruptly stop and stare was a flicker of recognition in the back of his brain.

It flashed behind his eyes only for a beat, almost like a twinge of déjà vu, but not quite, as he stared at his baby vanishing into the pitch-black shadows at the end of the property line, where a forest of hardwoods lay choked with weeds and foliage. In the dark of night, the woods looked as cavernous and black as a leviathan's mouth which was, at this very moment, about to devour Grove's baby.

It was happening as savagely and suddenly as a giant fly trap closing around its prey. But there was something else about that image—a helpless infant voluntarily slipping into absolute darkness—that paralyzed Grove for the briefest moment, until he finally found his voice.

"Aaron!"

Grove dashed across the dew-slick lawn in one continuous headlong rush and scooped up the baby in a single fluid motion with the muscular grace of a juiced-up halfback retrieving a live ball at the buzzer. Grove only slipped once, just a few centimeters on his back heel as he was lifting the child, but he managed to keep from falling as he cradled Aaron against his heaving chest. He found his footing and stood there a moment in the darkness with the baby in his arms and his heart pounding out a tarantella.

Aaron seemed oblivious. He wriggled and made squeaking noises.

Grove started to say something to his baby son when he abruptly stopped. The sound of the telephone had pierced the silence behind him in the kitchen. An instant feeling of apprehension stabbed at Grove's solar plexus. Something was wrong. It was too late for anybody in law enforcement east of the Mississippi to call him, and since he had just talked to Cedric and Hollister in California it was doubtful that it was the west coast. That only left two possibilities: a wrong number or his mother.

"Please God, don't make it my mom," Grove muttered under his breath as he carried the child back toward the house. The kitchen was dark and cold. Grove answered the phone on the fifth ring with the baby still in his arms.

It was his mother.

"Let me guess," he said, after detecting the note of somber dread in his mother's greeting. "You're working on another one of your premonitions?"

The silence that followed could have chilled the earth's core.

SIX

Around 10:00 the following morning, just outside Belleville, Illinois, a garishly painted panel van wended its way up the narrow switchback road that rimmed the Fenster Maximum Security Facility. The van had a small satellite dish mounted to its roof, and the NBC logo emblazoned across its bulwark. WJID-TV ST. LOUIS was stamped across its hood, and the driver wore a WJID windbreaker buttoned up to the collar, a Cardinals hat pulled down low against his dark glasses to mask his bloodshot eyes. The driver had spent the previous evening kidnapping, binding, torturing, and killing two nursing students from St. Vincent de Paul College in East St. Louis because the compulsion had washed over him again. But unlike his previous kills, *this* time he decided to bury these subjects in sealed oil drums in the barrens along the Mississippi south of Carbondale. Splet could no longer afford to play games with the media, or leave his victims in plain sight.

He felt the heat of law enforcement on the back of his neck like the breath of an avenging angel.

It was time for drastic measures.

Now Henry Splet approached the outer security gate at Fenster with heart thumping, palms clammy, and knuckles white against the steering wheel. He pulled up to the guard booth, which was fortified with riveted steel framing and razor-wire borders. He rolled down his window and stuck his head out. "WJID Action News."

The guard, a pear-shaped black man with a bald head like an artillery shell, shot a look out the pass-through at the van's empty passenger seat. "Just one this time?"

"Yes, sir."

The guard looked nonplussed. "You got clearance from the warden's office?"

Splet had been there only a month earlier, but that time he had accompanied the lovely and annoying reporter, Anna Fong, on a routine background piece. Splet now gave the guard a cursory nod. "Just a follow-up with Milambri."

A long pause. The guard shrugged and vanished back inside the booth.

The gate groaned open. Splet eased the van through the opening, then putted across the staff parking lot, searching for a parking place.

The granite edifice rose in the middle distance like some funereal pueblo, casting its sullen shadow everywhere you looked. A massive U-shaped fortress, it was like some great and hellish oven into which society's rejects had been shoved to stew in their own juices. Chimney stacks gurgled black smoke from its many corners, and not a single window adorned its Gothic ramparts. Concertina wire gleamed dully along the imposing outer fences like desiccated spun sugar. There were no sinister gun turrets, no potbellied guards out of central casting, just a general stillness born out of soul-numbing despair.

Splet parked near the service entrance, got out, and carried his briefcase along the east wall, walking with an officious-looking posture and gait. He wanted to give the impression that this was just another ridiculous follow-up assignment, an errand so ephemeral and routine that the station hadn't even bothered to send talent—only a lowly cameraman serving as an ersatz stenographer.

Inside the main entrance—a moldy-smelling foyer painted baby-vomit green—an obese black lady guard in cat's-eye glasses stopped Splet with a hamhock arm. Splet told her whom he had come to see. The lady cast an incredulous glance down at Splet's laminated press card. "Y'all talked to the warden about this?"

"Yes, ma'am."

The lady guard kept staring at that ID tag as though it might blink with subtitles. It was true—*technically*—that Splet had talked to the warden's office. Maybe that was four weeks ago, and about a different matter, but he had indeed talked to them. Today, however, Splet was banking on the fact that this heavyset woman in the horn-rims was too lazy to get on the bitch-box and confirm things.

A big sigh from the fat gal. "Alright . . . I'm gonna need ya to step over to the window. Remove all metal objects, your shoes, and your belt."

Splet did as he was told. Another guard, a middle-aged man with a buzz cut and hulking shoulders, came out of an inner office and patted Splet down. Meanwhile the fat lady opened the briefcase and made a feeble search. She looked at the notepad, the carton of cigarettes, the tape recorder, then sniffed absently and latched it shut.

"Gonna have to meet in the general population," she informed Splet with a nod toward the corridor to the left. "Visitation block."

"That's fine. Thank you," Splet said and smiled.

"Officer Tomkins will escort you to the cafeteria where y'all will have ten minutes, no more, no less."

Splet gave her a polite nod. "I understand, thank you."

"You may not pass anything other than documents or cigarettes to the inmate. You may not take anything."

"I understand."

"You may not touch or come into contact with the prisoner at any time."

"No problem."

"Officer Tomkins," the big gal nodded at her associate, and the beefy guard in the buzz cut grunted something that Splet didn't understand, then started toward the E-Wing corridor to the left.

Splet followed.

They passed through a series of steel-riveted doors, the monkey-house noises of the cafeteria rising and bouncing off the iron walls like sonar blips in a submarine. The air was close and smelled of BO and bleach and fear. The two men did not speak. Splet's heart was beating faster now. The noise rose and rose, until they finally entered the main cafeteria—Visitation Block E.

It was like a scene out of Dante's *Inferno* performed by a trailer park full of crystal meth addicts. Hundreds of families and couples of all shapes and sizes, including errant children, milled around long tables arrayed across the football-field-size cement floor. The cavernous room, with its low ceiling of exposed plumbing and fluorescent lights, stank of fermented grease and urine, and positively vibrated with squeals, shouts, howls, laughter, and sobbing. A sense of *fatigue* pervaded the room, from the faded inmate togs to the angst-ridden faces.

Splet took a seat at the end of a nearby table, and the guard told him they would bring Milambri down.

The guard left, and Splet waited patiently with his heart pounding and his briefcase latched securely in front of him. The only other occupants of the table were an elderly couple at the opposite end, holding hands and scowling at each other and saying nothing. The old man, dressed in wrinkled orange garb, looked wizened and gray and tubercular, as though he had only weeks to live and was just waiting for the time to elapse.

"The hell *you* want?"

Splet whirled at the sound of Big Ben Milambri's bourbon-cured voice.

The gray-haired man stood behind Splet, towering over the table, a potbellied golem in flame-colored fatigues. The man's craggy face was a relief map of wrinkles, his dark Sicilian eyes like two salt-cured olives set deep in their sockets. His massive forearms were profusely tattooed and crawling with wiry black hair.

"Mr. Milambri, hello, good to see you," Henry Splet offered, rising to shake hands.

The big man made no effort to shake the cameraman's hand. "I was in the middle of a game of Texas hold 'em and I was winnin' so I will ask you one more time: What. The. Hell. Do. You. *Want?*"

"Please, sir, have a seat." Henry motioned at the folding chair next to him. "I promise this won't take more than a minute or two."

Milambri glanced around the noisy hall. Fifteen feet away, against an adjacent wall, a morose guard was chewing on his fingernails, pretending that he cared about what was going on around him. At a neighboring table, a woman in hair curlers busily masturbated an inmate through his pants.

"Aw, what the hell," Milambri grunted, and sat down in the folding chair, making the legs creak with his weight. "What difference does it make?"

Henry Splet measured his words. "Do you remember me?"

"Sure, you're the little hemorrhoid with the camera."

"That's right."

Milambri grinned. His front tooth was rotten, capped in dull gold. "Came with that Oriental broad, what's her name."

Splet told him.

"That's the one . . . Anna Fong . . . nice little piece of Chinese chicken."

"She's Thai, actually."

Milambri fixed his dead stare on Splet, the same stare last seen by over three dozen mob enemies targeted for assassination by the Chicago outfit. That same empty, curdled stare proved to be the last thing each victim saw before expiring. "What do you want, dickhead?"

Henry casually opened his briefcase. Fifteen

feet away, the guard stopped biting his nails and watched. Henry pulled out the tape recorder and the carton of Camel straights. The guard watched with mild interest. Henry gave the guard an earnest, questioning look, pointing at the cigarettes. The guard shrugged, then went back to his cuticles.

"Those for me?" Milambri inquired, smacking his lips, a negotiation pending.

Splet pushed the carton across the tabletop. "They're all yours."

"You gonna turn that thing on?" Milambri was pointing at the tape recorder.

Splet smiled. "Actually . . . no."

Milambri waited.

Splet went on: "There's a photograph sealed inside that carton." Splet didn't point, didn't look at the guard, didn't even take his eyes off Milambri, just kept smiling his courteous frozen smile. "Go ahead, take a look."

Milambri frowned, furrowing his brow skeptically. "What the hell is this about?"

"Go ahead."

Milambri sighed, turned the carton over, and thumbed the cellophane open where it had been carefully steamed off and then reglued. He tore the seam and noticed a foreign object pasted to the underside of the packs. Milambri glanced up, looked around, looked at the guard, then looked back down at the cigarettes.

- • There was a wallet-size photograph nestled inside the carton. It was a Xerox carefully trimmed and glued onto card stock, probably taken from a JPEG off a public Internet web site. The picture was of a slender, handsome black man in his early forties.

Splet kept smiling. "Mr. Milambri, meet Special Agent Ulysses Grove."

The big man looked up. "Who?"

"Grove. Ulysses Grove. He's a criminologist, a psychological profiler for the Bureau."

After a long moment the hit man said, "And why the hell do I give a shit about this?"

Splet lowered his voice slightly, his tone becoming faintly conspiratorial. "You should care because I will pay good money to have this gentleman ... eliminated."

Milambri cocked his huge head. "Eliminated?"

Splet licked his lips. His smile faded. "'Whacked' is the word, right? Whacked?"

Three hundred miles to the north, at that very moment, Chicago was sweltering in an August fever. The heat from a high pressure cell off the prairies had slowly, incessantly, drew across the city like an invisible shroud. It was only 10:00 A.M., and the mercury had already risen to ninety-five. Asphalt along the Kennedy Expressway simmered and cooked. The neighborhood directly east of the highway, a gray enclave of New Deal tenements gone to rust known as Uptown, cooked in the humidity like a fragrant pot of dirty socks.

On the eastern edge of the neighborhood, just off Clark Street, an odd clicking noise pierced the customary rhythms of the street—the traffic, the birds, the sirens, the distant car alarms. This incongruous sound might easily be misidentified by harried passersby as a ticking engine or a loose gate banging in the breeze. But upon closer observation this *click-click-click-clicking* noise was revealed to be the tip of a wooden cane tapping the surface of a slate porch.

The cane belonged to an elderly Kenyan woman who was currently sitting on her porch rocker, waiting in the heat for an airport taxi to arrive, a shop-worn valise at her feet. The woman gave off an air of broken-down royalty, like some lost queen of a forgotten banana republic. Her porch was crawling with ivy, riotous with trumpet-pitcher vines and herbs and dried medicinal flowers. The cane itself was a doozy: a long spiral length of shellacked wood from a baobab tree, its handle carved from genuine ivory that had worn down over the decades to the color of rotten milk. She wielded it like a sword.

Vida Grove had just turned eighty last month and still smoked, her ubiquitous Camel straights tucked into a pouch that hung from a cowhide strap around her neck. This morning she wore a traditional floral kente dress with scarlet do-rag wrapped around her ashy silver braids. Her long regal face was the color and texture of arid earth, cracked and pocked with hardship. Her brown eyes, deep set and huge in her face, scanned Clark Street with sober wariness.

One of the reasons for Vida's nervous sobriety—and the tapping cane—was the fact that she hadn't been sleeping well lately. Occasionally she went through a period of insomnia not uncommon for a woman her age. *White nights*, she called them. But once in a while the sleeplessness coincided with a bout of visions. They would come unannounced—sometimes appearing in the very bedroom she occupied in that three-flat building—like ghosts. They would flicker at dusk or flash in the darkness of a closet, and they would invariably take Vida's breath away.

But these recent ones had done more than that; they had taken her back to her days as a young mother in Kenya.

The vision that bothered her most was almost like a memory, but not exactly. It was more like a snapshot of her past twisted and distorted through the lens of a carnival mirror: the sight of her only son, Ulysses, when he was a mere toddler, wandering off into the blue darkness of the Chalbi desert on the edge of their village. Something like that had actually happened years ago, but it had been fleeting, a minor incident. Vida had managed to immediately rescue the child.

But in *this* vision, unlike the actual event, the darkness of the desert coalesced into a shadow-figure, an incarnate of pure evil, who suddenly grabbed the child and vanished with him into the abyss without a sound. And Vida was helpless, mired in terror as though her feet were sunken into cement.

And that was why Vida had called her son last night, and that was why she now waited for a cab to take her to Midway Airport for a cheap flight to Virginia. It wasn't merely time for a visit. It was time to warn her son: these visions were more than prophecies, they were warnings.

And that was why she kept tapping the tip of that baobab cane on that stone porch. Most of the time she wasn't even aware she was doing it. The tapping was akin to a nervous tic or a habit, like biting one's fingernails. But it was also possible there was more to it than mere nerves. Perhaps the tapping primed some deeper rhythm in Vida's soul, perhaps it touched off some mystical reserve.

Regardless of the reasons, however, she was tapping like crazy now, and she would keep tapping that cane until she knew for sure that her son and his family were safe.

Click-click-click-click-click-click-click-click-click-click-click-CLICK!

"Gimme a smile, you stupid piece of rat shit," Big Ben Milambri uttered under his breath, boring his gaze like twin augers into Splet's skull. The prison lounge undulated around them with milling bodies, the din of voices waxing and waning.

Splet frowned. He was confused. "I'm sorry . . . you want me to what?"

"Smile, you idiot." Milambri glanced over his shoulder, then looked back at the photograph pasted inside the splayed cigarette carton like it was radioactive. "If you don't smile in two seconds I'm gonna shove this carton down your goddamn throat, you goddamn faggot."

Splet managed an awkward grin.

Milambri kept nodding at him with a weird, fake smile, his eyes as dead as buttons. "Now chuckle like we're just sitting around the cracker-barrel sharing a dirty joke."

Splet let out a dry chuckle.

Voices bounced off the painted cinderblock walls. It sounded like a monkey cage in there. The air reeked of old sweat and ammonia. Milambri cupped his hand over the photograph of Ulysses

Grove and closed his fist. "Yeah, that's a good one," he said with a laugh, loud enough for the guard to register nothing out of the ordinary.

Splet looked down at the crumpled little photo. "Is there a problem?"

"Shut the hell up."

"Did I say something wrong?"

"Shut your hole, dickhead," Milambri growled, still displaying his yellow teeth in that bogus grin. "And lemme explain something to you."

"I'm sorry if I—"

"You bring that shit in here when I'm looking at a goddamn nickel without possibility of parole?"

"I didn't mean to—"

"Shut up, faggot. And listen. And learn. I will erase your family . . . you bring that shit in here when I'm up for review in two weeks."

Splet swallowed drily. "I'm sorry."

"Shut your mouth," Milambri said, his grin changing to more of a yellow rictus. He ripped the photo from the carton and shoved it back at Splet. "I don't know where you got the idea the Outfit was some kinda drive-up window for faggots looking to wax some G-man . . . but lemme set you straight. Tagging somebody in the Bureau is like popping a priest. *Comprende*, dickhead? You follow me?"

Splet nodded, putting the picture in his shirt pocket. His voice softening. "Yes, I follow you, sir . . . absolutely, yes."

"Get that shit outta here."

"I'm sorry I—"

Milambri had already pushed himself away from the table, and had risen to his full six-foot-plus height, the carton of cigarettes under his massive tree trunk of an arm. He nodded at the guard. The guard came over, and the two men strode away without a word, without even glancing at Splet.

The animal sounds echoed. An obese woman cackled in one corner.

Splet let out a long, anguished sigh.

He left the building with the crumpled picture still in his pocket.

SEVEN

Around 5:30 that afternoon, Grove met his mother at Reagan International, and they hugged each other warmly, exchanging banalities. It felt good to see the old girl again, despite the rancid memories that she stirred in Grove, and he told her she was looking too skinny, and she should eat more of that kashishi stew she always used to foist on the neighborhood kids.

They walked out of the airport arm in arm. In the parking garage, Grove piled her things—her valise, her shopping bag of half-eaten sandwiches, trinkets, and empty water bottles—into the Blazer.

For much of the ten-mile hop back to Alexandria, they rode in awkward silence. Along the way, Grove would catch a glimpse every few moments of Vida in his peripheral vision, her proud Nubian visage raised against the overcast daylight, her long, wattled neck as brown as tobacco leaves. She looked as though she were summoning some kind of celestial energy from the clouds as she chain-smoked

her filterless Camels, the ashes flecking and tossing in the wind.

Grove had seen that look on her face before. It
usually meant trouble. That defiant gaze aimed up
at the heavens, eyes narrowed, brow furrowed and
crinkled with loose skin. Those looks usually pre-
ceded some kind of metaphysical proclamation
about the crops failing or locusts coming or rivers
running red. Grove had fought those old supersti-
tions for most of his life. He'd been embarrassed
by them as a child, and rebelled against them as a
young man. But nowadays he was a different person. He was a believer. Vida had saved his life on
more than one occasion with her mysterious juju.

In fact, for years now, Grove had been formulat-
ing a new unified theory of his work as a profiler,
his efforts to confront evil, his place in the cosmos.
He had become more and more interested in his
African heritage, and had started collecting spiritual ephemera, charms, talismans. He had secretly
become obsessed with the notions of black magic,
dark forces in the universe, and hell. Especially *hell.*
Not the Hollywood version, but the intricate, pro-
tean territory first depicted by Dante Alighieri in
The Divine Comedy, and later by Milton in *Paradise
Lost.* He had begun to believe in the existence of a
literal hell. Perhaps it was located in invisible re-
gions, perhaps merely in the convolutions of the
human mind, but he was more and more certain it
existed. And all the requisite denizens—the fallen
angels, the demonic entities—were as palpable as
the ragged souls he hunted. And somehow, in some
inchoate way, his mother served as connective tissue to all these unseen realms.

"What's wrong, Mom?"

The old woman turned, the wind from the open window tossing her tiny kente braids. She proffered a dignified smile. "Nothing's wrong. Why do you ask such a thing?"

Grove drove for a while. "I heard it in your voice last night. Something's bothering you."

She shook her gray head emphatically. "Nothing is bothering me, Uly. This is all in your mind."

"Then why the surprise visit?"

"Uly!" She shot him a look. "I did not teach my son such bad manners."

A ragged sigh from Grove. "Okay, okay . . . play it your way. Everything's peachy."

"That's right."

Grove looked at her. "And you just came down here on a moment's notice with the heat and with your arthritis and your sciatica because you wanted to burp your grandson and play another round of gin rummy with me and Maura."

Vida looked out the window with an implacable little smile on her ashy lips. "I could not have said it better myself," she mumbled.

"Alright. Fine. Whatever. It's good to have you, Mom." Grove searched the hazy distance for his exit. "There's a lot of burping to be done."

Vida smiled and said nothing . . . just kept staring out the window at the afternoon's lengthening shadows.

Far to the west, the rains rolled into the Mississippi River valley. Gray sheets billowed across the metro St. Louis area, flooding back alleys and low-lying gullies along the river. Steam oozed from the cracked thoroughfares and pocked asphalt. Lightning veined the heavens and volleys of thunder crashed over the Gateway Arch like an aerial dogfight.

Henry Splet witnessed most of the storm through the narrow windows of his equipment room at WJID, sitting at the coffee-stained editing bay, angrily burning copies of a public service announcement for the station manager. He seethed with anger as he sat there twisting knobs and poking buttons, staring at the cathode ray screen, not really seeing anything, and whenever an assistant came in to help, Splet would snap at them to get the hell out.

It went on like this for most of the day, the passage of time losing all context for Splet. He felt as though he were floating above his body, buoyant with hate and contempt. It all just seemed so unfair. All he wanted to do was hire somebody to kill a Fed. You would think he asked Milambri to hit the Pope. What was the big deal?

By six o'clock that night, Splet needed to feed the furnace inside him—the one in his brain—the smoldering embers inside his mind-space. He needed to answer the compulsion. But this time, he dispensed with the watching ritual. Instead he called Helen and told her he had to put in an all-nighter at the studio, then he went down to the warehouse district along the river and waited for a prostitute to approach.

The first one came off the stroll like a clerk in a fresh produce department—a heavyset black woman that didn't quite fit the profile.

Henry shooed her away.

Finally, around 9:30, a lanky young white girl accosted Henry, and he gave her a courteous nod, then led her around behind the Pillsbury building where he drove a screwdriver through the base of her neck with one easy thrust, sending her into paralytic shock against the side of the building like a dying moth. Then he dragged her around behind a Dumpster and removed her eyeballs, using a surgical instrument that resembled a baby spoon. The entire procedure took less than three minutes.

From there, Henry drove out to the storage facility with the souvenirs next to him.

The eyeballs floated in olive jars filled with saline, each jar nestled in a newspaper-lined Chinese carry-out box. Henry felt anxious and jittery knowing he was about to visit his secret place, his place of dark wonders. But that was okay because he needed to think, he needed to strategize, he needed to figure out how to eliminate this dapper fed . . . this *Agent Grove*. Special Agent Ulysses Grove. He would find somebody to do it.

Somebody.

That much was certain.

That night, Grove couldn't sleep. While his mother, wife, and child slumbered in the shadows of the little colonial, he paced his kitchen, and squeezed his rubber stress ball, and waited for Cedric Gliane to call from the Bureau lab. The DNA tests were taking longer than expected, and Grove felt like a walking fuse, his nerves sizzling, flaring, and sparking. He had tried calling Los Angeles repeatedly but each time he had gotten Gliane's voice mail.

Now he had a terrible feeling something was wrong. The calm around him—the ebb and flow of the air conditioner, the hum of the refrigerator—had started to mock him, taunt him, call out to him: *Be careful, Old Hoss . . . them is Injuns out yonder in the dark.*

Of course, Grove didn't know it yet, but his intuition was correct. There *was* something gathering out there in the night, far to the west.

But it was not even *remotely* like anything he would have expected.

EIGHT

The U-Store-It mini-warehouse was located out on Old Six Mile Road, north of the pine barrens along Pickman Creek. The area was a ramshackle wasteland of landfills, fallow fields, dilapidated barns, and abandoned cement foundries. As far as the eye could see, the rolling hills lay scabrous and strewn with discarded car chassis and refrigerator boxes. Shreds of truck tires littered the skeletal woods. In the wee hours, the distant horizon glittered with broken glass.

Henry Splet drove down the access road to the east, then pulled into U-Store-It's gravel lot. The crunch of the SUV's tires pierced the silence.

Headlight beams fell on an automatic gate, which was shrouded in fog, the dull gleam of concertina wire curling along the pinnacles. The rusty guard shack, now boarded and empty, flanked the left side of the gate. Henry slammed the SUV into park, left it running, and climbed out.

Glancing over his shoulder, making sure he was

alone, he strode over to the magnetic reader. He snapped his card through the slot, and a tiny green light winked. The gate began to rattle open.

Henry pulled the SUV into the labyrinth of narrow blacktop paths that ran between the low-slung tin buildings.

If most self-storage complexes were like honeycombs of low-rent neighborhoods, U-Store-It was like a rotting Calcutta slum compressed by a great garbage compactor. The corrugated roofs were buckled and dented and pocked with bird shit. The pavement was cracked and ulcerated and whiskered with weeds, and the endless rows of garage-style doors were all slathered with graffiti. In the dark it virtually glowed with methane and filth. Henry's unit was in the last building.

He parked near the access door, turned off the SUV, and got out. Then he carried his souvenirs—still packed in their white carryout boxes—through the rusted door and into the darkness of the building.

He found the light switch, turned the timer dial to sixty minutes, then watched the fluorescent lights sputter on—most of the ancient tubes nearing the end of their lives, flickering and stuttering and sending nickelodeon shadows down the long narrow corridor of vertical accordion doors.

Henry walked the length of the corridor until he reached unit 213. One more glance over his shoulder. Something rattled in the distance, a muffled thump somewhere hundreds of yards away. There were others somewhere on the property. Henry would have to be careful. He fiddled with the padlock, and finally got the vertical door to rise.

The odor of ammonia and quicklime greeted him. He squeezed into the pitch-dark cell and lowered the door behind him for privacy. He pulled a string that dangled by his face. A bare incandescent bulb shone down from the low ceiling, illuminating the battered road cases containing his cameras, his beloved surgical instruments, a tattered Barcalounger armchair, canisters of film, unopened bottles of chemicals, boxes of pornography, and his vast collection of old yellowed Polaroids.

The pictures lined the walls, showing countless pairs of terrified human eyes in extreme close-ups, horrorstricken, forced open by makeshift retractors.

He went over to the miniature refrigerator in the corner, knelt down, and opened it. He put the human eyeballs on the bottom shelf, right next to the Mason jar filled with other eyeballs floating in formaldehyde. There were other souvenirs in there as well: some eyelids in a Tupperware container, one of them still sporting its long fake lashes, and a tiny gray tendril of tissue that Henry believed was an optic nerve.

The pièce de résistance was a gray, egg-shaped organ extracted from a victim's skull, lovingly sealed in a pickle jar, suspended in mineral oil. Henry was convinced the organ was the occipital lobe, the part of the brain that records, calibrates, and interprets visual information. The human camera. This little piece of neurological anatomy fascinated Henry so profoundly it was almost erotic.

In fact, at this very moment, Henry felt the urge to look at the thing . . . so he pushed aside the other souvenirs and carefully pulled the pickle jar from the back of the shelf. He held it up to the light, and he shoved his free hand down the front of his pants.

He was just beginning to masturbate when he heard the noise out in the corridor.

It came from far away, through the walls, from the depths of the building, a familiar squeak and maybe a yelp. The telltale sounds of other doors opening. It made Henry jump slightly. He wrestled his erection back into his pants, then put the jar back in the fridge.

Henry cautiously raised his door—the rusty pulleys screaming—and he peered around the corner of his unit. In either direction, beyond the fluorescent tubes, the corridor stretched into shadows. Henry looked around. To his left was the entrance. Nothing moving there. But to his right, maybe fifty yards or so away, at the far end of the hall, glowed a dull orange light. It reflected off a spray-paint-ravaged door, where the corridor made a ninety-degree turn.

Somebody was in the adjacent wing.

Swallowing his panic, Henry stepped into the hall, carefully lowering and locking the door to his unit. He took a deep breath and started toward the light.

As he approached the bend, he heard other noises. Some he recognized. Some he didn't. There came a low, intermittent buzzing noise drifting through the silence, and the low, distant drone of voices. Henry turned the corner and saw the slum

section stretching as far as he could see. The slum
section had earned its moniker for obvious reasons, but most tenants preferred to simply call it
the wing.

Henry stopped and gaped.

He had seen this corridor before, in all its ragged,
squalid pathos—the trash drifting against the walls,
and the endless rows of discount storage units with
their cheap particleboard doors resembling some
hellish dormitory—but he had never seen it this
crowded.

Crowding every other doorway, it seemed, was
a silhouette of a nodding junkie, or a zoned-out
prostitute, or some poor obese welfare mother with
her barefoot urchins scurrying around her. Times
were tough. People needed shelter. An electric bug
zapper crackled fifty feet away, and somewhere a
transistor radio sizzled with Mexican music. The
stench of urine and scat and scorched plastic—the
smell of discarded crack pipes—hung in the air.
Somewhere an unseen woman sobbed.

Henry strode down the hall, throwing furtive
glances into each open unit as he passed. He recognized many of these poor lost souls: the Circus
Lady, Mister Klister, Arturo the Graffiti Artist. Some
of them were asleep. Some might be dead, for all
Henry could tell.

In one unit cowered a waiflike young boy of no
more than seventeen, his long oily locks dangling
across his face as he crouched in the corner of a
squalid little hovel brimming with old magazines,
candy wrappers, and paperbacks. Garbed in a tie-
dyed T-shirt and jeans with more holes in them
than a slice of Swiss cheese, he trembled as he

crouched there in the dark. His name was Angel. Henry had always felt sorry for the kid, but never probed any deeper than hello.

"Be careful, Henry," the boy muttered under his breath, barely looking up from his rolling papers.

"Hi, Angel—whattya mean?"

"Just be careful."

"Of what?"

The young man shrugged and didn't say anything.

"Angel?" Henry stared at the waif. "Is there something wrong?"

No answer.

Henry just shrugged, turned, and started back toward the main wing, the crackle of the bug zapper making Henry's skull throb. Walking briskly now, fists clenched, a knife edge of nervous tension pressing against his sternum, he needed to get out of this place. Right away. He needed to get out of this forlorn, pathetic place.

And he almost made it. He almost reached the bend in the corridor, which was maybe ten feet away, when he heard the voice of the woman he knew as Nurse White.

"Hennnnnn-reeeeee."

The sultry croon drifted out from the shadows of an open unit to Henry's left.

Henry could not resist pausing, and gazing in at the shadows. "Hey, hello . . . uh . . . how's it going?"

"Better now that you're here, Henry."

He looked away, his face warming.

"Come a little closer," she coaxed from the dim light of a single forty-watt bulb. She was sitting in the corner of a cluttered storage unit, still dressed in her nursing whites, perched on a lawn chair in front of a battery-operated shortwave radio.

An incorrigible alcoholic, Nurse White was a middle-aged woman with enormous doughy white cleavage spilling out the top of her partially buttoned blouse. Her wrinkled eyes were caked with mascara, and her lips had so much scarlet-red lipstick she resembled a partially finished clown. "You want to hear something crazy?" she said dreamily, pointing at her shopworn radio, an empty bottle of cheap bourbon on its side at her feet. "I can get Paris, France, on that thing. Or maybe it's Paris, Texas."

Her brittle laughter could have peeled paint.

"I'm going to need to be going, Nurse White," Henry informed her.

"You need any help tonight?"

"No . . . no thanks. I'm all set."

"I can be very handy."

Henry blushed again. "That's great, I'm just . . . I'm all set tonight. Thanks."

"Just be careful, Henry."

Henry wondered what she meant. "I will. Thanks." He started to turn away.

"He's here tonight."

Henry froze. He turned and looked at the nurse. He knew exactly what she meant. "Excuse me?"

"He's here."

A long pause. "Are you sure?"

"Go look. His light's on."

Henry thought about it for a moment. "Nah, that's okay, I don't need to—"

All at once Henry stopped and stared at her, a realization sparking in the back of his mind. An idea. Why hadn't he thought of this earlier? Of course. *Of course!* The perfect man for the job, the perfect way to eliminate Special Agent Ulysses Grove!

"What is it, sweetheart?" Nurse White was watching him with a lascivious smile on her painted lips. "You look like you swallowed a canary."

"You know what . . . maybe I will go talk to him," Henry murmured.

He turned away from the nurse's lair, took a deep breath, then proceeded to the end of the corridor, where a large, scarred wooden door was hewn from filthy slats. Henry could barely see through the slats into the pitch-black emptiness of an ancient service elevator. He could smell the moldering, dusty stench of what lay below.

Every fiber of his being told him *not* to get in that elevator.

He reached down to the leather strap and yanked up the vertical slatted door. It rose on squealing pulleys. Henry took one last deep breath and stepped into the dilapidated conveyance, pulling the door down behind him. His heart hammered in his chest as he glanced around. The plank walls were lined with tattered canvas. He found the rusted iron lever and slammed it down . . . and he rode to the basement.

Some folks believed the subterranean sections of U-Store-It were once the labyrinthine honeycombs of a salt mine. Others claimed the original owners had civil defense in mind, especially since the place was built just after World War II. But all Henry knew was that the basement of the facility was a horrible place, and it seemed to have only a single tenant.

"Hello?"

Henry's voice echoed dully as the elevator reached the bottom, and the door jiggered opened on to a passageway. The stone walls were sweating. The air was thick with mold. A single bare light-bulb hung from the stalactites thirty feet away, casting a thin beam down the seemingly endless tunnel. Country music played somewhere.

"Hello? It's Henry. From upstairs. Unit 213!"

No answer, just the faint weeping of a steel guitar from some old Hank Williams tune crackling from a tiny speaker somewhere. It made Henry's flesh crawl as he moved deeper into the passageway. A bruise of light could be seen maybe fifty feet away where the wall opened up like a wound.

"Anybody home?"

Henry approached the opening and looked in at the darkness of the storage unit.

"Two thirteen? What the hell you want?"

The disembodied voice was deep and sepulchral, coarsened from a lifetime of Lucky Strikes and sour mash whiskey, cured in the twang of Kentucky coal mines. Henry could see the glowing orange tip of a cigarette floating in the dark, and not much else.

"I have a . . . I have . . . I . . ."

"Spit it out, son."

"I h-have a job for you." Henry's bladder threatened to loosen and give way. His heart galloped. "That is . . . if you're interested."

At last the shadows moved and coalesced, and a

large human form emerged into the yellow half-light. "Might be and might not be . . . keep talkin'"

They called him The Hillbilly, and he had been skulking around down here for as long as any other aboveground tenant could remember. He stood a full seven feet tall, and was gaunt as a scarecrow and covered with jailhouse tattoos. He stank of BO and had nicotine-yellowed skin. Above his five o'clock shadow and sunken cheeks were two mean little eyes as hard and black as Indian corn.

Henry swallowed his nerves. "There's s-s-some-body . . . s-somebody I need you to kill."

The Hillbilly smiled, revealing a row of green, rotting teeth like tiny tombstones. He pulled a massive bowie knife from his belt and commenced cleaning the dirt from under one of his yellow nails.

"I'm still listenin' . . ."

PART II
Through the Caul

"Good and evil lie close together."
                    —Lord Acton

NINE

The next day, Grove's little colonial two-story was awash in the laughter of women. Vida made a big deal out of how huge the baby had gotten in the months since she had laid eyes on him. For most of the afternoon Vida sat in the bentwood rocker in the living room and bounced the plump little infant on her knee. She cooed Swahili lullabies to him in a hoarse voice that sounded like Tiny Tim with a hangover, while Grove shuttled back and forth from the kitchen, doing the prep work on an elaborate dinner. Maura looked on with weary amusement, every once in a while asking Vida about life in Chicago, her diabetes, her parakeet, and her back problems.

Grove had a hard time concentrating on all this while he basted his Greek chicken. He could usually lose himself in his cooking—he was practically a three-star chef—but not today. Today he went through the motions of roasting the garlic and making the lemon-rosemary reduction and adding the cornmeal to the bits of rendered bacon while ruminating on the Mississippi Ripper. Gliane's rapid DNA tests on the St. Louis scene had been inconclusive. More tests were being conducted. Grove had been compulsively checking his e-mails all day, but nothing had come through yet. They would come soon enough, and they would match up with somebody, and Grove would find this mother. Very soon.

It was all Grove could think about anymore. Which was fine. Perfectly fine. As long as he didn't discuss it with his wife. He knew Maura was at her wits' end with Grove's workaholism, but that was okay because Grove could segregate the different parts of his life into compartments in his brain. When he was home, he would not talk about his work. He would keep his file folders locked up in his office credenza. All the gruesome crime scene photographs and diagrams of entry wounds and pathology reports and horrendous details of off-the-scale madness were tucked into secret slots. His family would never come into contact with it. His wife and child were safe. When Grove was home he was a doting father and a loving husband . . . and now a dutiful son.

"Mom?" He called out from the kitchen. "Can I get you a glass of wine?"

"In a minute, Uly," she replied. "Right now Granny must go out and smoke one of her nasty cigarettes."

Grove went over to the threshold of the living room and watched his rheumatoid mother heft herself out of the rocker and hand the baby back to Maura. Then Vida creaked and shuffled across

the room toward the front door. Grove wiped his
hands on a towel, then turned and followed his
mom outside.

They both sat down on a wrought-iron bench
that was nestled in a patch of morning glories. At
length Vida snubbed out her filterless Camel on
the bench's leg. Sparks fell into the flower bed. "I
have not been completely truthful with you, Uly, I
must tell you."

"Uh-huh."

"The truth . . ." Her voice trailed off. She seemed
to be groping for words.

"Uh-huh." Grove waited patiently. He didn't know
exactly what was coming . . . but he had an idea.

Best not to rush it.

At last Vida looked at him with her sad, soulful
eyes. "You are in danger, Mwana."

"Hmmm."

"I cannot explain how I know this, but I do, I
know you are in danger."

After a long pause Grove asked her if *that* was
the real reason she came down to Virginia, to warn
him.

"I am afraid so . . . yes."

Grove looked at her. "More visions?"

"Yes."

"Figured that was the case."

Vida looked worried. "After all we have been
through, you're still the great skeptic?"

"I didn't say that." Grove kept his gaze leveled at
her. "I'd be an idiot not to take your visions seriously, Mom. It's just that . . ."

Now it was Grove's voice that trailed off.

Vida waited. "Yes, Mwana?"

Grove looked into her eyes. "I'm supposed to be in danger, Mom. That's the way it works. We've talked about this. You've seen it. Whether it's my bloodline, my destiny, whatever. This is what I'm supposed to do."

"I never said—"

"There are people out there, Mom, people with one prime directive—"

"Uly—"

"These people are rare. Okay? Thank God. But they're out there. They feed off pain and misery and death. And they have to be weeded out and removed, and I know how to do it. I don't know why it happened but it did. I was born into this." He softened then, and he put his hand on her bony brown arm. "You were the one who taught me that."

Vida looked at him. "I understand all this, Mwana, believe me, I do."

"Then what's the problem?"

She licked her gray lips. "It is not only you who are in danger this time, Uly."

Grove stared at her. "What do you mean?"

"It's your family this time."

A stab of dread ran through Grove's guts like a hot poker. "My family?"

Vida nodded slowly, deliberately, her gray eyes glinting in the failing light.

TEN

The dinner hour came and went in a series of awkward silences, and once again the Grove household settled down for the night. By eleven o'clock, Ulysses Grove found himself alone in the kitchen, sitting at the island counter, drumming his fingers on the marble top, watching his cell phone as though it might sprout wings and take flight at any moment. It sat on the counter in front of him, next to the remnants of the night's dinner, the wadded napkins, the polenta-crusted plates, and water rings. Moonlight streamed in through the Levolor blinds and, under an adjacent counter, a single fluorescent tube added a cold blue cast to the room. Grove kept staring at that infernal wireless phone.

A watched pot never boils.

A watched cell phone never rings.

Grove was about to crawl out of his skin with nervous energy. Still nothing conclusive from Gliane at the Bureau lab. No results. No DNA matches. And now Vida had dropped her bombshell that Grove's family was in danger, and it might have something to do with the Mississippi Ripper, but she had been maddeningly vague. Grove had prodded her, demanded to know what the hell she was talking about. But all she could tell him was that it had come to her in a vision, another vision, something about a shadowy figure on the edge of a desert. How the hell was Grove supposed to use *that* little nugget of information? Go station a surveillance van at the local beach? Stake out the sand traps at the local golf course?

"What are you doing?"

Maura's voice startled him, and he turned with a jerk. "Oh . . . sorry . . . I was just . . . thinking."

"Thinking, huh?" She crossed the threshold of the kitchen, her bare feet padding silently on the cool adobe tiles. Maura was draped in an oversize fleece sweatshirt, nude underneath, and her porcelain pale flesh looked almost luminous in the gloom. "I was doing a little bit of that myself." She paused at the end of the island, hands on her bony hips. "Always a dangerous proposition, all this thinking going on."

Grove turned back to his vigil with the cell phone. "I promise you my mom'll only be here for a few days."

"She can stay as long as she likes." Maura rubbed her neck. "That's not the problem."

"There's a problem?"

She let out a big sigh. "God, no. What gave you that idea?"

"What's on your mind, Mo?"

"*That.*" She pointed at the cell phone as though

it were a termite infestation. "We've talked about this, Uly . . . how many times now?"

Grove shrugged. He knew this was coming, and yet he felt an odd sort of fatalistic calm. He had segregated these components of his life so rigidly that they now felt like different TV stations in his head. He had just been enjoying the Rattled Criminologist Show and now, as abruptly as the click of a remote, he was tuning into the Henpecked Husband Hour. He wiped his eyes. "Tell me we're not gonna go through this again."

"Correct me if I'm wrong, Ulysses." Maura spoke evenly, a trace of weariness in her voice. "We agreed the weeknights are ours."

"I'm here, aren't I?"

"Actually you're still on the banks of the Mississippi."

He looked at her. "You know how close I am to grabbing this guy?"

"And you *will*, I have no doubt."

"Then what's the problem?"

A long pause here, Maura letting out another sigh and trying to put something very thorny and complex into words. After a moment she said, "Maybe I'm feeling a little needy tonight." Her voice softened. She came around the counter, and she put a hand on Grove's tense shoulder. "Postpartum dragons rearing their ugly heads again maybe."

"Maura—"

"I know what I signed up for, Uly. I know you're going to catch this one." She came around behind him and put her arms around him. "Matter of fact, I'm planning on doing an article about it for Graydon over at *Vanity Fair*. It's not the job. You know I'm proud of the job. I'm just asking you to give it a break for one measly night."

Grove drank in her scent, the powdery melange of lotion, milk, patchouli oil, and sweat. He closed his eyes. Cradled her hands against his chest. "You're right. I'm sorry." He closed his eyes, leaning his head against hers. He could detect a faint hint of cigarette smoke. "You're absolutely right."

She gently turned him around, faced him. Her nipples had stiffened under her nightshirt. The gray cotton material clung to her now. "Aaron's out like a light," she said, reaching up and touching Grove's grizzled brown cheek. Her hand was warm on his face. Her breath smelled of toothpaste and musk. "And your mom's dozing in the rocker in his room."

"Mom's asleep?" Grove said, his nerve endings down in his solar plexus waking up.

"Dead to the world," Maura whispered, planting a kiss on Grove's neck, then under his ear.

"Hmmm."

"Let's turn the phones off," she uttered, nibbling Grove's earlobe, flicking her tongue across his ear.

"Best idea I've heard all day."

"You know me, always thinking."

"An honest-to-goodness genius." He put his hands under her sweatshirt and found her heavy bosom. He kissed her, his tongue probing, his hands cupping her warm, swollen breasts. His erection strained at the seams of his boxers. "I'm nominating you for the Nobel."

"Mmmmmmm . . . put the cell phone on vibrate,

Uly." A tiny, slender hand squeezed his crotch. "Then put it between my legs and call me."

One hand still on her breast, he fumbled blindly in the moonlight for the cell phone. He snatched it up and thumbed it into the silent mode.

Somewhere in the back of his mind he told himself he would check it before he fell asleep that night.

"Do me on the family room floor."

Their lips stayed locked as they edged their way across the kitchen wall, knocking a bowl of apples to the floor. Grove's shoulder nudged the wall phone off the hook. The receiver dangled as apples rolled across the tiles.

They stole down the basement steps, pulling off each other's clothes.

By 3:00 A.M. the stillness that precedes the dawn had plunged the house into a deep, dark well of silence. The drone of crickets and cicadas outside had dwindled now until only the ceaseless cycling of the central air conditioner stirred the tomblike quiet of the two-story.

On the second floor, three souls slumbered deeply, barely making breathing noises.

Maura, nestled in her customary tangle of sheets, lay in the darkness of the master bedroom. She dreamt a fragmented mosaic of images, sensations, fleshy moments from Aaron's birth; a strange nude shopping expedition; and a disturbing vignette of her husband accompanying her to a funeral of an old high school friend. At the visitation, Ulysses excused himself and went up to the altar, where the closed casket sat on its flowered bier. He glanced over his shoulder, and then inexplicably opened the coffin and climbed in. Instead of a body, there were stairs inside the enclosure, and Grove descended those stairs into the dark unknown until Maura finally rolled over and fell into sub-REM sleep.

Outside her door, down the second-floor hallway, in the darkness of the baby's room, two separate noises ebbed and flowed in syncopated rhythm: Vida's soft snore and little Aaron's quick, faint sleep breaths.

Swaddled in a Winnie-the-Pooh blanket, his downy hair shimmering in the moonlight streaming through the blinds, the baby was curled against the side of the crib, fetal style, tiny moist thumb in his mouth. Across the room, Vida slumped in the rocker, her leathery brown face lolled to one side. A Pennsylvania Dutch quilt tented her lap—Maura had draped it over her earlier that night—and now Vida's ancient adenoids and nasal passages burbled noisily as she slept.

Vida's dreams had a mythic quality, as though they were stanzas from a book, or dark biblical psalms. She dreamed of Africa, of her arid little village, of miles and miles and miles of dead, shriveled, black baobab trees. She dreamed of a demon on a black horse tearing through a hamlet of grass huts, trailing fire from its tail like golden ribbons. And she dreamed of her baby boy, her little beautiful baby boy, wandering into the dark distance of the Chalbi at sunset. It was a moment burned into her subconscious: the little brown child in a stained potato-sack tunic, head cocked high and brave, vanishing into a black hole of shadows as deep and opaque as a solar eclipse.

But at some point in this macabre recurring dream, for the first time ever, Vida caught a glimpse of something new: Just before disappearing into the void, the boy turned and glanced over his shoulder. For the briefest moment he gazed back at his dreaming mother.

The boy's face was inhuman: contorted with rage, cut with deep creases, eyes as yellow as a jackal's.

The image nearly rattled Vida awake, but not quite. She merely snorted, repositioned herself on the rocker, and burrowed her gray, nappy head deeper into the throw pillow that Maura had gently placed there hours earlier. Within minutes she was snoring again.

All of this went fairly unnoticed by the only semiconscious individual in the house.

Grove lay in his underwear, two stories down, on the sofa in the basement, tossing and turning in the silent shadows. His notebook was on the floor next to him. Only a couple of hours earlier, on that same sofa, he had made fierce love to his wife. Afterward they had lain there for quite some time, contentedly talking of ordinary things, household things, their bodies clammy, their sweat cooling in the dank cellar. Maura had finally excused herself to go check on the baby. Grove decided to open his notebook back up and make some more notes on the Ripper profile. When Maura didn't return, Grove figured she must have dozed off up there. Probably for the best. This way, Grove wouldn't bother her with his compulsive chicken scratching in his notebook.

Now, Grove had been wavering in and out of slumber for what seemed like an eternity.

Sleep had always come uneasily to Grove. When he was involved in a case, it came over him like a poorly tuned shortwave radio station, gradually washing over the noise of his thoughts in fits and starts. When he was off duty, or on vacation, or spending a rare holiday with his family, it came even harder. He would stare at the ceiling for hours, thinking of work, thinking of what he *should* be doing. The doctors have a phrase for people like Grove.

Slow sleepers.

Which is why he was partially awake when the first noise came drifting across the backyard.

At first, it hardly registered. In fact, Grove wasn't even sure how long he had been listening to it. It sounded like a branch tossing in the wind out in the woods beyond the property line or maybe leaves rustling. He tried to ignore it, rolling over and pressing his uncooperative eyes shut. But the noise persisted.

It was muffled and distant, but it seemed to be changing shape, coming into focus, refining itself. It had an awkward rhythm, like a faint snapping noise, a jittery tattoo . . . and as it clarified itself in Grove's groggy ears, he became aware of something vaguely troubling about it.

It seemed to be approaching the house.

ELEVEN

Looking back on that tense moment in the basement—specifically the point at which Grove recognized the noise was coming from the backyard—he would be hard pressed to precisely recount all the subsequent details. It was as though some silent alarm had sounded inside him, drowning all his other senses, even eliminating his awareness of the passage of time. It seemed like an eternity between the moment he sat up on the sofa . . . and the point at which he finally rose on creaking, sleep-numbed legs to pad over to the window.

There were two narrow, horizontal basement windows, both of them on the west wall facing the backyard, one at each end of the room. The windows were shuttered and positioned near the ceiling. Each looked out upon a little gravel concavity, which was slightly below ground level, drastically hindering the view across the lawn. Maura had planted a clutch of multicolored petunias in each window well, further obstructing the view. At night, shadows latticed the little wells. The flowers looked black and funereal.

Another eternity passed as Grove peered through the nearest window, seeing nothing but moonlight and dancing shadows out on the lawn, his head cocked with the rigor of a satellite dish, listening for that sound, that arrhythmic noise which had halted, for the moment at least. For an interminable length of time Grove stood wondering if he was hearing things. He wondered if the noise had been part of a dream. Maybe he was still dreaming. He didn't want to turn on a light. Something told him to stay immersed—at least for the moment—in the safe anonymity of darkness.

How long he stood there at the window, waiting for that maddening noise to return, would never truly be known. Maybe five minutes, perhaps less.

Grove rarely lost track of time like that. In fact, if pressed, he could recall only two or three times in his career that he got so panicked or involved in the moment that he felt time slow down to a crawl. It happened in Alaska a couple of years ago, on a mountainside, when Grove finally came face to face with Richard Ackerman. Ackerman had been crazy as a loon, but also had displayed something behind his eyes which Grove had come to think of as Factor X.

Factor X could turn a meek, persnickety accountant like Ackerman into a dangerous psychotic. Or transform a frightened Tulane grad student like Michael Doerr into a ritualistic killer. Factor X existed, it seemed, solely in order to turn people into puppets, make them perform off-the-scale evil acts. A Catholic might have called it a demon . . . but Grove believed that such an assessment was

too easy. He believed that the jury was still out
about Factor X's true nature.

Maybe this was why Grove, over the past two years,
had become such a homeschooled expert in de-
monology and gnostic depictions of evil. After por-
ing over the ancient texts, from the Greeks to the
medieval period, he moved onto the modern
acolytes such as Aleister Crowley, Bertrand Traviere,
and Winston Baines Walker. Grove then created a
virtual database of occult connections to the modern serial murderer. He saw consistencies in Old
Testament passages about evil recurring down
through the centuries, in the Kabbalah's discussions
of shattered psyches and violent internal schisms,
and even in Islam, in the *jahannam*, with its complex political view of evil incarnate.

Simply put, it seemed to Grove there existed a
monolithic-antagonist—an alter ego that resurfaced
down through the ages and hijacked the weak—
that ultimately focused its bloody exploits toward
some esoteric, cosmic purpose. Grove could even
see evidence of this in the feverish paintings of
Hieronymus Bosch and William Blake, the flayed
bodies of the damned and the contorted expression on the faces of the fallen angels. The demon
face was so familiar to Grove. It was the face of utter
bloodlust—cruel, cold, impassive—possessing an in-
satiable hunger. He had seen it on the face of more
than one killer in his day, and he believed he might
have once even worn the expression himself.

In Alaska, when Grove had managed to become
infected by this powerful force—or at least that was
the consensus of those who had been present—he
had ended up in the mental ward. That was an-

other occasion during which Grove had lost track of time. He had floated in a dark abyss inside himself for nearly a week, until his mother and a small team of clergy and spiritualists had exorcised this new personality—*or whatever it was*—out of Grove. But the experience had changed Grove, galvanized him, made him realize his true nature: he was the polar opposite of Factor X.

He was Factor *Y*.

And now it felt as though another battle between the two polarities seemed to be brewing. It felt as though a horrible, inexorable dance was about to begin. Grove felt it in the pulse of his blood, the quickening beat of his heart, the humming in his bones.

And right now, an invitation to that very dance was out in the woods behind his home, coming this way, coming toward his house.

The noise had returned. Closer. This time it was unmistakable: the snapping of a twig. Footsteps. Grove stiffened, and felt the skin of his neck prickle. He peered out the window and saw what was making the noise.

A man with a gun emerging from the woods. Coming this way.

Maura stirred. Still half asleep, still in the throes of that weird dream of her husband vanishing down the black void of an empty coffin, she turned onto her side. The blurry, glowing numerals of a digital clock appeared in the gloom. They seemed to float in the void: 3:13 A.M.

She swallowed an acrid taste in her mouth, and

rubbed her eyes. She looked at the clock again. 3:13? Had she only been asleep for a couple of hours? She felt as though she had been sleeping all night. Had she heard a noise? Was Aaron crying? She had no idea what had awakened her.

She rolled onto her back and stared at the ceiling, trying to gather her bleary equilibrium. The room was bathed in shadow, almost completely dark except for the dull red glow of the digital clock and a strand of moonlight adhering to the ceiling like a brushstroke.

Gradually the events of that evening returned to her in stages. She remembered making love to Ulysses in the basement, and she remembered putting the quilt on Vida and kissing the slumbering Aaron good night. She looked at the other side of the bed. The huge queen-size comforter and sheet were still tucked neatly into the mattress.

Where the hell was Ulysses?

Maura remembered lying with him down there in the afterglow, softly talking, then telling him she was going to go check on Aaron. But then what? Didn't he say he was going to make a few notes and then come up to bed? Or was she supposed to come back downstairs? She couldn't remember. She supposed he was still down there; probably dozed off at the desk.

Rolling back onto her side, she stared at the clock and considered getting up to pee. Her bladder was full, but she was so exhausted she could barely move. Ever since she had given birth to Aaron—a difficult cesarean—her energy level had been nil. Unfortunately her bladder had also been compromised by the incision, and she knew if she didn't get up right now and go to the bathroom she would wet the bed.

At last she climbed out of bed, then trundled across the room and out the door.

When Grove, now dressed in his pants but still barefoot, reached the master bedroom on the second floor, he took a deep breath before pushing open the door. He knew that Maura was a light sleeper. The slightest creak would wake her. But he also knew that time was of the essence. The man he saw only moments ago, emerging from the woods behind the house, had been moving slowly yet steadily toward the two-story with obvious malice. It had been too dark to make out the man's features, or to see much of what he was wearing, but the object cradled in his arms was unmistakable: either a cut-down shotgun or some hot, filed-down assault rifle.

On one level, it seemed preposterous to Grove that somebody would be sneaking up on him in this fashion, guerrilla-style, in the dark of night. Burglars don't operate like that. Burglars will case a place, and then look for a window—both of opportunity and of egress—through which to slip in and out unnoticed. Veteran burglars, in fact, usually don't even carry firearms. In the state of Virginia, breaking and entering is a fairly mild class 3 felony . . . unless the perpetrator is armed with a deadly weapon, which bumps the penalty up to a class 2. This man coming toward Grove's house was definitely *not* a burglar. Just exactly *what* he was, would remain undetermined for the next few critical minutes.

The reality of this situation, though, was that

Grove did not have the luxury or the time to rumi-
nate on the intruder's nature or motives. Too
much was at stake. The clock was ticking. *It is not
only you who are in danger this time, Uly.*

He pushed the door open and glanced around
the dark bedroom and stopped cold. The bed was
empty. The baby monitor was off. Maura was gone,
the blankets tossed and shoved toward the foot of the
bed. Grove stared, momentarily paralyzed. His heart
raced. For some reason, right at that moment, it
didn't occur to him that she could be in the bathroom. Perhaps it was the adrenaline humming in his
system. Or maybe it was the urgent need to get to
the closet.

For a brief moment he considered calling out
for her, but nixed the idea when he realized it would
cause more problems than it solved. It would not
only wake the rest of the household but also alert
the intruder.

Grove had two guns. One of them—a Charter
Arms .357 Magnum Tracker with a 6-inch barrel—
was at his office at Quantico, quaintly locked up in
an antique glass case behind his credenza. His co-
workers in the Behavioral Science Unit often teased
him about that, calling him Barney Fife, claiming
that locking up his gun like that looked like something out of a Norman Rockwell painting. But they
didn't know what the gun meant to Grove. It had
been a gift from his late partner, Terry Zorn. Grove
owed his life to that gun. He had cornered Richard
Ackerman on the summit of Mount Cairn with that
gun. The speed-loader had frozen that day, and in
a desperate gambit Grove had literally hurled the
weapon at his adversary.

Later, the CSI unit had retrieved the handgun from a rocky buttress and eventually returned it to Grove.

The second gun in Grove's collection was safely locked away in his bedroom closet. It lay in a storage case, unloaded, oiled, and disassembled.

Grove padded across the dark bedroom and threw open the pocket door, revealing the spacious closet full of tailored finery. He and Maura shared the large walk-in space, and Grove had to reach up and push aside the hatboxes and the Pendaflex files of old letters to get to the black vinyl briefcase pushed against the back wall.

The gun was inside, broken down into pieces, each metal component nestled in its spongy nest. Huddling in the darkness, heart thumping, the floor cold on the soles of his feet, Grove uprooted the grip from the case, the odor of machine oil wafting up at him. The barrel felt like ice in his clammy hands. The snapping noises seemed outrageously loud in the silent closet as Grove assembled the .44 Special Bulldog. His hands did not shake, and he remembered the procedure better than he would have guessed, but still, the entire process, from the moment he reached the closet to the moment he got the weapon put together, chewed up at least two minutes. Ordinarily that would be pretty impressive for a nonshooter like Grove, a man with one blind eye, who hadn't touched a gun in months, but tonight the minutes were deadly. In less than two minutes the intruder could reach the back wall of the house. Another two and he could be inside.

Grove spun around with the .44 in one hand and the speed-loader in the other.

Maura was standing in the doorway, agape. "Where *were* you?"

"Listen, uh, listen—" He turned and glanced around the room, his mind racing. What should he tell her? Did he want her scared and alert . . . or oblivious and quiet?

"I thought you were gonna come back up," she said in a groggy wheeze, apparently still half asleep, coming toward him.

"Listen—"

"What is *that*?"

"Okay, now let's not—"

"Is that a *gun*?"

"Maura—"

"What the hell is going on?" She had stopped midway across the room, her pale green eyes looking like Buffalo nickels in the gloom. "Why do you have a gun?" She swallowed hard, and Grove took a step toward her, and she backed away. "Why are you holding a gun?"

"Okay, I'm going to need you to stay very quiet."

"What's going on? *What the hell's going on?*" Her voice had raised an octave. Her fists clenched.

"Listen to me, listen to me." Grove went over to her, shoving the gun down the back of his belt. "It's gonna be okay, everything's okay."

"Then why do you have a gun?"

"Take it easy, come on." He put an arm around her. "It's probably nothing."

"Don't patronize me, goddamnit! Is it a burglar?"

"I don't know yet, I'm going to need you to stay here, and don't move no matter what."

"Did you call 911?"

"Maura, just stay here!" He went over to the door and locked it from the inside. "I'll be right back."

"Wait!"

He was already through the door, and he turned and quickly pulled it until it clicked.

Then he quickly crept down the hallway to the nursery. A quick glance inside confirmed that his mother and the baby were still asleep, safe and oblivious.

He locked the inner lock, then pulled the door shut until it clicked.

Then he headed for the stairs, pulling the .44 from his belt and thumbing back the hammer.

TWELVE

Outside, in the mist, the man in black reached the southeast corner of the two-story and paused with his back pressed against the flashing. He was breathing hard. Hard and loud.

He stood there for a moment, gathering his thoughts, cursing his forty-seven-year-old body, his girth, his two-pack-a-day habit. Once upon a time he had the ability to slip up on a domicile with the stealth and silence of a panther. Not now. Not anymore. Too many highballs, too many burritos. The man in black was an old shit now with a paunch and bursitis in one shoulder and clogged arteries. Now all he had left was the longing, and the piss and vinegar to kill without hesitation.

Glancing over his shoulder, he quickly surveyed the back of the house. Everything was still and silent. So far, so good. Overhead, the dead night sky was low and dark with very little moonlight. This was good. The darkness would help. It would help with the element of surprise.

Darkness was comforting to the man in black.

He yanked the cocking mechanism on the cut-down .45 caliber rifle. It made a dull *clunk* that sent shivers up his back. The Ingram M10 was a very heavy weapon—over ten pounds fully loaded—and he had to grip it with both hands to keep it level. The magazine had thirty rounds in it. He raised the bead to his eyes and kept it trained on the back door . . . as he began to move.

It took Grove maybe ninety seconds to get back down the stairs and across the first floor to the rear of the house. During that brief transitional period, padding across cold hardwood floors, Grove found his mind racing with panicky undercurrents.

He searched his memory for the last time he had fired his weapon in the line of duty. Was it in New Orleans a year ago? Profilers rarely pulled the trigger on anybody. Profilers were desk jockeys, professors, consultants picking through the aftermath of crime and delivering PowerPoint presentations. Grove found himself wondering, after all the therapy and medication of the last year, whether he still had the steely nerves to throw down on somebody.

As Grove neared the kitchen, he lowered himself to a semi-duckwalk, staying behind the center island for cover, staying just under the angle of the kitchen windows. He gripped the Bulldog one-handed, steadying himself with his free hand on the floor. The Bulldog was a single-action pistol—meaning it required no cocking, just a simple squeeze of the trigger to fire. Grove had forgotten about this in all the excitement, and already had the hammer cocked.

The .44 was now hair-trigger ready.

Grove peered over the top of the kitchen counter. The windows revealed nothing but a black shroud of a sky and the distant tops of basswood trees and hickories swaying in the predawn breeze. Grove held his breath. Waited. Watched. Nothing out of the ordinary yet. *Where the hell did that son of a bitch go?*

Right then, an errant thought crossed Grove's mind with the suddenness of a circuit breaker snapping: *9-1-1*. Maura had asked him if he had called 911. Neurons fired in his brain as he thought of this and realized it was a good question. He then realized that his house's phone had been off the hook and his cell phone had been in silent mode since eleven o'clock, and now something about it tweaked at his memory.

A shadow moved across the windows.

Time stuttered again like a broken clock as Grove watched the shadow slide toward the back door. Grove raised the gun. He leaned around the edge of the island and drew the front sight down on the vertical screen of the back door.

The figure appeared outside the door.

Grove held his breath. He cocked his head so that his one good eye was staring down the muzzle, and aimed the tiny blade of steel at the end of the Bulldog at the figure. The sight was pointing directly at the figure's heart—a kill shot.

Grove curled a finger around the trigger . . . but in that millisecond before he squeezed he heard other noises out in the backyard.

Radio sounds?

* * *

The gray-haired man in the London Fog coat, three hundred yards to the west, pacing near a government Humvee, lost his patience finally and thumbed the walkie-talkie's send button. "B-Team, move in! Now! Move in!"

"Copy that," came the crackling reply, and the deeper shadows to the east began to shift.

Bushes trembled, and limbs bullwhipped with movement, as the Tactical group started toward Grove's house. The gray-haired man chewed his fingernail as he watched the reconnaissance unfold in time-lapse slow motion.

"Engage only on my signal!" he barked into the radio.

"Copy."

This all happened within the space of seconds. But just as Grove had temporarily lost his sense of time, the man in the topcoat had lost track himself. He paced and paced, his thumb poised on the radio.

He could see personnel fanning out through the woods, slithering toward the clearing along Grove's property line. They looked like ghosts, like moving shadows against the black canvas of trees and foliage. Twigs snapped. Fabric rustled. Breaths puffed.

A Cyclone fence jangled, and the team finally emerged into Grove's backyard with weapons raised.

The night seemed to hold its breath.

At that moment three things happened very quickly inside Grove's kitchen. One: Grove heard another noise behind him that pierced his aware-

ness of the footsteps and radio voices outside. It
was Maura. Gasping. She had just crossed the living room, and now stood in the kitchen archway in
her underwear and nightshirt. Taking one look at
the armed man outside the screen door, she had
sucked in a startled breath and then stood there,
paralyzed with terror.

Two: The man in black opened the screen and
kicked the door in with a single, efficient slam of
his jackboot. It was done with such precision and
decisiveness that the metal hinges simply popped
like corks. The door slapped down hard, thunder-
clapping on the floor in a puff of plaster dust.

Three: The Bulldog went off, the muzzle flashing in the darkness.

The blast went into the intruder's shoulder.
Maura screamed, and the man in black jerked
backward, pinwheeling through the gaping doorway in a gout of smoke. His gun went flying, then
clattered to the tiles.

He landed outside with an anguished grunt on
the flower bed next to the porch.

Silence crashed down on the house.

Whether or not Grove willfully fired at the man
in black would be the topic of much speculation—
even between Grove and Maura—for months to
come. The Bulldog's hair trigger responds to the
slightest pressure or the minutest movement and,
of course, there was the handicapped eye. There-
fore, the debate would be relegated to Inconclusive Evidence for the foreseeable future. The
question of intent was mitigated by the fact that

Grove, only seconds later, crouched in the darkness beside the counter, head spinning, began to realize that things might not be as they appeared.

Right now: Ears ringing, his good eye momentarily flash-blind, mouth dry from the adrenaline, he turned and rushed over to Maura, who still stood stone-frozen in the archway.

"Down! Down—get down!"

Grove reached her and literally lifted her wan, hundred-and-ten-pound body off the floor. Then he lurched behind an armchair in the living room and laid her on the carpet. She was kicking and yelling in garbled, inarticulate yelps by that point— a mixture of rage and panic.

More figures had arrived at the back door by then. They came systematically—two on each flank with government-issue assault weapons. They wore the standard black Kevlar vests and paramilitary-style night suits. Thin beams of infrared light pierced the cordite, gunsmoke, and dust. A leader called out over Maura's protests.

"STAND DOWN, STAND DOWN! HOLD YOUR FIRE!"

Grove stayed crouched and coiled over Maura like an animal protecting its brood.

"EVERYBODY IN THE HOUSE—I WANT TO SEE HANDS UP AND WEAPONS ON THE FLOOR, PLEASE!"

Grove could not move.

"NOW, GODDAMNIT, OR WE DROP EVERYBODY WITH A PULSE!"

At last Grove managed to slide the Bulldog across the floor and on to the kitchen tiles.

A beam of red light glimmered off it.

The leader, a broad black man, roared into the kitchen with his M10 assault rifle nose up, boots squeaking, legs wide and bent at the knees. He came over to the archway and made eye contact with Grove and Maura in the living room. "DOWN ON YOUR STOMACH NOW! HANDS LACED BEHIND YOUR NECK! NOW! NOW! NOW!"

"It's okay, Mo, it's okay—"

"DO IT!"

Grove did as he was told. He could smell the old carpet fibers like moldy hay, and he tasted the metallic tang of blood in his mouth where he had bitten his tongue at some point in the struggle. Maura lay next him. She was shivering or crying or both, Grove couldn't tell which.

The sound of the Bulldog's cylinder cracking open, bullets spilling on the tiles, bouncing like coins.

"CLEAR!"

Grove heard others approaching out in the backyard. Police radios. Somebody calling for a paramedic. The big black man with the assault rifle was standing over him now. "You're Agent Grove? Ulysses Grove?"

"That's right," Grove grunted into the carpet.

"What the hell is going on?" Maura's voice was reedy and thin.

"You can put your hands down now. Sorry about that. Is there anyone else in the house?"

Grove sat up, then helped Maura into a sitting position, then gaped up at the SWAT leader. "Are you ATF?—Tactical? What are you doing?"

"Sir, is there anyone else in the house?"

"No, I mean yes . . . just the baby and my mother. Upstairs."

"Is that them?"

Grove swallowed hard and gazed across the living room. At the base of the staircase, Vida was standing with the baby in her arms, looking aghast. Grove nodded, then turned toward the back door. The man in black was still lying in the flower bed, a paramedic administering CPR.

The medic pumped the man's chest, while strands of saliva glistened, and radios crackled, and voices hollered in the distance.

"Oh, no—"

"Agent Grove—"

Grove rose on his wobbly legs and started toward the back door.

THIRTEEN

"Don't tell me . . ." Grove approached the man in the flower bed. The man lay there in his black field garb, a paunchy, middle-aged Tactical officer with a receding hairline. He looked like a decent man, probably a father. A small black starburst scorched his shoulder. Grove felt his gorge rising. "Don't tell me . . . shit . . . *don't tell me.*"

The officer coughed. Once, twice . . . choking on his own saliva . . . but alive.

Grove's eyes welled up with relief.

"He's back," the paramedic commented under his breath, looking into the man's eyes with a penlight. "Normal sinus rhythm."

Grove knelt down by the man. "Thank God, thank God, thank God."

"Get this goddamn thing off me," the wounded man in the petunias groaned.

"Dig the slug out, somebody," a voice came from behind Grove.

"Marty, get the slug out and bag it," somebody

else ordered. Another balding man dressed in street clothes—a sport coat with a CSI tag hanging around his neck—suddenly appeared in Grove's peripheral vision, snapping on a pair of surgical gloves, opening a Swiss Army knife. More figures were emerging from the woods to the north, a few lab techs, another Tactical group, a few guys in suits. The noise rose around the house. Grove wiped his eyes as the balding man knelt down by the flowers and ripped open the Tactical officer's shirt, popping three of the top buttons.

The Kevlar vest underneath was dimpled with a tiny puck of charred steel. It looked like a miniature silver egg nestled in a tiny crater. The tip of the pocketknife rooted at it for a moment until it finally wiggled free.

The slug went into a Ziploc bag.

Grove helped the man in the flower bed sit up. "You okay, brother?"

"Little bruised, little pissed at myself . . . but fine." The paunchy sharpshooter looked as though he were trying to catch his breath. He shrugged off his heavy, armored vest. He rubbed his sore collarbone. "That's the second time that goddamn thing has saved my ass."

"I never should have—"

"Don't sweat it."

"I didn't realize—"

"Forget it." The officer waved it off. Wiped his face. Took a deep breath. "Feces occurs."

"Yeah, feces occurs," Grove concurred. "What the hell are you guys doing rushing my house?

The Tactical officer took a steadying breath.

"Threat of an Unknown Subject. Your phone was off the hook."

Grove looked at him. "Unknown what?"

"Obviously we take that shit seriously."

Grove was nonplussed. "Threat of an Unknown Subject? You mean—"

"Agent Grove?"

The voice came from behind him, the baritone growl of the group leader.

Grove spun around and looked directly into the cold, implacable brown eyes of the broad-shouldered black man. Grove gave him a deferential nod. "Yes, sir?"

"This is just a formality," the big man said, almost apologetically, pulling a nylon strap from his belt. "Due to the shot fired, gonna have to ask you to go ahead and put your arms behind your back."

"Excuse me?"

"Gonna have to cuff you up."

"Um, yeah, okay . . . yeah." Grove complied, turning his back to the leader, crossing his wrists against his tailbone.

Grove felt the cold nylon ribbon lick across his skin as the leader started fitting the shackle. Grove tried to gather his thoughts. He still wasn't thinking straight, his mind still revving from the assault on his house. *Threat of an Unknown Subject?* Were they talking about the Mississippi Ripper? And what kind of threat?

Glancing over his shoulder at the group leader, Grove started to ask, "Does this mean—?"

A voice called out from the lawn. "What the hell are you idiots doing?"

Grove looked out at the yard and saw a group of suits approaching across dew-slick grass. They came like a brigade of bankers in their expensive raincoats and Florsheim wingtips, all of them unfamiliar to Grove . . . except one. The one out in front. The one with the graying temples and aging athlete's build, the one with the angry gait of a college football coach whose team just fumbled . . . *that one* was instantly recognizable.

"Take those goddamn things off him!" Tom Geisel ordered as he approached the porch.

"Sorry, I was just—"

"You were what? You were *what?*" The Section Chief reached Grove and touched his shoulder reassuringly. "This man was protecting home and hearth, and now you're gonna bust him? Take those goddamn cuffs off him."

"No problem. They're off." The big man flung the nylon strap across the porch. It landed in a hedge of roses. The leader backed off.

Grove looked at Geisel. "You want to tell me what's going on, Tom?"

The Section Chief rubbed his neck, glancing across the porch at the ruined back door. Inside the dim shadows of the house, Maura, Vida, and the baby were barely visible, huddling in the kitchen, watching wide-eyed at all the lights and noise. A uniformed policewoman stood nearby, watching over the traumatized women.

Geisel turned back to Grove. "You're not going to like it, kiddo. Let's go take a walk."

FOURTEEN

In the hardwood forest north of Grove's subdivision, rays of early morning sunlight threaded down through the gauze of mist and cobwebs clinging to the trees. It was still cool in the shadows of those ancient hickories and walnuts, and the air smelled new and bitter and green along the narrow hard-dirt path. Grove wished he had brought along a jacket—he still wore only a T-shirt and jeans—but the current conversation was keeping his embattled brain occupied enough to distract him from the chill. "This contract, the original conversation that took place . . . what prison was it?"

"The Bureau snitch was from Southern Illinois Max in Carbondale," Geisel replied, his collar turned up. He was using a dry kindling branch as a walking stick. "But we don't think the original conversation happened there. We're leaning toward Fenster in Missouri."

"Missouri?"

Geisel nodded. "We're thinking it's somebody

with an old grudge. Anatoly, maybe. Kaminsky's at Fenster, Ulysses. Maybe it's somebody from the old Joliet gang."

Grove didn't say anything.

Geisel went on: "They go to some wiseguy at Fenster, and then the news spreads across the system through trustees and guards."

Grove nodded. "Great fun for the skells and lifers, news like that."

"Can you imagine? Gossip like that? Makes a great late-night kibbitz around the old crack pipe."

Grove walked silently for a moment. "What about the Ripper?"

A long pause, then a grudging nod from Geisel. "We thought about that, Ulysses. It makes geographical sense but does it fit the profile?"

"Absolutely it fits. This is exactly the kind of thing our boy would do."

"How's that?"

Grove looked at him. "This guy is about control, Tom. It's all about the grand gesture with this guy. Something like this . . . ?"

"I don't know."

"Trust me, boss. This is our boy. I feel it in my bones, I really do."

Geisel smiled then. Not a mirthful grin, but one filled with exhaustion. "Far be it from me to argue with your bones."

Grove walked a little bit more, thinking. His stomach clenched. "Fenster has video in its lounge, I assume?"

"Yes and no. We got all kinds of surveillance tapes, but they're sporadic. Lots of dead air, dropouts."

"Lemme guess, the pen's underfunded. Tax cuts chewing into resources."

Geisel shrugged. "We're still reviewing tapes but it's not looking good."

"I assume we're interviewing guards at Fenster?"

"Yep, same problem. They're stretched thin."

Grove let out a pained sigh. "I hope we're sweating the likely candidates."

"You mean at Fenster?"

Grove nodded. "Scumbags, wiseguys, and such."

"We're already compiling a list: cowboys, meth heads, independent contractors. Anybody you might hire for some wet work."

"Bill Menner out of St. Louis would be a good guy to do the Q&A."

"Yeah, well. Prisons aren't the only ones with funding cutbacks."

Another sigh from Grove. "Lemme guess, you got Menner pullin' OT already."

"He's into golden time, Uly. I got sixteen field offices in the central Midwest working a grand total of thirty-four active cases. And that's just the central Midwest."

They walked in brisk silence for a moment.

Grove gazed up at the steeples of white pine and hickory overhead, the early morning sunlight slicing down through the leafy netting of branches and cobwebs, but Grove was hardly able to focus on it. His midsection burned with anger, his gut squeezing and turning. The break in the Ripper case that he was waiting for finally presents itself and all Geisel can do is talk budgetary cutbacks? It was baffling, and yet there was another layer to it, a deeper vein of outrage, cured in an autoclave of fear: harm was seeking his *family* now. Just as Vida had prophesied. His wife, his little baby. His *son*. The thought of it ignited a column of flame up his gorge, so hot and intense that he felt dizzy, nauseous. The footpath wavered in his vision for a moment.

"You okay?"

Grove snapped out of his momentary daze. "Yeah, sorry . . . I'm good."

Geisel said something else but Grove didn't register it. He was considering something important now, something that had been in the back of his mind since they had embarked on their little walk a half hour ago. This was war now. No holds barred. He had to protect his family with any means necessary—including any fancy African hoodoo he might be able to drum up.

This made him think of one of the most interesting case studies he had run across in his recent, obsessive research—a reference that would forever be etched in his memory. It was a twelfth-century volume complete with startling woodcuts called *Locus Pugnae* by a monk who called himself Brother Gueriana. Loosely translated as *The Battlefield*, the book told of an invisible, apocalyptic struggle between two fallen angels. The illustrations depicted lurid figures locked in mortal combat in the wilderness, in wastelands of razed villages, on mountains of burned corpses. The text and pictures had haunted Grove to the point that he had started dreaming of these eternal combatants—seeing them, of course, only through his blind eye.

"You okay with that?" Geisel's voice broke the spell.

"Okay with what?"

"The safe house. WITSEC. We're all set." Geisel gave Grove a sidelong glance. "You didn't hear a word I said, did you?"

WITSEC was the federal witness protection program which the Bureau used for informants, families of suspects, and witnesses in ongoing investigations who were under the threat of retaliation. At-risk families were whisked away to secret locations across the country and given new identities. Sometimes they stayed in the program until the perceived threat was neutralized. Sometimes for the rest of their lives. Grove had used the program on several occasions for his own witnesses and snitches. But he had never dreamed he would be a participant himself.

Grove looked at his boss. "WITSEC is a good idea, Tom. For Maura and Aaron . . . and Mom, too, maybe."

Geisel seemed relieved. "Great, great. You can rest assured, Uly, we'll get this guy. You'll be back home in a matter of months."

"I don't think you heard me, Tom. I said 'For Maura and Aaron.'"

"What are you talking about?"

Grove stopped walking. Geisel stopped as well. The two men looked at each other.

Grove managed a humorless smile. "I know you want me to go in, too . . . but I've got a better idea."

FIFTEEN

A thousand miles to the west, the gaunt, sallow-skinned man known to his acquaintances only as the Hillbilly stood in an airless chamber lined with moldy cardboard, trying to ignore the voices in his head.

(Kill 'em all!)

"Shut up," he murmured to the voice, and continued preparing his hit kit, sorting through the various rusty blades and duct-taped handguns with nicotine-stained fingers. The instruments of death were spread out in front of him on a length of black canvas beneath a narrow slab of cracked, dirty mirror.

The mirror was framed in a cheap particleboard frame, and hung off a bent nail. The Hillbilly had found the mirror a little over a year ago in a Dumpster behind the storage facility, and had brought it down to his lair on a whim. He didn't much like looking at himself. He had a harelip from a congenital defect. And his thinning hair, recently dyed black, looked ridiculous. In the unflattering light of that single bare forty-watt bulb, which hung to his right, he looked freakish.

That's exactly what you are—a freak!

"Shut up!"

He shook his head violently as though shaking off a cloud of killer bees.

But the voice was right. It was always right. He had felt like some kind of freak for most of his life, ever since he was a teenager and grew to the freakish height of six feet, nine inches. All the high school kids back in Arkansas had started calling him names at that point: Stretch, Stick Man, Beanpole, Freak. It didn't matter though; he had never cared about schooling.

His size certainly came in handy years later in the joint. The brothers left him alone, and the Aryan Nation welcomed him with open arms. They needed a guy like him, a guy who could take a life with his bare hands without hesitation, a guy who was an equal-opportunity killer. Men, women, children—it didn't matter—the Hillbilly was good at one thing, and that thing paid well.

Now he was about to take off on his biggest target yet—a goddamn G-man—and the risks were much bigger, the job more complicated. But what the hell did the Hillbilly care? The payoff was a lot bigger as well. He was going to make a wagonload of bread for this job, and that's all he cared about.

Kill the fed! Spread his brains on toast and eat him!

He carefully rolled the weapons up in the black cloth, and tied them securely: an old switchblade, three bowie knives for up-close situations, a cheap .38 Smith & Wesson for point-blank head shots, and an old Army .45 with a homemade suppressor for making sure the son of a bitch was dead. He shoved the weapons in a tattered duffel bag, along with a change of clothes, then turned off the light, and ambled out of the locker toward the elevator.

A gangly tattooed freak in a cowboy hat can raise a few suspicious glances from passersby. That's why the Hillbilly usually only came out of the warehouse after dark, when it was easier to blend in with the weirdos and whores and street scum that came out from under their rocks every night. But right now, he was emerging into the hard, pale sunlight of a Missouri morning, and it made him blink and squint just to see his hand in front of his face.

He crossed the adjacent bean field on foot, the sun beating down on his neck, the wind smelling of cow shit, hot tar, and garbage. He reached the nearest train station in less than half an hour. Located just north of Pickman Creek bridge, the Amtrak depot was a lonely brick outpost with a single bench and a public restroom.

Sitting there, waiting for the 11:15 to arrive, the Hillbilly thought he heard a strange noise around the corner of the building. Like whispers, and maybe the scuff of a shoe. Could somebody be following him? He went over to the northeast corner of the depot, and he peered around the edge of the building and saw nothing but weeds and trash and a few discarded tires. Could it be that idiot Splet?

Not now—Not yet!

The Amtrak train bellowed into the station a few minutes later, and the Hillbilly climbed on board with his duffel bag slung over his back and his flask of whiskey sloshing in his pocket. People stared as he searched for a seat. He finally found one in the rear of the last car and settled in as the train barreled eastward on its clattering course.

Eastward toward Virginia.

"I understand about the safe house, I do . . . I understand all that, Uly." Maura was sitting on a blackened stump at the edge of the front yard where the lawn service had been wrestling with a stubborn tree that had died the previous summer of Dutch elm disease. The afternoon had turned blustery and overcast. She wore dark sunglasses and a denim jacket, and compulsively dragged on a Camel Light between sentences. "I just want to hear from you why you're not coming with us."

Grove, garbed in his FBI jacket and beret, paced across the grass in front of her, hands in his pockets, as Behavioral Science Unit task force members went in and out of the front of the house. Most of the operatives wore standard-issue Bureau windbreakers, and most carried computer equipment and roadcases filled with Tactical gear. "I'm not going to lie to you," Grove said at last. "It's all a long shot but I'm staying for a reason."

She looked up at him. "Let me guess."

"Maura—"

"You're the bait again."

"Mo—"

"Here we go."

Grove stopped pacing and looked at her. "I'm going to be surrounded by the—"

"I don't want to hear it." She waved his words away like a noxious breeze in her face. "I don't want to hear how safe it is, and how you're going to be in the rear and out of the line of fire, and all that *bullshit.*"

A moment of strained silence, then Grove nodded. "Okay, straight talk."

"Go on."

"I need you to go to the safe house right away because we are putting out the welcome mat for this guy."

"So I was right."

Grove swallowed his nerves. "Yeah . . . we're thinking maybe he'll try to put the tag on me here, and we can track him back to the source."

Maura smoked and thought about it for a second. Grove noticed her hands were shaking. Finally she said, "You have a child now, Ulysses."

"I'm aware of that fact."

"I just want you to remember that."

Grove sighed. "And his father works for the FBI, and people are going to die no matter what we do, and tax time is going to roll around again next year."

Maura gave him a hard look. "Thank you, Farmer's Almanac."

"Baby—"

"Look, I know it doesn't matter what I say, I've played this record before."

"It *does* matter what you say."

"Let me talk."

Another sigh from Grove. "Sorry . . . go ahead."

She dropped her smoke to the dirt, ground it out with the toe of her Converse All-Star. Then she looked up into her husband's eyes. "I saw the wire photos of those Memphis murders, and the Davenport scene. The way he tortured those two poor nurses. I saw it. I'm a journalist, Ulysses, in case you forgot. I was there in New Orleans. In Alaska."

He gave her a deferential little bow. "And thank God you were."

Maura took a deep breath. "I saw what this monster did to those girls in St. Louis. I want you to get him more than anybody. I don't give a shit *what* I have to do—take the baby, hide in a hole in the ground, *whatever.*"

A pause here, Grove cocking his head at her, a little nonplussed. "Okay, now I'm kind of confused. What are you saying exactly?"

She rose and went over to him. She touched his cheek, then she hugged him, tightly, longingly. She uttered softly in his ear, "What I'm saying is I'm proud of what you do, and I want you to catch this guy by any means necessary, just don't *lie* to me about it."

He held her in his arms for a long, nourishing moment. "Copy that."

"Catch this guy, Ulysses," she whispered. "Then come back to us in one piece."

Around two o'clock that afternoon—after Grove had cradled his son in his arms for endless minutes, planting kisses on his downy head, nuzzling his little plump caramel cheeks and whispering tender good-byes—Maura and the baby unceremoniously departed with a Federal Marshal for an undisclosed city in the Midwest. By that point the Grove house had transformed into a giant Trojan horse. Surveillance cameras had been installed. Trip wires along the edge of the property. Wireless bugs at strategic points. Sensors. Infrared. Inside the house, Tactical specialists were positioned in rooms on every floor like pawns on an elaborate game board. When it was all up and running and operational, Geisel toured the various rooms with Grove and ran down all the contingencies. "Of course, he may never show up," Geisel was saying as he paused near the front door. "And I'll have to justify all this to the director at the oversight meeting next month."

"We'll cross that bridge when we burn it." Grove glanced over his shoulder at the winding staircase. "Have you seen my mom?"

"She's upstairs packing her bags. Great lady."

"Yeah, she has her moments."

"We're going to escort her back to Chicago, put a uniform on her house for the duration."

"Sounds good." Grove wiped his mouth. His stomach tightened a little. He needed to negotiate a tricky subject with his mother before she left. "Excuse me for a minute, I'm going to go say good-bye."

Grove went upstairs and found Vida in the guest room, zipping her worn leather satchel, preparing to leave. The creases around her brown eyes looked as though they had deepened overnight. Her salt-and-pepper braids were drawn up on her head like coils of rope. "There is my brave boy," she said with a wink.

"Ready to roll, Mom?"

"I think. Finally."

"Mom, before you go . . . can we talk?"

"Ulysses, of course."

"C'mon, I'll walk you to the car."

They went downstairs, and Vida said good-bye to Tom Geisel. Then Grove ushered his mom out into the gray daylight, her brittle bones creaking as she descended the porch steps. The wind tossed her braids, and Grove put his arm around her to steady her. The unmarked Bureau sedan was idling over by the massive weeping willow tree at the end of the driveway, waiting for her.

"Mom, um . . . something I want to ask you," Grove said, pulling Vida to a gentle stop. They stood just out of ear shot of the middle-aged female field agent leaning against the unmarked sedan, reading a newspaper, about thirty feet away. "You remember when we talked about the summoning."

A dark shade passed over Vida's expression. "You are talking about Alaska?"

"That's right."

"How could I forget?"

"Yeah . . . yeah, anyway . . ." Grove wiped his mouth nervously. Two years ago, clinging to the side of that mountain in Alaska, locked in a mortal standoff with a psychotic killer, Grove had resorted to the same brand of African hoodoo his mother had been shoving down his throat all through his childhood. He had broken down and recited an ancient incantation, a litany *summoning* a monster out of a madman.

It worked.

The entity had been hooked and pulled out of

its host like a parasite burned out of a gangrenous wound.

Today Grove had a new perspective on his mother's spiritual tool kit. "I remember years ago, you talking about a different kind of summoning, a kind of . . . connection with a higher plane. Something like that? Something called a *hirizi*?"

She gave him a look. "You mean *uzuri*—a talisman?"

"*Uzuri*, right. I couldn't remember exactly what it was."

Vida frowned. "Ulysses—"

"Wait, hear me out, please. This is my family, Mom. I don't know if this latest scheme is going to work, but I'm willing to try anything to protect them."

A pause, Vida looking into his eyes. "You are a very special young man."

"Mom, c'mon."

She touched her spindly, brown fingers to his face. "Unfortunately, I'm not sure you grasp the power of this *uganga* yet."

"Teach me, then."

"I'm not sure that's a good idea. A man must discover these things on his own."

Grove swallowed the urge to raise his voice. "I need something else, I need an edge."

A long pause here. Vida looked into her son's eyes. "A man finds his own way to this *juju*, Ulysses."

"Show me, then. Gimme a map, gimme directions."

She stroked his cheek with wrinkled, tea-colored fingers. "You have very special blood running through your veins, my baby boy."

Grove let out a sigh. "You're not going to help me. Are you . . . ?"

Vida's face darkened. "I cannot speed the process. You must connect with it your own way."

"Okay, whatever. Message received."

She smiled. "You'll get there."

They embraced then, the embrace of a mother hugging a soldier bound for war.

SIXTEEN

That night, Amtrak Zephyr 312 out of St. Louis, Missouri, thundered into Washington, D.C.'s Union Station. Cones of magnesium-blue vapor lights shone down on the rails as the train flickered and sparked into the switchyard, taking its place at the block-long berth along the southeastern edge of the depot. The cars jerked to a halt. Compressed air hissed. Doors rattled open, and a platoon of redcaps and porters emerged first with handcarts and portable steps.

At length, the passengers disembarked.

The last figure to emerge was a gentleman dressed all in black with a cowboy hat. His surly expression kept most of his nosier fellow travelers at arm's length. He carried a heavy canvas duffel.

The Hillbilly took his time that evening. From the switchyard platform he proceeded across the echoing marble walkways of the station out into the sultry night and down the street. He had never been to D.C. but he felt very little anxiety. He found a small diner on H Street, went in, and took a seat at a window booth. He ordered scrambled eggs, bacon, pancakes, toast, and coffee, and he sat there eating his dinner with his knives and guns securely tucked away in the duffel at his feet. He only heard the voices in his head once during his meal, something about tasting the blood of an African.

After supper he asked the waitress where he might catch a bus or cab into Virginia. She told him, and he thanked her with a cold smile and a 12 percent tip.

The trip downriver to Alexandria took about twenty minutes, and the Hillbilly spent most of those twenty minutes sitting in the darkness of the cab's backseat, studying the folder full of information that Splet had given him. The file included newspaper clippings about Ulysses Grove, stillframes from news footage tapes, printouts of background material on the profiler from the Internet, and the most important piece of the puzzle: a photocopy of a Rolodex file card with an address scrawled in ballpoint. 2215 Cottage Creek Drive, Alexandria, Virginia, 23445.

Splet claimed that he got the address from the WJID producer who interviewed Grove.

It was nearly 2:00 A.M. when the cab finally crossed over the border of the subdivision known as West Knoll. The Hillbilly asked to be dropped off a quarter of a mile east of Grove's home, near a lonely, deserted bus stop. The cabbie—a nondescript man in a Redskins cap—pulled over, took the fare, and left without saying a word.

On his way across the sleeping streets of West Knoll, the Hillbilly strode along calmly, casually, whistling a tune as if he belonged there. He was a returning soldier, a beloved son, a second-shift worker, a butcher, a baker, a candlestick maker. He was everyman. He heard voices in his head telling him to suck the eyeballs from the skulls of the dead. He heard other voices telling him he was weak, dirty, and pathetic. He blocked it all out of his mind.

He was almost there.

The first landmark loomed up ahead: a tiny red reflector poking out of the cattails and saw grass. Then came the mailbox, materializing in the moonlight like a ghost: a simple aluminum box with a little red flag mounted on an iron post. No name, just the address. 2215 Cottage Creek Drive. The Hillbilly walked past the mailbox, past the driveway, then past the property . . . until he reached the gully on the west edge of the property.

The Hillbilly paused and glanced over his shoulder. The street lay in shadows. Nobody in sight. Houses shut down for the night, windows dark. The Hillbilly turned and carefully slipped into the darkness behind the foliage.

A footpath sloped steeply down into a dry creek bed that was choked with wild undergrowth and weeds. In the absolute darkness it was difficult to make out anything but a jungle of limbs. The ground was strewn with stones and corrugated with roots. The Hillbilly moved cautiously through the dark, squeezing his way between branches with the duffel bag over his shoulder, catching on thorns and snagging limbs along the way. In time he reached a clearing near a little moraine of land that jutted off the northeastern corner of Grove's property.

A pause here.

He gently set the duffel bag down on the spongy ground. The zipper came open slowly, silently. A small penlight came out, and he clicked it on and put it in his mouth. He dug deeper into the bag. The massive .45 caliber Army automatic appeared like a shiny gray slug in the tiny circle of light. He took the gun out and screwed on the homemade suppressor, a ten-inch-long contraption that looked like a tin can painted black. A black coat hanger served as a shoulder brace.

Something caught his attention to his left, a shiny thread in the corner of his eye.

He looked down and saw the trip wire. It wove through the milkweed about eight inches above ground level, barely visible in the darkness, but shimmering like corn silk in the beam of the penlight. How old was it? Had Grove installed the security measure years ago?

Or had he done it recently?

The Hillbilly was sweating now, shaking, dizzy all of a sudden. He quickly rooted the other weapons out of the duffel bag: the bowie knives, the switchblade, the .38 Police Special. He shoved the smaller gun behind his belt. The knives went in his socks, in his sleeves. Two extra magazines of hollow-points were slipped into his back pockets. Time to put this nosy fed's hair on the wall.

Creeping sideways, staying low, moving through the foliage at a parallel angle along the edge of the property, the Hillbilly paid close attention to the trip wires until he reached another clearing off the northwest corner of the yard. Now he paused and girded himself. He jerked the hammer on the .45, tightened his grip, and took a deep breath.

Showtime.

He slipped out of the woods, then hopped over the Cyclone fence with a single bound. His weapons rattled and his knees popped, but he kept going. The grass was slick, and he nearly slipped as he made his way toward the house. It was maybe fifty yards away, now thirty, now twenty.

Now fifteen feet.

He dove to the ground near the foundation, the odor of something doughy and sweet filling his senses. A light burned behind the sliding glass doors off the patio. Muffled music played behind one of the walls. A wave of hate swelled inside the Hillbilly as he lay there on the cold ground, breathing manure and oily grass.

He crawled toward the sliding doors, belly pressed against the ground. He reached the doors and peered over the top of the steps.

Inside sat an old black woman in a rocking chair. The room was cozy, a fire burning. The woman held a baby, and it looked as though she were humming to it. Maybe singing a lullaby, the old filthy whore.

The Hillbilly tasted sulfur on his tongue. He wanted to vaporize this old mammy and her little mongrel baby. He rose to a crouch and raised the gigantic barrel of the silencer until it rested against the glass. The liquid-tip loads would cut through the glass like butter, and the retooled mechanism would send a burst of eight rounds into the home in less than three seconds.

He held his breath and started to squeeze off a shot when all at once—inside the house the old woman jumped out of her chair.

And the baby fell to the floor.

And a black handgun appeared in the old lady's hands, the cocking mechanism chucking loudly.

It happened so quickly and unexpectedly that the Hillbilly had no time to react, had no time to fire, had no time to retreat; he merely flinched backward as though splashed with cold water, and whirled instinctively, blinking and reeling at the harsh light flaring in his eyes from the backyard, and the noises, voices, and loud clanging of bullet chambers coming from all directions, and the bizarre image now lingering like a sun dot on the Hillbilly's mind screen: *the baby bounced!*

The baby just fell to the floor—
—and it bounced!

"Stand down, goddamnit! Hold your fire!"

Grove came around the southwest corner of the house with his .44 Bulldog clenched in both hands, his Kevlar Second-Chance vest bunching around his neck, dragging on his lungs. He had been sitting in Geisel's control van, fidgeting restlessly the whole night. Now his heart pumped and his boots slid on the wet grass as he lined up the intruder in his sights, his brain blazing with contrary flashes of thought: *Bag this mother!—Goddamn idiots were supposed to wait till he gained entrance!—What went wrong?*

The first shot rang out—a great watery boom—sending Grove to the ground as though he were sliding into home plate. The muzzle flash came from the backyard, from one of the SWAT guys from the Alexandria PD, a silver pop that lit up the sky and sang in the high tension wires.

Glass exploded.

The sliding doors went away, and the intruder rolled across the patio in a hailstorm of diamonds, unaffected, still clutching that contraption in his hand, that stupid goddamn redneck repeating gun. Less than fifteen feet away, in the shadows of the lawn, Grove struggled to his feet and started waving off the troops, screaming at the top of his lungs: "Hold your fire! Get back, goddamnit! Stand down! Stand down!"

The second volley came from the intruder *himself* as he rose to a kneeling position in front of the jagged broken patio doors and aimed at the figure inside.

Five quick thumps of air—*fffhht-fffhht-fffhht-fffhht-fffhht*—burst out of that homemade gun, trailing silver rosettes of fire.

Grove cried out from the lawn but it did no good. The large-caliber blasts tore through the family room and also through Special Agent Harvey Moshman with the relentless buzz of locusts. Agent Moshman—who was a veteran with Quantico Tactical, and was skinny enough to pass as an old lady—now jitterbugged in a cloud of red mist just inside the gaping doors, as the hollow-points tore through his fake dress and his African beads above his vest and sent the back of his head spraying across Maura's Hepplewhite oak cabinet.

Outside, on the periphery of the lawn, heavily armed figures began converging on the house.

Panicking, acting mostly on instinct, Grove managed to climb back to his feet in that split second of silence and raise his Bulldog before the barrage started. But Grove didn't fire at the intruder. He didn't fire at anyone. He pointed the barrel skyward, and he squeezed off the contents of the cylinder: the Bulldog barked fire—five enormous *BLATS!*—into the black heavens like Roman candles.

Then Grove hurled himself to the ground, careening down the wet slope.

Almost simultaneously the intruder spun around with a .38 in his hand and was firing in Grove's general direction as Grove covered his head as he slid against a hickory trunk. Bullets chewed through the air above him. A ricochet punched the dirt near his face and sprayed his eyes, but nothing hit him, and he ducked around behind the back of the tree.

Now the air lit up with high-caliber suppression fire from the trees, from the bushes, from the second-floor windows, from the shadows to the west of the property. The sound was tremendous and horrible—an earsplitting fireworks display—and the corresponding blasts strafed the edge of the patio in a continuous string of firecracker explosions, sending puffs of brick dust into the night air.

But through it all, blinking away the tears of adrenaline and the *schmootz* in his eyes, Grove could see the intruder slipping away across the lawn, scurrying toward the shadows of the woods like a rat fleeing a sinking ship. Good! That was exactly what Grove wanted. He had one chance. *One chance.* And it all depended on this redneck getting away.

In the distance the hit man vanished into the shadows of wild grass and foliage.

Meanwhile the black-clad figures started after the gunman. One of them—a younger officer with a jarhead haircut and steroid-marinated muscles—

charged toward the woods, raising his M1 to his eye line.

Grove leapt across the patio with his Bulldog gripped in both hands. "Back off! Back off! Back off!"

The jarhead hesitated near the edge of the woods, nearly losing his balance on the wet grass. He spun around and gazed thunderstruck back at Grove, while a dozen or so other Tactical officers fanned across the lawn, either crouching down in firing positions or reloading their speed cartridges. Grove madly waved them all back as he hurried toward the woods.

"He's mine! He's mine!"

Grove plunged into the darkness of the forest with his Bulldog sticking out in front of him like the shaky prow of a ship. He could hear frantic breathing and churning footsteps up ahead, a shadow retreating into the blackness. The hit man had gained maybe a hundred-yard lead, but Grove had advantages: he was in terrific shape for a man his age, his cholesterol down, his weight a consistent 175 pounds; plus he had been trained by Bureau specialists back in the Academy in the art of tracking someone.

But most importantly he knew shortcuts.

SEVENTEEN

West Knoll, Virginia, is laid out in the style of a great medieval embattlement. Cross Creek, a narrow tributary of the Potomac, curls around three sides of the community like a moat. A swath of dense woods lines the inner banks of this waterway not unlike an impenetrable bastion. Inside these woods, the fortresses rise in all their glory—split-levels, ranch homes, Victorians, and massive Empire-style mansions whiskered in bougainvillea and ivy. Grove knew the southern edge of this kingdom well. He took his early morning runs around there sometimes, and he and Maura had looked at a house down there a year ago. Along the southern-most edge, the woods abut a tree-lined boulevard called Pilson Avenue, a sleepy cobblestone road that channels slow-moving traffic and tourists in horse carts toward Interstate 95 to the west.

At night the mercury vapor lamps blaze down on this lonely thoroughfare like votive candles in a silent chapel.

Grove reached the Pilson end of the woods—a mere thirty feet from the road's pea-gravel shoulder—then paused inside the hickories, breathing hard, his pistol still clutched in both hands. His sweatpants were grass-stained and torn where he fell, his leg skinned and bleeding underneath. His Kevlar vest weighed a ton. His heart hammered. He could barely see the road through the foliage, which stretched into the distance to the west.

Pilson was deserted, litter skidding along the night wind like tumbleweeds. It was so quiet Grove could hear the buzz of sodium lamps . . . and the faint sound of sirens coming from the east, probably heading toward the shootout at 2215 Cottage Creek Drive. He squinted to see down the street. The assailant was now just a shadowy figure a block away, limping hurriedly along. Grove reached down into his pocket and found a small flat device about the size of a pack of cigarettes.

"Mobile One, this is Grove." He murmured very softly into the walkie. "You copy?"

"Copy that," a voice crackled.

"Shit." He turned the volume down. "Listen . . . stay back at least a couple of miles. I don't want him to hear even an *echo* of a chopper."

"Yeah, copy. We got you on the GPS, we'll wait for your signal."

Grove clicked the radio off, shoved it back into his pocket, then pushed his way through the webbing of branches.

The humid breeze hit him in the face as he emerged from the woods. The air smelled of the Potomac, fishy and piquant. He took a deep breath and crept silently westward along the gravel shoulder, staying low, keeping his gun down but ready. A block and a half away, the shooter had turned a corner and was now heading south on Wabash Drive.

A row of dark storefronts loomed, lining the intersection of Pilson and Wabash. Grove slipped behind a dry cleaner's, then hurried silently down an alley, past festering garbage and drifts of moldering trash. He thumbed the hammer back on the Bulldog as he approached Wabash.

The first shot rang out as he was emerging from the mouth of the alley.

Grove lurched behind a mailbox as the blast ricocheted off the cement with a dull crack, missing his right leg by mere inches. His ears rang. *Shit!* The assailant had already made him, and now it was a horse race. Grove peered around the edge of the mailbox and saw the shooter hobbling away, heading toward a row of low-slung warehouses.

"Shit!"

For one frantic instant Grove stayed there, crouched behind that mailbox, frozen with indecision. He could try for a head shot but what good would that do? DNA might identify this guy but it was unlikely such information would lead to the Ripper. A nonfatal wound might yield better results—they could sweat the information out of the bastard. But even *that* was doubtful. The best option was surveillance.

Grove sprang to his feet, then sprinted after the son of a bitch.

At the end of the block the assailant darted between two canning plants.

Grove raced after him. He reached the canneries in seconds flat, hurling around the corner of one building, and then into the dark gap between the two edifices. Leading with his gun, Grove ran with such hell-bent fury down that narrow passageway crowded with Dumpsters and pallets that he nearly cracked his teeth. He tasted the rusty tang of blood where he'd bitten his tongue. He gasped for breath.

Fifty yards ahead of him, the gunman vaulted over a rusted chain-link fence and vanished.

They had just crossed into a transitional area bordering the two main commercial districts of downtown Alexandria. Urban renewal and 1960s social programs had made feeble attempts to beautify the area, but the last few decades had taken their toll, and now the play lots and parks were riddled with decay. Behind the canneries lay a vast, littered abandoned baseball field. Grove landed on the other side of the fence and immediately noticed a lone vapor light shining down near the chainlink backstop, and it was directly at this pool of light that he aimed his .44.

The assailant was waiting for him.

Gunfire erupted like heat lightning.

Grove flung himself to the ground while simultaneously squeezing off an entire cylinder of rounds. The air boiled. Large-caliber blasts popped and thumped in the earth, as Grove rolled out of the line of fire. His .44 roared, the muzzle flashing brilliant florets, each concussive blast further deafening his ears with the impact of dynamite in his skull. Somehow Grove managed to roll behind the cover of a discarded oil drum near the right-field wall.

The barrage lifted.

The Bulldog clicked and clicked and clicked in Grove's hand, as he instinctively kept squeezing the trigger long after the cylinder had run dry. He was out of breath, and deaf, and he had to huddle there behind that oil drum for a moment just to get the air back into his lungs.

Another moment passed. Grove peered around the edge of the barrel.

The assailant had vanished.

"Shit—*shit!*"

Grove sprang back to his feet, fumbling with the speed-loader as he hurried toward the empty pool of light behind the backstop. The air seemed frozen with echoes and latent violence. Grove finally got the bullets into the cylinder, snapping the .44 closed and tossing the empty loader. He reached the backstop and stayed low, coming around the left side, gun raised, hammer thumbed back.

The shooter was gone.

The stillness mocked Grove as he turned around and around, 360 degrees, searching for a receding shadow, pointing the gun at the empty night air. He became very still. He listened, and he heard something trailing off in the middle distant: frenzied footsteps.

Somebody running away.

Grove launched in to a dead run, charging after those fading footsteps.

The neighborhood to the immediate north was dense with gentrified condos and boutiques and artificial playgrounds for yuppie children with too much time on their sticky little hands. At night, the district rolled up its sidewalks. Most businesses closed at 6:00. Bars shut down by midnight. By 3:00 A.M. the place was a dark labyrinth of deserted storefronts and empty sidewalks.

At the intersection of Hamlin and Orchid, where the high-rise developments towered over manicured parkways of boxwood and lilies, and the quaint wrought-iron street lamps threw pools of yellow light on the cobblestones, Grove paused, his rasping lungs heaving for breath. He realized he couldn't hear the footsteps anymore. It was over. He had lost the intruder—the only sure chance he had of finding the Mississippi Ripper.

Grove realized he had blown it.

That's when he saw the object on the sidewalk.

At first, glimpsing it out of the corner of his eye, he thought it might be a dead animal, a squirrel or a raccoon flattened by a taxi, but upon closer inspection, he realized it wasn't animal *or* vegetable. He gaped at it. He shoved his gun behind his belt, and quickly plucked a pair of rubber gloves from his back pocket.

He knelt down by the pile of fabric, pulled a pen from his vest, and carefully lifted the thing up for a closer look. He stared at it. And stared at it.

"What the hell?"

He shoved the shirt inside his vest, and continued on down the deserted sidewalk.

A block west of there he found another pile—a wadded pair of pants; black denim, 36-inch waist, threadbare. He folded the pants and shoved them inside his vest next to the shirt. A block and half farther he found the assailant's footwear: a pair of black leather cowboy boots with pointed steel toes. Grove stood there for a moment, gazing at the shabby boots. What the hell was going on?

The man's underwear lay half a block west of there. Grove forgot all about his stiff legs, his skinned knees, his aching lungs, his ringing ears, and the coppery taste of blood in his mouth. Sirens were closing in. Grove stared at the underwear.

A cascade of thoughts streamed through Grove's mind. The clothing would yield a bumper crop of DNA. The chances of matching a logical candidate seemed more than likely now—the behavior alone would add reams of pages to the case files. Plus: How far could this lunatic get, walking around naked as a newborn? This notion instantly flooded Grove's brain with another wave of troubling, half-formed possibilities. Was it a trick? Was there a deeper symbolism here? Did it have something to do with Factor X? And the worst part: *If* and/or *when* the man was apprehended, there was still no guarantee that he would lead them to the Ripper.

Grove pulled his radio out. "Base, this is Grove. You copy?"

Static sizzled out of the speaker for a moment. "Geisel here, talk to me."

"Tom, I lost him."

Pause. "Where the hell are you? I warned you about this cowboy routine."

"Tom, listen to me——"

"How many times do I have to tell you, Sport," the speaker squawked, "you are not Tactical. I cannot afford to go through another New Orleans."

Grove thumbed the button and said as calmly as possible, "I'm just east of downtown. Cannery district. But there's something else. We're gonna need to get a bulletin out on this guy. Right away. Redline it."

"Already on top of it," the voice crackled. "Got a good, clean image of the prick. We'll get him. Get your ass back here. We've got a casualty, and you're gonna need to be in Q&A all day tomorrow."

Grove swallowed hard, then thumbed the send button, and calmly told the section chief about the perp's clothing strewn along the road like the shed skin of a snake.

There was a long pause on the other end. At last, Geisel's gravel-throated voice returned: "What is it with you and these freak-show cases?"

Grove let out a sigh, and started to answer, when a scream rang out.

Grove froze.

The voice from the walkie-talkie crackled: "What was that? Grove? What was that noise?"

The noise had come from the west, rising above the sirens, a shrill, piercing keen that instantly raised Grove's hackles. He shoved the radio in his vest pocket, drew the .44 from his belt, cocked the hammer, and started westward, jogging along the sidewalk with both hands clutched around the grip. His jaws throbbed with pain.

"Grove? What's wrong?"

The muffled sound of Geisel's voice served as a weird counterpoint as Grove moved faster and faster toward the sound. The scream had already started to dissipate. It seemed to be emanating from the shadows of a narrow alley a block away. Grove raised the gun as he approached. His ears still rang, but he had good enough hearing to make out mewling noises coming from the alley.

"Goddamnit, Grove! Answer me!"

Grove paused outside the alley, pressing up against the adjacent brick wall, wrapping his finger around the trigger, taking steady, deep breaths. Sobbing noises echoed within the alley. The sirens rose and wailed. A nearby street lamp threw a jagged beam of light in to the alley.

With one fluid movement Grove swung around in front of the alley and aimed the gun.

"Grove?"

He saw the assailant's handiwork on the ground by a stack of broken pallets.

"Grove?"

He saw the source of the screaming, and he let up on the trigger.

EIGHTEEN

The gruesome contents of the alley registered in Grove's midbrain in stages. The woman to the left was alive, on her knees, fully clothed in the squalid rags of the homeless, her stringy hair dangling across her filthy, grease-stained face. Probably in her fifties, but now appearing much older, she was the one who had screamed, her raw, parboiled eyes averted now like a punished child's. The woman on the right was either dead or very close to expiring.

"L-ll-look at her eyes," moaned the homeless gal on the left, her face trembling.

Grove moved in. "It's okay, I'm FBI, it's okay, stay back, ma'am, stay back now."

"Oh, l-ll-look at what he done to her eyes . . . oh sweet Jesus, Jesus!"

"It's okay, stay back now." Grove knelt down by the woman on the right. There was nothing he could do. He still had his rubber gloves on so he felt for a pulse. Nothing. The nude wreck of a woman had been hastily assaulted, stripped of her clothes, and then mutilated. She lay in a pool of her own blood, still so fresh it was steaming in the wee hour chill. She looked to be in her midsixties, maybe a prostitute, maybe just a street lady; it didn't really matter.

Grove's brain reeled. This made no sense. Hit men did not behave this erratically. Private contractors might be nasty, but they weren't psychopaths. Grove looked at the dead woman's face. Her eyes were gone, removed quickly, with very little finesse, leaving behind two sockets of red pulp. Twin rivulets of blood ran down her face, dripping off her chin.

Grove turned to the lone survivor. "We're gonna get help right away, sweetheart. Can you tell me your name?"

"D-doris."

"Doris. Okay. You saw the man do this, Doris?"

The homeless woman nodded.

"Was he naked? Was the man naked?"

Another nod.

The sirens had almost reached them, the keening wail penetrating the alley. Grove rose on unsteady legs. He found the radio and thumbed the call button. "Tom, it's me. You copying this?"

After a moment of static, the voice crackled: "Chrissake, it's about time! What the hell is going on?"

Grove stared down at the nude, crumpled remains of the homeless woman. His voice softened. "Scratch that last transmission, Tom."

Through the speaker the voice asked him what the hell he meant by that.

Grove let out a pained sigh. "I don't think our boy's naked anymore."

The next morning, in a quiet suburb of St. Louis, Missouri, Helen Splet stood in her damp, moldy basement laundry room, tears burning her eyes, as she worriedly ironed her husband's oxford-cloth shirts, ruminating on his whereabouts. Henry had called on Monday evening from the station, claiming that he had to work all night on a bunch of WJID public service announcements. He had told her not to wait up for him. But that was two days ago, and now the kids were starting to ask questions. Where's Daddy? When is he coming home? Helen had been telling them he was on assignment for the station, a big news story that required all the camera operators to work overtime. But she wasn't sure how long this ruse was going to keep the children placated. Caleb suspected something was wrong. And little Ethan had cried himself to sleep last night. Now Helen was getting desperate. Nobody at the station knew where he was, and the private investigator whom Helen had hired last year to confirm her suspicions that Henry was having an affair had come up with nothing.

Helen sprayed starch on another collar, dragging the iron, spitting and hissing, across the fabric. The house above her was as quiet as a coffin. Caleb and Rachel were both at school, and Ethan was at a playdate over at the Wilkinsons'. Helen felt the loneliness pressing down on her.

She wondered if she should pray harder. She

tried not to bother Jesus with trivial matters such as her arthritis, or Ethan's day care, or the overdrawn bank account, or Rachel's braces. But this was different. This was her marriage. This was her family's future. If her husband was having an affair, then she and the Lord would deal with that. But the uncertainty was killing her, these disappearances tearing her apart inside. She had to know. She had to know the truth, and she asked Jesus Christ, her Lord and Savior, on a daily basis, to keep her strong, to keep her focused on her family.

Hanging the last of the oxford-cloth shirts on a wire hanger above the old iron sink, Helen decided to pray once again for strength. She wiped her eyes and took a deep breath. But just as she was kneeling down on the cold cement slab to talk to the Lord Jesus, the phone rang upstairs.

She sprang to her feet, then hurried up the steps. She figured she better answer it in the unlikely event that it was Henry. She crossed the kitchen and grabbed the receiver on the fourth ring. "Hello," she said, her voice sounding wooden and falsely hopeful to her own ears.

The flat baritone on the other end was familiar. "Mrs. Splet?"

"Yes?"

"It's Ray Reinhardt again, ma'am. Sorry to bother you. Do you have a second?"

"Oh. Yes. Mr. Reinhardt, what is it?"

Helen's stomach tightened. Reinhardt was the St. Louis investigator whom Helen had been paying a hundred and fifteen dollars an hour plus expenses, off and on for over a year now, to get to the bottom of her husband's mysterious behavior. Helen had talked to the man yesterday morning when her husband had not come home, but Reinhardt had offered no help.

"Mrs. Splet . . . um . . . this is going to sound kind of odd," the voice said.

"Odd?" *Here it comes,* Helen thought. *Please, Lord, help me be strong.*

"Yeah, um, look." Reinhardt sounded hesitant, uneasy. "This is highly unusual, a case like this."

There was a pause.

Helen gripped the receiver tighter. "Mr. Reinhardt, is my husband having an affair?"

Another pause. "You know . . . it might be easier if we sit down face-to-face. Any chance we could meet today?"

Helen swallowed the taste of acid in her mouth. "Mr. Reinhardt, I asked you a question. Now, *is* he or is he *not* seeing someone?"

"Ma'am . . . there's something you need to know. But it's way too complicated to tell you over the phone."

"I don't . . . I don't understand."

"Ma'am, is there any way you could come by my office today? There's something you really need to know about your husband."

Helen licked her lips. "All right, fine. I have to pick up the kids from school first. Then I'll try to get a neighbor to babysit."

Grove spent the balance of that day at Quantico, the sprawling Virginia campus situated about thirty miles south of Alexandria, on a hundred wooded acres, which served as the central headquarters for the FBI. Most of the day was spent in meetings with bureaucrats. The endless procession of stoic Justice Department men in suits sat across from Grove in white acoustic-tile rooms, asking the same questions about who authorized the trap, and why wasn't Grove in the WITSEC program with the rest of his family where he belonged, and what evidence did he have that this assailant had *anything* to do with the Mississippi Ripper. Grove took it all in stride, dutifully telling them what they wanted to hear.

By dinnertime, he had run the entire gauntlet, and had finally stolen away to his private little corner of the BSU office.

His cubicle was next to a window overlooking the tree-lined campus. A cluttered warren of bulletin boards, light tables, and haphazard stacks of files, the office, at first glance, seemed better suited for an overworked actuary or film lab manager than a senior profiler with the FBI (a famous one, at that). The swivel chair was tattered and squeaky, the old Steelcase desk slumping with the sediments of past cases. Many of the black-and-white photos tacked to the corkboards were of mutilated corpses, scourged faces, eyelids mangled or ripped away. All that misery, all those bereaved families.

Both of Dina Louise Dudley's parents were still alive, as well as her sister and ex-husband. Jennifer Quinn had a five-year-old son. Both of the nurses came from big families. These wrongful deaths would haunt the generations, they would scar entire extended families. Murder is viral. Especially motiveless serial murder. Pain and survivor guilt and ceaseless grief and soul-deep trauma would haunt these families for decades. Something had to be done. The universe insisted upon it—a response.

Lab results had determined that the substance on Dina Dudley's cheek was indeed Perfluoron, or artificial tears. The makeshift ophthalmic procedures, the involvement with the eye area, the obsession with watching—all of it would eventually lead the FBI to the Ripper. But something was wrong. Somehow the puzzle pieces did not quite fit. Something kept nagging at Grove, something just beyond the reach of his conscious mind.

The hitter who had come after Grove—this cowboy lunatic bent on destroying Grove and his family—he had left a message. The gouged eyes of the homeless woman were no mere coincidence. Had the Ripper ordered such mutilations? Was it part of another elaborate ritual? In the back of Grove's mind, deep in the tangled synapses of his lower brain, he sniffed a familiar stench. It reeked of decay, the dry stink of the grave, the odor of ancient shrouds and ceremonies and black magic. It strummed some buried chord in Grove, like a tuning fork vibrating at a subsonic level, and it triggered feelings and sensations beyond logic, beyond physics, beyond the mundane protocols of psychological profiling.

Grove was thinking about Maura and Aaron—stranded somewhere to the west, at this very moment, in some innocuous community, the identity of which even Grove was unaware—when he noticed a rectangular box on his desk that hadn't been there the day before.

"What's this?" Grove picked it up and looked at

the address label. It was the standard red, white, and blue overnight postal box, dated yesterday, the return address written in the flowery script of his mother: 7716 Lawrence Avenue, Chicago, Illinois 60617.

It weighed very little in his hands. He hurriedly tore open the perforated strip and looked inside. Something flat and papery was wrapped in tissue. A small watermarked note fell out. He looked down at it.

The message bore Vida's distintive, careful hand:

My Dear Baby Boy,
On my way home yesterday I felt a change of heart. You asked me for help, and now I present you with the most powerful uzuri of them all. Many times you have heard me speak of your troubled birth. You were, as the shamans say, a caulbearer. I have never shared this with you until now. When you came out of me, you wore a veil, a part of me, over your face. A child born with a caul has a special destiny. They have the sight. Use it, as you were born with it, Uly. But use it wisely for it can reach places best left unreached. I love you, Uly. I pray for you.

Grove read the note a second time before once again peering inside that box as though it held something that might bite. He pulled the tissue-wrapped object out of the carton, pushed his files aside, and laid it on the desk blotter. Then he carefully peeled the paper away.

At first glance it looked like a deflated bladder, or a purse of ancient linen from some musty display case in some esoteric old museum. It was the color of old parchment, and marbled in delicate intertwining capillaries that were long dried and desiccated into blackened threads. Grove found a fold along one edge and spread it open like the seam of an enormous pita. The caul had apparently been stretched and tanned. It smelled of alkaline and old cinnamon.

Somewhere in the back of his mind Grove recalled reading about this little-known anomaly of childbirth.

The amniotic sac envelopes all fetuses and usually breaks free during labor. But in rare cases—something like one tenth of one percent of all births—this thin, almost transparent membrane covers the face of a newborn like a fleshy mask. The phenomena has inspired a large body of folklore. In Victorian times sailors took dried cauls with them on long voyages as preventives against shipwrecks and drowning. Cauls were used for centuries to heal, to conjure, to tell the future in arcane potions.

Grove carefully folded the membrane, put it back in the tissue, then slid it back into the mailing box.

As the dying light threw long shadows through the dusty blinds flanking his cubicle, and the raw Virginia sky, just visible at the top of the window, turned the color of ash, Grove leaned over the table and punched the intercom button on the desk phone. "This is Grove, if it's okay with the team, I'm gonna head home now."

A moment later he turned off the lights and walked out with the caul safely tucked away in its shipping box, stowed neatly inside his attaché case.

NINETEEN

"Come in, Mrs. Splet, have a seat." The private detective rose up behind his cluttered desk, extending his meaty, callused hand to the haggard woman coming through the door.

"Oh . . . thank you." Helen Splet paused in the vestibule for a moment, shaking his hand and gazing around at the tawdry little office, which was gloomily lit by fluorescent overheads. The three-hundred-square-foot hovel was crowded with computer desks, metal shelves, file boxes, and filthy motel-style furniture coated with decades of dust. The grimy front window—formerly the storefront of a pawnshop—was printed with the words REINHARDT INVESTIGATIONS UNLIMITED, and lined with steel mesh. A second person, a slender, severe-looking middle-aged woman, sat on a folding chair behind Reinhardt.

"Over here?" Helen gestured at a swivel chair next to a file cabinet.

"Please." Reinhardt motioned at the chair. He was a big, gangly man with receding hair and a taste for collegiate clothes. Tonight he wore an orange and blue silk jacket with the University of Illinois emblazoned on the back. "I'd like to introduce you to Doctor Boeski."

"Hello, Helen." The woman rose and came over with her hand extended. She wore her shiny coal-black hair cut short in a 1920s-style pageboy, and sported a shapeless black dress and horn-rim glasses. Her bony hand felt cold to the touch. "Susan Boeski. It's a pleasure."

The two women shook hands, and then Helen sat down, nonplussed.

Reinhardt and the skinny doctor scooted their chairs closer so that they were flanking Helen with nurturing, sympathetic looks on their faces, as though they were high school guidance counselors about to dispense some tough love.

"You're a doctor?" Helen asked the Boeski woman.

"Susan's a psychotherapist and an MD," Reinhardt said.

"I know this is a very difficult for you." Dr. Boeski patted Helen's knee. "Information is power in these types of situations."

Helen looked at the doctor, then glanced at Reinhardt. "I'm confused. I'm sorry."

Reinhardt sat forward. "Mrs. Splet—"

"What type of situation *is* this?" Helen felt anger turning in her belly. "My husband is missing. Do you have information on his whereabouts?"

A pause, Reinhardt measuring his words. "Actually, no . . . we don't know where he is. He could be anywhere."

"Then shouldn't we go to the police, and fill out

one of those—those missing person reports or what-ever?"

Reinhardt glanced at the doctor. "Dr. Boeski? You want to . . . elaborate?"

The doctor took a deep breath. "Helen, the thing is . . ." She paused. "May I call you Helen?"

"Sure, sure."

"The thing is, Helen . . . I'm breaking the rules by telling you this but I'm going to anyway . . . your husband's been a patient of mine for a little over a year now."

An awkward moment of silence as the doctor let this sink in. Helen stared at the psychiatrist. The anger stirring in Helen instantly congealed into fear. "What? He never said . . . he's been seeing you?"

"Since last January, actually." The doctor shot a nervous glance at Reinhardt.

Helen felt woozy. "I don't—I don't understand. He's a patient of yours? He's seeing a psychiatrist?"

"Helen, I need to ask you something."

"Go ahead."

"Are you familiar with the phrase 'doctor-patient privilege'?"

Helen felt as though she were floating. She began wringing her hands, squeezing so tightly her knuckles began to whiten. "Not really . . . I've heard it before . . . but I never really knew what it meant."

"It means that what I'm about to tell you is completely confidential."

"I would never—"

"I realize you're his wife," the doctor went on, her jaw set with tension, "and I suppose you have a right to know your husband's medical issues, but what I am about to tell you is private information, and you must, must, *must* keep this completely confidential or I will lose my license. And worse than that, I will lose your husband as a patient."

Helen clenched her fists. "Please tell me—what is going on?"

Reinhardt spoke up then: "Mrs. Splet, take it easy. We're going to work this out. I promise. We just have to take this one step at a time. Now, the whole reason Doctor Boeski is here is because I followed your husband to her office one night. I followed him to other places, too."

Helen interrupted: "What are you telling me? What are you saying?"

"Mrs. Splet, your husband is very . . . ill." Reinhardt gazed into her eyes. "*Mentally* we're talking about here. *Mentally* ill."

Helen swallowed a lump in her throat. She refused to cry again. She had already burned out her tear ducts, and besides, as long as she walked with Jesus, she could handle any curveball the world threw at her. "Okay, I'm listening. Please tell me everything. Please don't leave anything out." She looked at the doctor. "I can handle it. I can. I need to know what's going on. He's my husband."

Boeski and Reinhardt exchanged another glance. At last the doctor looked at Helen and said, "You feel up to taking a ride across town? There's something we'd like to show you, something that might help us find your husband."

That night, two unmarked squad cars sat outside 2215 Cottage Creek Drive, parked single file against the curb. Each car had a pair of occupants—

two uniformed officers equipped with 12-gauge shotguns—and each vehicle was connected via satellite to the FBI command post at Quantico. Behind the two-story colonial, in the shadows near the tree line, sat a pair of Tactical officers, one on each corner of the property. None of these officers expected further assaults on the house; perps, like lightning, rarely struck the same place twice. Inside the unmarked sedans, where silent men played cards and smoked cigarettes and absently fingered the stocks of their weapons, minds began to wander, thoughts turning to upcoming vacations and worker's comp for sprained knees, and office politics.

The house at the center of this vigil was mostly dark, a single light burning behind a second-floor window, the sound of someone furiously typing away at a keyboard.

Behind that second-floor window sat a lanky, good-looking black man in khakis and sandals. He sat at a desk, pecking at a laptop. The room was littered with files, photographs, and maps. The typing noises were accompanied by the soft drone of a Dexter Gordon CD. Grove loved the iconic jazz saxophonist's lazy, round tones—they reminded Grove of summer rains and Sunday mornings—and right now the music was imperative. Grove needed it to concentrate, to clear his head.

The Ripper investigation had mysteriously stalled, despite the recent attack on Grove's home. Cedric Gliane's lab people had been testing and scrutinizing the assailant's clothing for several hours now, but other than isolating the genetic material, there wasn't much to be learned. "Armed-and-dangerous" bulletins had been sent out—even suggesting the possibility of a fugitive in bag-lady drag—but the shooter had evidently vanished into the hinterlands. And even with the plethora of evidence—including clean DNA sequences off the hair at the Adams County scene, shoe prints, fibers galore, and a psychological profile that was getting big enough to publish in two volumes—the case had simply hiccuped in the eleventh hour.

Agent Menner's temporary task force had come up with exactly zero likely candidates from area mental institutions, and nothing out of the ordinary on the thousands of rap sheets provided by regional violent crime divisions. Dr. Booth from Iowa City had uncovered not one suspicious ophthalmology student. Nor had the IBI found anything of interest in the network of field offices investigating similar crimes. No parolees, no scumbags with criminal jackets out on bail, no suspicious behavior noted on any police blotters. This was always the central problem with genetic results: Without persons of interest to compare and contrast the DNA samples to, the lab results were essentially about as valuable as the paper they were printed on.

The feeling of stalemate lay in Grove's belly like jagged glass as he madly searched the VICAP site for *anything* suspicious, any sign whatsoever of a logical candidate. Deep down he knew the real problem was the nature of outwardly motiveless killers: They were ciphers. Everymen. Shy, withdrawn, introverted nerds. People who blended into the scenery.

Grove pushed himself away from the desk and paced the room. He paced and paced, clenching his fists, concentrating on the Ordinary Person who could do something like this. The Ripper was out there somewhere, the faceless guy in the crowd, the worker bee in the office cubicle, the guy in the fast-food uniform asking if you wanted fries with that. He was out there in the great vast nowhere, waiting for news from a hit man, waiting to hear about another butchered family.

"Shit!" Grove stormed out of the room.

The caul was waiting for him out in the kitchen, on the counter.

Grove had put the box in there when he got back from Quantico, having second thoughts about using it. Now Grove opened the end of the shipping box, pulled out the membrane, and unwrapped it. In the low light it looked like a flattened, dried fish. He picked it up and smelled its musty, peppery aroma.

Should he mess with this stuff, this old, old magic from his mother's world?

He stared and considered, and found himself thinking of that nameless everyman preparing to bring more hell into the world somewhere in the Midwest.

The parking lot behind the boarded-up Piggly Wiggly flickered in the light of a broken vapor lamp. Mayflies swarmed through the aluminum-silver funnel that shone down on the cracked asphalt. An echo of a scream that only moments ago filled the night air now faded away into silence.

The Hillbilly crouched on the north edge of the lot, wiping the blade of his tarnished bowie knife on the hem of his skirt. Still garbed in the ragged pinafore dress of the homeless woman, the Hillbilly rose to one knee and wheezed with exhaustion. His face was streaked in grime and sweat. He was not as young and facile with close-contact killing as he used to be. Killing people hand to hand had gotten to be a labor.

He stared at the fresh kill lying facedown on the pavement a few feet away.

The corpse, still warm and twitching, had been a night watchman who had snuck up on the Hillbilly a few minutes ago, surprising him in the shadows of the deserted lot. The Hillbilly has quickly and decisively slashed the man's throat, but the ensuing struggle had also taken the Hillbilly by surprise. The dying man had grappled and wrestled and swung wildly at the Hillbilly despite the subsequent strikes of the blade, one to the man's neck, severing his carotid, another to the femoral artery in his leg. The man dropped after that, but he had bled like a pig due to all the exertion.

Now the Hillbilly watched a pool of blood spreading under the corpse, creeping across the blacktop. In the darkness it was the color of India ink. And for some unknown reason, that shiny puddle of blood made the Hillbilly feel strange, uneasy, edgy.

He looked down at the blood.

He jerked back with a start.

In the dark pool he could see his reflection as clearly as if he were looking in a mirror, and he couldn't believe what he was seeing. It was a trick. He must be hallucinating. The sight of his contorted reflection made his innards squeeze. His head spun with dizziness.

He was looking at his reflection but it *wasn't* his

reflection. It *wasn't* a gaunt, middle-aged cracker from the hills of Arkansas. It was a reflection of someone *else*—a doughy, balding man with pale skin.

The face in the puddle, the one staring back at the Hillbilly, was the face of Henry Splet.

TWENTY

"He's an MPD."

The dashboard light glowing off her gaunt face, Dr. Susan Boeski spoke in low tones. She sat in the front passenger seat of Reinhardt's war-battered sedan. The detective was hunched behind the wheel, steering the car up Old Six Mile Road, just north of the wild forest skirting Pickman Creek. Deep black shadows rushed past the windows like ghostly veils unfurling against the sky. It was nearly midnight.

"Highly functional, too, with components of delusional psychosis." The doctor glanced over her shoulder at the backseat. "Are you familiar with the term MPD, Helen?"

"No, ma'am." Helen Splet felt like a prisoner being led to the gas chamber. Alone in the backseat, clutching herself as though she might fall apart at any moment, she looked out at the barren landscape. She wanted to die. She wanted to crawl into a hole.

"It means Multiple Personality Disorder." The

psychiatrist looked owlish in the green glow. "It's quite rare, actually. But we do see it occasionally. And I'll be honest with you, we still have a lot to learn about this disorder and what makes it tick."

Helen managed to croak, "You're telling me my husband is . . . *schizo* or something?"

"Not *schizo*, Helen. Schizophrenia is much more common. The schizophrenic hears voices, has trouble connecting with reality. The MPD, on the other hand, is literally a series of different individuals competing with each other."

Helen swallowed. "Competing for *what*?"

"Dominance, control. They're called alters, as in *alter ego*. Some alters are dominant, some are submissive. And some are so deeply buried in the patient's brain they surface only under controlled hypnosis. To me, though, MPD patients are quite heroic. Their brains are amazing corrective mechanisms, fractured early on."

"What do you mean, 'fractured early on?'"

"Childhood trauma, usually. The different alters become defense mechanisms. One thing we've noticed, though, with functional MPDs—especially those who keep the disease a secret like Henry—is that they have a place they go to when they feel a 'switch' coming on. It's the *locus convertere*. The place of change. Sometimes it's a secure room in their house, an attic, somewhere private. Henry has a place like that. Way out in the country. It isn't foolproof. Sometimes he experiences blackouts. Wakes up someplace unfamiliar. But most of the time he keeps his transformations hidden inside this one location."

After a lengthy pause Helen said very softly, "That's where you're taking me, isn't it?"

Boeski shot a glance at Reinhardt.

"Almost there," he murmured.

Boeski looked at Helen. "About a year ago your husband came to me for something very straightforward. He couldn't sleep. Nightmares. He wanted a quick fix. We tried hypnosis, and it was during one of those sessions that another personality tried to come out."

Helen made a moaning sound.

The doctor went on: "I haven't even told him yet. It's very delicate, introducing the dominant personality to his alters. I was about to tell him when he disappeared."

Helen looked at the back of the doctor's impeccably groomed head. "You're telling me he doesn't even *know?*"

Boeski nodded. "It's a process, a very delicate process. That's why we want you to take a look at this place. Maybe give us some insight."

Reinhardt took a left turn at an unmarked farm road. The lack of streetlights instantly plunged them into darkness. On either side of them, as far as the eye could see, stretched vast landfills and fallow cornfields. "It's right up here, around this corner."

Chills crawled up Helen's spine as they rounded a bend and the building came into view.

The barn rose in the murky middle distance like a ghostly monolith, its warped siding and rotten roof gable silhouetted against the black sky, the sole manmade structure for miles. It sat back from the dirt road on about half an acre of scrub grass and weeds, surrounded by a broken-down barbed-wire fence. In the darkness it looked like a rheumatoid beast, slumped and sagging.

A sign posted near the dangling, broken gate—once printed with UNITED STATES IMPLEMENT AND TRACTOR—was now so sun-faded only these letters remained:

U   ST E I   T

Reinhardt pulled up to the gate, put the sedan in park, and got out.

Helen watched from the backseat, chewing her cuticles, as the private investigator shoved the gate open, then climbed back in to the car and carefully pulled into the weed-whiskered gravel lot. Tires crunched, the roar of crickets coming through Reinhardt's open window. They parked in front of the barn and Reinhardt turned the engine off.

The silence hummed in Helen's ears, raising gooseflesh on her arms. She glanced out the window to her right. "Oh my God, there's his car!"

In the darkness to the west, the SUV was canted across a bald patch of earth under a mammoth oak tree. The satellite dish on the roof, the road cases in back, the WJID decal prominently visible on the driver's door.

"Been there since Tuesday," Reinhardt said as he climbed out of the sedan with a groan.

"It's okay, Helen, no reason to be afraid." Dr. Boeski unbuckled her seat belt, then got out. "It's possible your husband hallucinates when he's here, sees this place as some significant milestone from his past."

Helen Splet reluctantly opened her door and stepped out into the night air on wobbly legs.

She followed them across broken glass to the double door. Upon closer inspection Helen could see that the barn was padlocked. A rusty Yale lock secured the ancient latch. She felt faint, standing there, shivering, staring at the padlock. "You're saying Henry comes here and . . . *changes personalities?*"

"At first I didn't even believe it myself." Reinhardt stood behind her and lit a cigarette, the tip glowing in the darkness. "He goes in, futzes around, comes out a different person, different clothes sometimes. Once I saw him come out dressed in a nurse's outfit."

"That's enough, Ray," Boeski said. "Helen, I have to ask you a question."

Helen Splet was on the verge of tears. "I don't think this is a good idea."

Boeski put a hand on Helen's shoulder. "Helen, did Henry ever tell you much about his childhood?"

Helen shook her head. "I don't know. Some."

"Did he ever tell you about a bad thing that happened to him at one of those self-storage places?"

A tortured pause, Helen trying to remember. "His foster father was . . . not a nice man. He got physical with Henry." She thought about it some more, wiping her eyes, looking at that forlorn building in front of her. "Never told me anything about a storage place, though."

"The reason I ask is—"

The doctor abruptly fell silent. A noise had come from the other side of the barn, the faint crunch of gravel, then silence. Reinhardt wheeled around, then became very still.

Helen listened. "What was that?"

Dr. Boeski shrugged, trying to appear calm, but her eyes burned with nervous tension. Reinhardt cocked his head and listened. It sounded as though something was skittering around inside the barn. A raccoon? Mice maybe. *Maybe . . .*

Helen's whisper was choked with fear. "Could that be—?"

"Sshhh." Reinhardt motioned for the two women to stay put, then turned and crept toward the northeast corner of the barn. Helen watched the detective vanish into shadows, heard his crunching footsteps abruptly halt.

The two women stood there, waiting for the investigator to return. At last, they heard his footsteps again, and saw him emerging from the shadows with a sheepish look on his face.

"Nobody there," he said, joining the women at the double doors.

Something moved inside the barn again. A puff of air, some muffled shuffling noises. The threesome turned toward the door. The shuffling noises persisted. Helen gaped, a deer-in-the-headlights look on her face now, her voice suddenly getting stuck in her throat.

It sounded like—

The double doors burst open, the padlock catapulting into the air like a mortar.

A massive shadow leapt out.

The group disabled the detective first, Nurse White surprising him with a knife to his throat. He was fumbling for his .38 (which he kept taped to his right ankle) when the big woman slashed a half-inch-deep cut across the bottom of his Adam's apple. Massive breast cleavage bouncing above her stained white togs, the nurse growled some inarticulate battle cry as Reinhardt staggered. Then she kneed the man in the groin, and the detective finally collapsed in a bloody mist of arterial spray.

Meanwhile the psychiatrist and Helen had finally snapped out of their horrified stupors. Dr. Boeski gasped, then whirled around and started running headlong toward the shadows of the neighboring landfill.

Helen Splet was backing away in the other direction in utter terror, her slender hand going to her mouth, muffling her agonized moaning and garbled attempt at speech. Another denizen of U-Store-It darted out of the shadows to her left. Knuckle crawling like a little baboon, chubby little pug-nosed face all screwed up with rage, Angel had a flexible motorcycle chain clutched in his sticky fists.

The chain whipped around Helen's shins as she tried to turn and flee. She stumbled, sprawling across the pavement, her breath knocked out of her lungs.

The feral child loomed over her. Helen tried to crawl away but the chain came down hard on the back of her head. The greasy linkage dug deep into her skull, bouncing her cranium off the asphalt. Dynamite erupted in her brain, and Helen was mercifully knocked out, her last conscious thought a jumble of regret and recrimination toward her God. How could the Lord let something like this happen?

Unfortunately these final thoughts would vanish like ashes in the ether, forever unanswered, as the razor-sharp chain came down on her skull and neck.

In the meantime the psychiatrist had gotten a head start across the northern edge of the property, and now was frantically scaling the steep hill that bordered the adjacent junkyard. She had kicked off her one-inch Fendi heels, and now was scurrying barefoot up the slope, a distant vapor light providing a dramatic bit of theater to the struggle. She reached the top of the berm and saw an ocean of wrecked vehicles and discarded appliances stretching out before her, the dented metal mosaic like a vast chipped-enamel sea.

Dr. Boeski paused at the apex to catch her breath when the shot rang out.

The blast struck her right shoulder just above the deltoid ligament. It felt like a fist punching through her bone, spinning her on a wild axis in a blood cloud, right before the second round struck her left temple, turning her power off forever. The psychiatrist crumpled, tumbling down the ravine into a gully of broken glass.

Her body did not lie there unobserved for long.

A figure appeared almost instantly at the top of the hill above her. Silhouetted in the arc light, the man was dressed in drag. He was a little thick in the middle, his posture slightly stooped, but mostly of average height and build. He looked a little ridiculous in the tattered dress—a fifty-seven-year old amateur transvestite.

Henry Splet gazed down at the carnage, still drenched in sweat from his long journey. His .45

handgun, with its homemade silencer, was still smoking.

Other figures joined him. One by one, they came up over the rise like phantoms and stood with Henry, a conquering army, the other tenants of the secret warehouse: Angel, the feral child; Nurse White in her blood-spattered togs; the Circus Lady; Mister Klister; Arturo, the Graffitti Artist; the Hillbilly; and others. Over a dozen of them.

They stood there, side by side, gazing down at the lifeless doctor.

A quarter of a mile to the west, amid the squall of barking dogs, the owner of Amalgamated Salvage came out of his shack and gazed off to the west. A squat, hairy Italian with a linebacker's neck, Sonny Massamore had been working on the last fingers of a bottle of Jim Beam and playing solitaire when he heard the two gunshots as plainly as church bells.

Now he was shoving his cell phone and his Glock nine into his jacket pockets as he raced over to his rust-pocked golf cart.

It took Massamore a little under a minute to wheel across the hardpacked road that bisected the junkyard. His little golf cart rattled over broken bottles and shredded tires, shaking him hard enough to crack his jaw. His heart pounded as he approached the westernmost edge of the yard.

He scudded the golf cart to a stop behind a tower of engine blocks and hopped out.

In that horrible, pregnant silence before Massamore noticed the body of Dr. Susan Boeski lying crumpled like a rag doll in the gully to his right, he saw two very odd things. The first was a sign way up at the crest of the hill, nailed to a fence separating his junkyard with the neighboring deserted farm. Somebody had doctored the faded, missing letters of the original United States Implement sign:

U   st OR e   i T

The second oddity was a solitary figure standing at the top of the hill—a man in a torn dress—looking down upon the salvage yard like he was surveying his kingdom, like some cardboard Napoleon commanding an invisible army. He held a big handgun at his side, and was talking to himself.

All alone.

Talking.

To himself.

TWENTY-ONE

A thousand miles and a million light-years away, at precisely the same moment Henry Splet was starting to clean up his mess at the abandoned barn, Ulysses Grove locked himself inside the basement of his Virginia home, out of view of the surveillance officers. Clad only in a T-shirt, khaki pants, and sandals, his .44 Bulldog snug against his ribs in a shoulder holster, Grove was about to give himself over to Vida's *uganga*.

It was something he had resisted for most of his life. He had resisted it as a child, growing up on the mean streets of Chicago with an eccentric Kenyan mother who insisted on dressing him in dashikis and putting chicken bones under his pillow. He had resisted it as a young, noncommissioned officer in the Army's CID unit when he started having prophetic nightmares of body dumps and evil urges hiding in ordinary people. But now, as he pulled the shades on the cellar windows, and turned off the overhead fluorescents, he found himself longing to be in that zone again, that borderland between two worlds.

One world was ruled by science, logic, the laws of physics, and the statistical predictability of human behavior. The other was ruled by invisible forces, by angels and demons, by spiritual warfare. Grove could not yet articulate his role in this latter realm, but he was convinced now that he belonged in this no-man's-land. His visions had taught him that. His mother's beliefs had led him to this place.

Over the last hour he had gathered a very special assortment of raw materials from his home office, a sort of makeshift collection of sacraments, some of them unholy and profane, some strictly forensic. He chose key pages from the Ripper profile: the "High-probability Traits," recorded in Grove's tightly woven handwriting, scrawled in ballpoint on legal pads. He neatly folded these into an empty cardboard printer box. He threw in a plethora of other items: several five-by-seven photographs of the Ripper's size-eleven triple-E shoe imprint stamped into a blood-streaked sidewalk at the Memphis scene; a close-up of the seventh victim's lidless, staring eyes; a wide angle of the body-dump along the river near Quincy. Also a small Ziploc bag with hair and synthetic fibers taken from the Davenport scene. Also numerous faxes of autopsy reports, DNA analyses, ballistics, latent prints, sketches of scene geography, trace residue tests, bloodspatter narratives, sweepings, dustings, ultraviolets, sonograms, X-rays, and tracings. All the most significant physical evidence. All of it went into that worn-out Hewlett-Packard box.

To these items he added a host of objects that

even Grove would be hard-pressed to explain. He was operating on sheer intuition now. He threw in a faded happy-face decal that a serial killer had given to him during a prison interview, the empty rictus of a smile and black-dot eyes always reminding Grove of the empty soul of a killer. He threw in a chipped, hand-painted clown figurine that John Wayne Gacy had presented to him during the filming of a Court TV documentary. He threw in a small, desecrated crucifix recovered from the home of the Hillside Strangler—spattered with dried human feces like blackface on the tiny Jesus—an artifact that radiated malevolence.

With the lights off and the shades drawn, the basement was now completely dark.

For Kwanzaa last year, Vida had given Grove a dozen ritual candles made from Sudanese beeswax, each one a different earth tone, each of which Grove now lit, placing them, one by one, on the carpeted floor in a large circle about eight feet in diameter. Ordinarily he would have been embarrassed by what he was about to do. He felt no such emotion right now. The candles filled the darkness with flickering yellow light.

Grove settled down on the floor in the center of the circle, legs folded Indian style.

He put the red, white, and blue shipping box in front of him. He rooted out the amniotic sac, peeled the tissue off, then placed it on the floor by the box. As an afterthought, for reasons he would never fully understand, he took out the desecrated Jesus and laid it to his right. He put the macabre happy-face decal to his left, and the clown figurine behind him. He also fanned a number of documents around the periphery of the circle, including the stark black-and-white images of scourged victims, mangled eyelids, macro close-ups of pupils that looked like marbles in aspic. Also positioned in clear view were the footprints, fingerprints, and DNA prints of the Ripper, shed like the ghostly skins of a snake.

Picking up the caul, Grove unfolded it carefully, like a bride's delicate veil. It crackled faintly, as though he were opening a sacred text whose binding had fossilized from neglect. It seemed to exhale a cloud of dust in his hands. He could smell the long-evaporated proteins like rancid cloves as he swallowed the last traces of fear and hesitation.

He put the caul over his head.

The first impressions that washed over him were odors. Memory is stirred best by the nose, and _this_ memory was prenatal, genetic, primal—a sort of unconscious déjà vu—galvanized by the leathery, grassy musk of that caul. It was a complex smell, a miasma of bitter old cinnamon, cowhide, and just a trace of dried urine. The next impression was visual. As his one good eye adjusted to the darkness inside the caul he began to make out the faintest trace of light spots.

At first Grove thought these spots were simply artifacts on the backs of his own eyes, the kind of luminous dots that appear when one's eyelids are abruptly shut. But these spots were a yellowish sepia color like van Gogh's stars, and swam slightly in the blackness of the mask. Grove realized he was looking at the tiny flames of his mother's ritual candles through the translucent membrane of her amniotic sac.

He focused his thoughts on the Mississippi Ripper, the hidden order to the murder scenes, the systematic torture, the meticulous clamping open of the eyes. He thought of the killer's home, an ordinary house on an ordinary street, and he focused on a face, on the flesh-and-blood features of a face. He concentrated and concentrated and—nothing.

All he saw were flickering dots floating in the limbo of darkness.

He felt feverish, his face flushing hotly inside the caul. He closed his eyes again and concentrated harder on the Ripper's face. What would it look like? Ugly? Handsome? Androgynous? Probably none of the above. This face was more than likely a banal, ordinary face. Come out, come out, wherever you are . . . whoever you are . . . whatever you are. In his imagination Grove conjured the Ripper's features as a mere silhouette, a dark cut-out, like a two-dimensional caricature.

An image sparked in the darkness of Grove's mind's eye for the briefest instant.

The image was accompanied by a snippet of a sound, like a single flash frame in a movie unspooling in Grove's brain. He jerked as though slapped in the face, blinking in the blind darkness.

It took him a moment to figure out what he had just seen, an image lingering like a ghostly after-negative on the back of his cornea: seeing through the eyes of someone buried alive, underground, in the dank, black earth with the worms and the roots. . . .

Henry Splet was dragging the third and final body—his wife's limp form—around the back of the barn, when he heard the first low, deep noises coming from inside the building. Actually the word *building* is insufficient. In Henry Splet's fragmented, disjointed brain, the solitary old barn had transformed once again into a place from Splet's past: the U-Store-It mini-warehouse complex.

In Henry's gaze, the front of the barn had melted into the front of the self-storage warehouse, complete with its graffiti-stained steel entrance doors and boarded windows. To the left, in his mind's eye, stretched the massive east building with its honeycomb of storage units. To the right, dominating the western horizon, lay the ramshackle Quonset-style structure that made up "the wing"—that squalid, slummy corridor where all of Henry's personalities lived. The long tin building was now cloaked in moon shadows just as it was way back in the late sixties when Henry was a kid in Peoria and his dad would take him out to U-Store-It for disciplinary reasons.

At the moment however, a terrible noise was coming from *inside* this hallucinatory world.

Actually the word *noise* probably also lacks the proper impact. An animal in the wild will hear subsonic vocalizations, tremors in the air that will send all manner of alarm across the feral synapses. But the noise that was emanating from inside this imaginary complex was more like a disturbance of air currents, a stirring of stillness at the bottom of a well, a warning growl so low and deep and basso profundo that it sounded at first like a gigantic diesel gurgling to life.

Henry dropped Helen Splet's corpse next to the others, which were neatly lined up on the gravel behind the complex like cordwood. He cocked his ear toward the noise. It sounded as though it came from inside "the wing" somewhere. Goosebumps slithered down Henry's back, under his blood-spattered dress. He felt woozy, faint.

He willed himself to walk around to the front of the building.

His key slipped into the padlock. Rusty hinges screamed as he opened the doors and entered the building. He found the timer switch, and turned the dial to sixty minutes. A single overhead tube sputtered and flickered dull light down on the dirt floor of a rotting barn, but what Henry saw was the tiled foyer of a warehouse, with its long narrow corridors spreading off on either flank, lined with vertical accordion doors. The hallucination was a remnant of his childhood, a memory made real, as real as a Technicolor movie in his brain.

In reality there was only that barn, and Henry's gruesome souvenirs, arranged in obsessive little piles and patterns in the spiderweb-clogged corners—those battered road cases containing his cameras, his surgical instruments, that tattered Barcalounger armchair, his canisters of film, boxes of pornography, and his vast, beloved collection of old yellowed Polaroids. But now, as always, he stood in that flickering horrible barn, and his head slumped, and he got very still as though he were sleeping standing up.

A voice pierced the silence in the imaginary corridor to Henry's right: "There's somebody new here."

In his shattered brain, Henry saw the endless row of accordion doors illuminated by flickering candles. The ghost of Nurse White, a social services worker, a woman who once took the young Henry Splet into protective custody, had materialized once again at the end of the hallway. She now stood like a phantom, staring balefully at Henry. "Did you hear what I said?"

"What do you want from me?"

"New tenant." She jerked a thumb toward the service elevator. "Wants to see you."

The low, sepulchral growling noises had risen, vibrating the air like the lowest stop of a vast pipe organ. They came from the elevator.

"Why me?" Henry wanted to know. He trembled convulsively, hands shaking out of control.

Nurse White let out a laugh, her pale cleavage rippling and jiggling. "Go find out for yourself."

"Maybe I will, maybe I'll just do that." Henry's voice was the voice of a frightened, brutalized little boy.

"What are you waiting for?" The nurse urged him with nod toward the elevator. "Go on."

In his imagination Henry started toward that hideous elevator.

He approached the door with its scarred wooden slats. Henry could see through the slats into the pitch-black emptiness. He could smell the moldering, dusty stench of death wafting up from the sublevel.

He pulled open the door and stepped into the dilapidated elevator. The growling noises engulfed him, penetrating his skull as he slammed the lever down . . . and rode to the imaginary basement.

* * *

The cascade of imagery took Grove's breath away.

At first it flickered across the back of his blind eye in staticky waves, a distant signal beyond his reach, a frequency not yet tuned to the proper wavelength. Very soon, though, he realized he was seeing something important in the fractured, jagged images coaxed out the void.

He felt himself rising up through dense, spongy geological sediments, leathery wings unfurling, enormous serpentine eyes blinking open in the ceaseless dark.

His heart palpitated with dread. He felt short of breath, his lungs laboring. Even his olfactory senses were filling up with the dank stench of black loam untouched by daylight and layers of shale and tangled roots. His brain swirled with questions. Was this coming from within or without? Was this natural or supernatural?

Ever the investigator, Grove felt compelled to follow it out to its logical extreme, play it out, see where it led. He took deep breaths and concentrated on the unbidden flicker-show crackling behind his blind eye.

He saw his own blackened, skeletal hands clawing their way upward, upward through an endless mine shaft, toward the surface of the earth, hungrily seeking the light.

Grove pulled the caul off his head. He couldn't breathe all of a sudden, the heat and closeness of it excruciating. But worse than that, far worse, was the Pandora's box that these hellish images seemed to be opening, crackling like lightning in his blind eye, imprinting the back of his damaged retina like radioactive afterimages burned into a photographic plate: Something nameless and inhuman crawling out of the netherworld.

Grove looked around the basement. The candles were sputtering, shrinking and bloating, waxing and waning as if in some invisible breeze. The very air seemed charged with static electricity. He felt his scalp crawling. How did this happen? He had set out to summon a killer into the light, but now it seemed as though he were unleashing something, loosening something from the earth. His solar plexus contracted and clenched as he remembered his mother's message.

"Use it wisely, Ulysses, for it can reach places best left unreached."

Science and the military called it "remote viewing." First studied by the Russians in the 1960s, and later recruited in this country in classified CIA programs, the remote viewer is a highly specialized psychic who can see "remotely" through the eyes of enemy combatants. The viewer can see inside enemy installations or aircraft or fortresses, gleaning invaluable data, describing in great detail the secret workings of the enemy. But what Grove was doing inside that caul was seeing through the eyes of something else altogether, some dark, sentient being coming out of the earth.

Was it Factor X?

Something deep down inside Grove's very being told him to put the caul back on.

He did.

A moment later he saw again through the eyes of something crawling out of hell.

"Hello?"

Henry's feeble voice echoed dully as the elevator reached the bottom of the shaft, and the door jiggered open onto the passageway.

The stone walls vibrated with monstrous snarling noises, which were now so loud they drowned the thumping of Henry's heart. A single bare light-bulb hung from the stalactites thirty feet away, casting a sickly yellow skein of light down the tunnel. The Hillbilly's door was open. Henry could see the dull bluish glow of a bug zapper flickering out of the opening. He passed the Hillbilly's locker.

The silhouette of a lanky, weathered hit man lurked in the corner, leaning against the wall, having a cigarette, the growling noise practically drowning his sleepy drawl. "Watch yourself, pardner."

"What is it?" Henry asked, pausing, staring in at the tall man.

The orange tip of the cigarette bobbed. "New guy. Very nasty piece of work."

Henry noticed something odd at the end of the tunnel, about twenty feet beyond the Hillbilly's lair. Up until tonight, the subterranean corridor had always ended at that very spot, terminating in a graffiti-slashed wall of stone. But now, as the inhuman growling noise rose to bone-rattling levels, Henry saw that a *new* storage area had magically appeared.

It lay in the shadows to the left of the dead end, a *fresh tunnel*, fringed in roots, and uneven, as though hastily excavated by moles from the *inside* out.

Something was emerging from it, something huge and dark and subhuman.

* * *

Grove didn't notice the air around him seizing inward like a bellows, making the tiny sacred flames wag in unison on the invisible currents. He didn't see the gelatinous substance oozing out of the walls like black sweat while his brain crackled and fizzled, a shortwave receiving some strange signal from the darkness and making the venetian blinds buzz like angry hornets. Even if he had seen all this, he wouldn't have cared by that point.

He was in some kind of hypnotic zone, his emotions syncing up with the invisible battle in his brain.

"Come out!" he called to the empty basement, rising to his full height, still blinded by the caul on his head. He staggered, struggling for balance, then turned slowly around like a boxer poised to fend off an onslaught, fists clenched tightly.

"Whatever the hell you are! Come on! Come out!"

The darkness around him shimmered and resonated like a tuning fork. The windows rattled and hummed. Grove's brain crackled with memories of Factor X, the pale, hideous face of murder-lust.

The face of the enemy.

"Come out, you son of a bitch!"

Henry moved toward the gaping hole in his hallucinatory world, at once repulsed by it as well as drawn to it. The opening exuded a sort of breath smell, a sharp musky stench like rotting meat or the inside of a garbage can. And that deep baritone growl, now reaching otherworldly proportions, issued out of the dark aperture like a hellish, amplified aria.

Part of Henry wanted to turn tail and run away, climb out of there as quickly as possible, but he could not resist taking those last few paces toward the newcomer's lair. The growling engulfed him like a poisonous liquid, seeping into his ears and his brain and marrow as he approached the opening.

The impossibly deep noise began to change, transforming into a hum that sounded as if it came from the ocean floor.

"Who—who's there?" Henry could hardly breathe as he stepped in front of the opening.

Grove flinched.

He ripped the caul from his head, dropped it to the floor like a dead leaf.

An echo of a scream had filled his brain, a *nonsound*, like a snippet of a tape recording running off the track, but very familiar. His brain swam with confusion for a moment, unfocused rage and fear making his eyes water, blinding him. Without warning the flickering yellow light from the circle of candles flared brightly, spontaneously bloating as though a power surge had jolted through the foundation. One of the candles fell over, sending a pool of wax across the papers. Grove gazed around the basement, too stunned to register what was happening. He felt a puff of heat on his face, his flesh prickling with the pressure spike.

What was happening? Warning alarms were going off inside him.

He smelled the smoke before he saw the flames. The caul lay on the floor, a few feet away from Grove, on top of a fan-fold of DNA results . . . smoldering. He stared incredulously at it for a moment, as though staring at a dream. The edges sputtered and curled and burned as though stoked by invisible wind. Grove stood there, paralyzed with awe as crackling sounds rose behind him, emanating from the rafters and the joists.

Grove's house was burning.

Henry looked inside the cave, and for one brief instant, he saw the figure—or the creature or the ghost or *whatever*—standing in the center of that empty crater like a blackened pit in the core of a rotten piece of fruit.

"Oh."

Henry froze. Stopped breathing. Eyes bugging. Flesh turning to ice. Staring, staring, staring for that horrible instant of absolute terror before something popped like a fuse overloading, and then something dark and glittery and weightless jumped out at Henry with cobralike suddenness.

Henry slammed backward as though struck by an invisible tank.

The dull light went out completely.

Darkness flooded Henry Splet, changing him forever.

TWENTY-TWO

By dawn, the indigo sky above West Knoll, Virginia, flared and flickered with brilliant tendrils of light. The fire was visible as far north as downtown Alexandria, and as far south as the hills above Quantico. Great heaving clouds of black smoke rose off the gabled roof peaks, choking the sunrise, staving off daylight, while a virtual armada of emergency vehicles surrounded the two-story, their chaser lights spinning luminous red and blue ribbons through the misty morning air.

It had taken less than an hour for the fire at 2215 Cottage Creek Drive to rage out of control.

In the basement, Grove had valiantly tried to snuff it out, first with towels from the wet bar, then with a small fire extinguisher that he found under the sink. But it had been futile. It was as though the caul had exuded accelerant across the scattered documents. Within minutes, the flames were climbing the walls of the basement, licking up the vent conduits and staircase.

At that point Grove wrapped himself in damp towels and escaped through one of the window wells.

When he got outside he realized there were others in harm's way. The Tactical officers watching over the backyard had come into the house through the back door, looking for Grove, their shouts drowned by the roaring flames. Meanwhile, in front, the patrolmen who had been absently watching the house had immediately called in the fire to 911, and then gained entrance through the front door. Unfortunately, by the time the beat cops met up with the two Tac guys in the kitchen, the fire, which had originated in the basement, had already reached critical mass. The floor under the stove began to cave. The joists were cracking, the smoke billowing up from the furnace registers.

Outside, coming around the side of the house, coughing up scorched air, Grove heard the first cries coming from the kitchen. The floor was collapsing. Grove immediately leapt up the porch steps and plunged into the tide of thick smoke roiling out of the living room.

The majority of all fire-related fatalities result from smoke inhalation. The poisonous cocktail of hydrocarbons, sulfur, carbon monoxide, and corrosive gases can disable a person within seconds, taking their life within minutes. These superheated toxins are often invisible, which is why firefighters commonly utilize breathing apparatus upon entry. Grove, unfortunately, had no such protection as he lumbered blindly across the smoke-flooded living room, a handkerchief pressed to his mouth, eyes stinging.

Timbers popped and cracked like pistol shots as the heat radiated down on him. He tasted bitter, charred almond on his throat as he searched the archway into the kitchen. Voices pierced the din. He saw the dull, bleary ghosts of men staggering toward him.

"Out! Get out now!"

One of the men hollered a hoarse warning as Grove reached the injured patrolman. The cop had fallen, had maybe broken his leg trying to save Grove. Grove put his arm around the limping patrolman and ushered him toward the exit. The others followed, coughing and hacking. These were seasoned law enforcement men, hardened cops who had seen all manner of emergencies, but not one of them had ever witnessed a house fill up with smoke and burn out of control this swiftly.

Grove and the others stumbled out in to the dawn, gasping for air, wheezing and coughing uncontrollably, as the building went up behind them.

The pale light of dawn shone down through skylights and reflected off the immaculate tiles of the new Eastern Missouri Amtrak Station, just south of St. Louis. At this hour, commuters were flooding the turnstyles, an orderly stampede of Brooks Brothers suits, briefcases, and folded newspapers, jockeying for position in front of the Texas Eagle 7:09. Voices echoed and bodies milled through the arched track gates, as plumes of vapor swirled along the platform. Nobody seemed to pay much attention to the apparently crazy, homeless man shuffling along the rear cars of the train.

Dressed in a stolen raincoat and scarf, the torn hem of a bloody skirt barely visible underneath, broken-down sneakers on his feet, the man seemed to be arguing with the voices in his head. He approached the steps leading up to the rear coach, and one of the porters, a big, stout-bellied black man in a smart blue uniform, put out a hand.

"Hold it there, cousin . . . afraid this here's as far as ya go this mornin'."

The mysterious man held out a hand. The porter was taken aback.

In the man's dirty palm was a ticket.

Grove watched the last pillars of his house go up in smoke from the back hatch of an ambulance. Ears ringing, nose and eyes stinging from the smoke, he had an oxygen mask over his mouth and a blanket draped over his shoulders. He was glad the mask was there, not necessarily because he needed the oxygen, but because he didn't want the good old boys to see him crying. The tears that tracked down his face under the mask were not from the smoke. He was sobbing, watching a part of his life vanish before his eyes—not to mention a quarter-million dollars' worth of FBI communication gear. Up in the flames went Aaron's crib; the wedding pictures; Maura's portfolios; old mementos from his late first wife, Hannah—things like anniversary cards and lockets and ties she had given Grove. Grove watched the maelstrom engulf the second floor and he sobbed. He sobbed for his past, he sobbed for his uncertain future.

At length, the grief passed through him like a

receding storm, leaving behind feelings scoured clean like bleached bones left on a beach at low tide. What remained in his guts was something like anger, but not exactly. His family was gone. His home was gone. An animal in the wild, when roused out of its nest, will bristle with fight instinct. Claws protrude. Eyes dilate. Grove knew in his marrow that he had awakened something in that basement, he had triggered something beyond his ability to understand or put into words.

Now he hungered to face it.

"Agent Grove?"

The voice came from behind the ambulance, and Grove whirled around in time to see Walter Maksym, a heavyset field agent from Quantico, approaching from the street. The morning sun, diffused by the smoke, put a halo behind the big, graying man as he approached in his ill-fitting sport coat.

"Got the section chief on the horn," he announced as he came around in front of Grove.

Grove peeled off his mask and took the cell phone. "Grove here."

"Jesus H. Christ in a handcart!" the voice boomed on the other end.

"Good morning to you, too."

"I can't leave for one day?"

"Like the man says, 'Feces occurs.'"

"What happened?"

"I don't know what happened."

There was a strange pause then. Grove could almost hear Tom Geisel's wheels turning. At last the voice said, "None of this is coincidental, is it?"

There was a muffled crash inside the house. Agent Maksym, who was watching Grove from a distance, flinched nervously. A fireman yelled. Grove let out a sigh. "As a matter of fact, Tom, no . . . it's not."

"Lemme guess: You can't tell me what's going on because you're not sure yourself."

"Something like that."

"You're sure you're okay."

"I'm still working the case, Tom." Grove wiped ash from his T-shirt. "Believe it or not."

"That's good . . . because there's been a break."

"Excuse me?"

"There's been a break in the Ripper case. St. Louis Tactical is processing the scene as we speak."

Grove shook his head, icy cold stabbing his gut. "Jesus. How many this time?"

"Three. But there's more to it."

"Excuse me?"

After a long pause, the voice said, "They found his souvenirs."

Grove gripped the cell phone tighter. "What are you telling me?"

"They found his lair, Uly. The sick shit. They got enough physical evidence now to bury him."

"Wait a minute, what are you saying?" Grove's chest tightened. "Are you saying we got a positive ID?"

"That's exactly what I'm saying. Now look. I want you to go down to—"

"I'm on my way." Grove dropped the cell phone, threw off the blanket, and started across the lawn. "Agent Maksym!"

"Sir?" The big man scooped up his phone, then hurried to catch up. "What's the deal?"

"Gonna need a chopper scrambled out of Langley on the double, got that?"

"Got it." Maksym was already punching in the numbers. "St. Louis, right?"

"That's right."

Grove was half way across the cul-de-sac when the roof of his house collapsed in a gusher of flaming debris behind him.

He barely noticed.

TWENTY-THREE

"Are you nursing, Miss Garnett?" The doctor was a painfully thin, balding man named Reichman who had been referred to Maura by the Federal Marshals. He was thumbing through Maura's fake chart, glancing over all the bogus background information manufactured by the Marshal Service.

"As a matter of fact, yes." Maura, dressed in floppy sweatshirt and spandex stretch pants, her hair pulled back, sat in a burnt-orange swivel chair across from the gynecologist's massive veneer desk. She felt like sitting on her hands; the shaking had gotten so bad. Her hands had *never* shaken like this. In fact, for most of her life she had taken pride in the fact that she was solid as a rock, had nerves of steel, could climb volcanoes, and interview world leaders and fly shotgun in single-engine puddle jumpers across Alaskan glaciers. Now she was reduced to a pathetic, scared lump of a women trapped in the witness protection program with a one-year-old boy, wondering if she would ever see her husband again. But the shaking had been the last straw. She hated it when her hands trembled like this. Why now? Was she a canary in a coal mine? Was it her intuition flaring up again? She missed her husband desperately. She felt like a big, greasy white whale. She hated herself. But all that was par for the course. It was the shaking that was bothering her the most.

Dr. Reichman kept looking through the file, mumbling as though talking to himself. "That's going to limit our options on the anxiety attacks—most of these medications can pass into the breast milk."

"Then I'll stop nursing."

He looked at her. "How old is your child?"

"Eleven months."

"That's such a cute age."

"Yeah, it is."

"Great, so . . ." He gave her a perfunctory smile, then wrote something on a prescription tablet, murmuring as he scribbled. "Let's get aggressive and start the tricyclic four times a day for the postpartum depression. You can go with the generic, if you like, or we have some Elavil samples to get you started. Then we'll also get you some antianxiety medicine you can take on an as-needed basis."

"Cool, thank you."

Maura Grove (now known as "Melanie Garnett") rose and extended her hand to take the prescription, but the doctor hesitated for a moment. He looked up at Maura as though he were seeing her for the first time. "You *will* call me, Miss Garnett, if there are any unexpected side effects? I can count on you to do that?"

Maura told him not to worry, he could count on

her, then she snatched the prescription out of his hand, turned, and got the hell out of there.

On the trip back to the safe house, driving her new government-issue Ford Focus, crossing unfamiliar tree-lined streets bathed in morning sunlight, consulting a map provided by the Marshal Service, Maura wondered what that last comment was all about. Did Reichman not trust her around her own child? Did the doctor think she was going to do something psychotic like drive herself and her kid into the lake? A single mother mysteriously appears in a small town. Edgy, nervous, reclusive, she doesn't show her face much except to go out to get more drugs. Who could blame people for being suspicious?

Maura felt another craving for a cigarette coming on as she turned onto her street.

She pulled in to her driveway and threw it into park, reaching into the glove box and rooting out a crumpled pack of cigarettes. One last soldier was buried in the flattened package. She guiltily lit up and puffed the stale cancer stick, feeling shame for not being able to quit, for her kid, for her own health. Her hands shook furiously as she smoked.

Screw it! What was she worried about? Some faceless serial killer would probably bump her off long before lung cancer had a chance to set in. She gazed through the windshield at her squat little brick town house. The home was built in the 1980s but looked as though it had seen better days. The wood trim was chipped, the chimney in bad need of tuck-pointing, the haphazard landscaping mostly dead or dying. The *safe house*, they called it, which was rich. There was nothing safe about it.

Maura smoked and trembled and ruminated another moment until she noticed the neighbor lady watching her with furrowed brow behind the window of an adjacent house. Vivian Cansino, a large, hirsute Italian matron, had lost her husband to a stroke three years ago. Now she was the only saving grace for Maura in this horrible new exile. Two days ago, the older woman had welcomed Maura to the neighborhood with open arms and a baking pan full of cheese manicotti, and it hadn't taken long for Maura to realize that this sweet-natured old lady had a heart as big as her gigantic bosom.

In just two short days, in fact, Vivian had won over Maura enough to entrust the woman with Aaron during a quick trip to the doctor.

Maura snubbed out her cigarette, climbed out of the car, and skulked up the Cansino's walk.

"Don't tell me, something's wrong," the old woman fretted, peering out her screen door with Aaron propped on her massive hip. The baby was suckling a rubber teething ring and looked happily oblivious.

Maura managed a smile as she approached the porch. "Nope . . . just . . . better living through chemistry."

Vivian pursed her lips for a moment, then softened. "Your little angel was just absolutely perfect. Just one little mess in his onesy, got it cleaned right up."

Maura gently shoveled her baby up into her arms. "Dere's my big man. Thanks, Vivian."

"Are you okay, sweetheart?"

"Yeah, fine."

"You don't look fine."

Maura let out a sigh. "Just a little . . . tired."

A long pause as Vivian regarded Maura for a moment. "Come in for a second."

"Thanks . . . but I need to get him down for a nap."

"It'll just take a second, honey."

Maura shrugged and followed the portly woman into the cozy warren of knickknacks and country antiques. The Cansino house smelled of potpourri and Ben-Gay, a pleasing mélange that reminded Maura of her grandmother's house in Seattle. Vivian led Maura into the kitchen.

"Put the little duffer on the floor for a minute," the woman urged.

Maura set the baby down on a braided rug.

"Before my husband Bill retired, he was a transit cop in Detroit." The big gal was reaching up to a cabinet over the Norge as she spoke. She pulled down a wooden case about the size of a lunchbox.

"I have cousins back there," Maura commented absently, looking at the case, hands shaking.

The old woman handed Maura the case. The varnish was rubbed off. It smelled like cedar and oil. "You've got some troubles," Vivian said. "I can tell when somebody's fur is up. The world on their shoulders. Nice girl like you."

"Vivian, the thing is—"

The old woman raised an arthritic hand, interrupting. "I don't want to know any details. I just want you to take this. It's better than any pill."

Maura flipped the latch and looked inside the case. Nestled in a molded concavity was a .22 caliber handgun, its dark blue steel shank as oily and smooth as sharkskin. It made Maura's neck prickle with gooseflesh.

The old lady smiled sadly, her gold incisor gleaming. "If you want to know how to use it, I can give you some lessons."

Grove gripped the arm rests of the Blackhawk as the aircraft descended through layers of turbulent clouds. Clad in a flight jacket he had dug up at Langley, his body hastily bandaged, he felt as though he were in some kind of metaphysical free fall, and it wasn't merely the gravitational forces working on the helicopter. Grove felt as though he was about to cross some kind of Rubicon, a point of no return. One thing seemed certain: the cycle was coming around again.

He looked down through the slice of grimy windshield at the landscape rushing under them: the snaking black waterway of Pickman Creek, dark as motor oil in the overcast daylight, bending its way around the wasted terrain of scorched-out dumps. Behind them, to the west, the gray skyline of St. Louis stretched across the horizon.

The chopper pitched. Grove dug his fingernails into the padding. The engine yowled and the aircraft banked over a patchwork of soybean fields. Grove saw the intersection of Highway 20 and Old Six Mile Road about a quarter mile away, a cluster of emergency vehicles like Matchbox toys circling an old barn, all the roof flashers spinning with the mad frenzy of Christmas tree lights.

"There it is!" Grove pointed at all the vehicles in the distance.

"Copy that, bro! Hold on!" The Blackhawk pilot, a wiry surf punk from Redondo Beach, barely out of his twenties, fresh from his second tour in Iraq, dressed in a camo suit and helmet, wrestled the chopper toward a flat plateau of bare earth just east of the barn. The salvage yard got bigger and bigger as the Blackhawk descended. The junk swirled and roiled in the chopper's backwash, car hoods flipping up into the air, wadded newspapers tumbling in every direction.

The chopper sank to the earth, and the skids hit terra firma, rattling Grove's molars. The entire craft groaned as the engine revved, and a series of beeps and bells signaled the end of the journey.

Grove struggled out of his harness, then climbed out of the chopper.

He stood there for a moment, getting the lay of the land, his pants legs flapping. His eyes burned from the dust and exhaust, and he could barely hear somebody calling his name over the ringing in his ears. About a hundred yards away, dozens of CSI people were already carrying Styrofoam hazmat containers out of the barn and across the gravel lot. Resembling macabre carryout food cartons, the white containers meant only one thing to the initiated: *body parts*. Ribbons of yellow crime scene tape fluttered in the breeze, crisscrossing the barn's fence, the entrance, the boarded windows. Cameras flashed silver in the dreary gray light, and a mixture of plainclothes cops, Bureau suits, and uniforms milled around the parking lot, some of them writing on clipboards, others getting metrics on the ground with tape measures or brushing surfaces for latent prints.

"Agent Grove!"

Big Bill Menner, his craggy face aglow with excitement, his houndstooth sport coat straining with the girth of his belly, came running up, ducking under the back currents coming off the chopper's rotor. He wore cotton booties over his shoes and had rubber gloves on. "Looks like we hit the mother lode!" he hollered over the rotor noise.

"Hundred percent it's the Ripper?"

Menner nodded. "Thousand percent! Wait'll you get a load of the physical—come on!"

The beefy field agent turned and ushered Grove down a rocky slope of crabgrass, then across the gravel lot toward the barn. They passed throngs of white-suited lab people and evidence techs taking step impressions. They passed another group doing a methane probe, poking the ground with instruments, searching the edge of the building for any hidden remains. Another cluster of technicians crouched in the shadows under one of the windows, spraying the glass with ninhydrin aerosol for prints. At least a dozen plainclothes detectives or field agents milled around the inner and outer perimeters, bagging, dusting, measuring, and notating. The country air buzzed with the smell of ammonia and nerves.

"Is Cedric here yet?" Grove asked, sidestepping a woman in a lab coat.

"On his way. So is Geisel."

"Who was first on the scene?"

Menner explained how the salvage yard owner, Massamore, had heard shots being fired, then called 911. The state police sent a trooper, who found three fresh victims stacked outside. "Right up yon-

der," Menner said, pointing at the white tape out-
lines on the hard stony ground by an ancient water
trough. The three corpses were neatly arrayed, side
by side. "Found a lot more goodies inside," the big
man went on. "No sign of the perp. Won't be long
now, though. Considering the time of death on
the vics outside, our boy couldn't have gotten far.
Salvage yard owner got a good look at him, got a
great sketch, positive ID. It's all good. Just a matter
of time."

Grove nodded. "Who is he?"

"Name's Splet, a local."

"Spell it."

"S-P-L-E-T. Henry Alan Splet. White, late forties,
father of four. Cameraman for the local ABC affiliate."

Grove stopped just outside the entrance to the
barn, pondering the name. *Henry Alan Splet.* The
name had no resonance, no effect. It set off no
eerie feelings of déjà vu. No sense of cosmic meaning, no inchoate connections to ancient struggles,
no vibrations whatsoever. Henry Alan Splet was
the ultimate everyman, the proverbial face in the
crowd, the ordinary schlub. In fact, there was something about this *lack* of resonance that bothered
Grove. Henry Alan Splet was a nobody, a human
black hole, and maybe that was the most terrifying
revelation of them all. For a man to be capable of
pinning open a victim's eyelids while—

"You okay?"

Big Bill Menner's voice brought Grove back to
earth, and Grove rubbed his face. "Yeah, sorry. Just
taking it all in. I assume you got the trooper on ice
for Q&A?"

"Yeah, well, that's another thing."

"What's the problem?"

"Trooper's just a kid, couldn't be more than twenty-something."

"Yeah, and . . . ?"

"He's kinda rattled. What he found in there . . . it put the hurt on him, messed with his head." Menner paused in front of the double doors. "Here we are." He pulled a pair of rubber gloves from his pocket and handed them to Grove, then pulled a pair of paper booties out and handed them over. "I think you'll see what I mean when you see this place."

Grove sighed and slipped the paper booties over his shoes, then looked up again at the barn's entrance.

The double doors, crisscrossed with yellow police tape, hung by the threads of broken, rusted hinges. Mold and bird droppings clung to the worm-eaten timbers. The doors looked as though they were welded shut with a patina of age, stuck together in the aspic of decay. They also looked strangely imposing, like a drawbridge sealing off some haunted, bewitched fortress.

For the briefest moment imaginable, Grove flashed on a line from the *Inferno*. In the story, Dante Alighieri sees a legend at the threshold of the underworld, warning off all who dare enter.

"Lay Down All Hope, You That Go In By Me."

"After you, Agent Grove," Big Bill Menner said at last, gesturing at the double doors.

TWENTY-FOUR

It took a while for Grove to discover the clippings, and the secrets contained within their wadded remnants. He was too busy taking in the banquet of evidence strewn about the barn, the amazing array of human dementia made solid. When he first entered the dark, cobweb-covered space, for instance, he immediately noticed the weird way the bales of straw were arranged across the floor. He had to step back for a moment in order to finally identify the purpose of the oddly shaped rows: Like a child's playroom, they formed imaginary chambers, secret hallways, private hiding places. Evidence flags riddled these areas where blood from multiple sources—of all different ages and stages of decay—had formed droplets and streaks and spatters. An expert would be able to recreate a death chronology from all those stains with the reliability of a linguist translating a text.

As he slowly walked through the airless, hidden world of a madman, gazing at everything all at once, Grove wished he had his equipment, a camera, and maybe a digital recorder. The barn was as silent as a library. A pair of forensic technicians, the only other souls currently in the place, quietly worked in one corner with an ultraviolet scanning device. Purple light pulsed. Menner followed Grove at a respectful distance, softly indicating key pieces of evidence.

"Horse stalls," the big man murmured at one point, tipping his head at the rows of wooden enclosures lining the barn's east and west walls.

Grove paused to take in the rows of stalls. The simple wood-framed cubicles were lined with moldy hay, and some featured the names of former equine occupants embossed on silver-plated plaques affixed to the doors: Angel, Nurse White, Circus Lady, Mister Klister, Arturo the Artist, and The Hillbilly. All the names had that whimsical tone that horse names often have—maybe they had been racing horses, maybe show horses. Everything was coated with a thick layer of dust and grime, and the air smelled of chemical rot and quicklime.

Upon closer inspection, Grove saw that many of these horse stalls had been doctored, cryptic numbers spray painted across boarded doors, the feeding troughs filled with garbage, tires, old bottles, shoes, and discarded articles of clothing. Somewhere down in the tangled ganglia of Grove's subconscious he recognized this honeycomb of vaults as the product of a madman's delusional world: a territory of the imagination, a *locus dementia*.

"We left the last one pretty much how we found it," Agent Menner was saying, indicating the last stall on the left where tiny red evidence flags spread in profusion off the base of the doorway. Red strings connected some of the flags with key blood smears, resembling a cat's cradle of forensic minutiae. The odor of formaldehyde hung in the air like a curtain. "Kept his collection in there."

Grove felt a chill pinch his spine as he approached the doorway to the stall marked 213 in black spray paint—a feeling not unlike biting down on crushed ice. He looked in and saw the tawdry, blood-spattered furniture illuminated by one bare hanging lightbulb, a thin film of print dust shimmering on most of the surfaces. Grove saw the road cases, the trays of surgical instruments, and the bottles of chemicals. But mostly he saw the pictures on the walls.

"Ophthalmic retractors," Grove muttered, flexing his hand inside its rubber glove.

"What was that?" Menner asked.

"Pictures on the walls." Grove hovered in the doorway, staring. "The eye thing. Forced the victims to watch. We were right about that one."

"*You* were right."

"Very sick individual, this guy."

"Yeah."

"What's in the minifridge?"

"Don't bother looking, IBI took it all to the lab. Body parts."

Grove kept staring at a poorly focused photograph of a dilated pupil, shiny with terror, wrenched open by razor-thin wire clamps. "What kind of body parts?"

"Eyeballs, mostly."

With a nod Grove stepped inside the cell, then turned slowly around, 360 degrees, in order to take it all in, hoping there might be some detail that would hasten the man's capture. This was a critical time in any manhunt, the point at which the beast has been flushed out of hiding, the most dangerous hours. Desperation sets in. The killer often goes on one last rampage. If Grove could absorb some tiny shred that would help find Splet, some infinitesimal detail, *something* specific, lives might be saved.

He turned and scanned and searched . . . until his gaze fell on the pile of litter.

At first glance the trash appeared random, just an assortment of wadded newspaper and crumpled documents shoved into the corner. But the more Grove looked at the papers, the more his gut tightened with recognition. The wads of paper lay within a circle of ash. Faint symbols rimmed the circle. Numbers. Pictograms, perhaps. Some of them scrawled in blood, some in soot or grime. Grove knelt and drew a rubber-tipped index finger across the ash.

It was still warm.

"What is it?" Menner wanted to know.

"Not sure." Grove picked up one of the wadded clumps of paper and opened it.

He stared at the wrinkled page torn out of a *Time* magazine. The headline said, "Superstar Profiler Zeroes in on Latest Quarry." Grove read the first few lines of the text, the bit about the "famed FBI criminologist" claiming he is about to nab another killer.

Gooseflesh trickled down Grove's back.

"What's the matter?"

Agent Menner's voice faded in Grove's ears as

he picked up another piece of paper. This one was a Xerox. It was made off a microfiche machine—a grainy clipping of a social announcement from the *Alexandria Arts Weekly*—showing Grove and Maura one year ago, on their wedding day, arm in arm, smiling stiffly for the photographer.

"Agent Grove?"

Pure, white-hot anger began to smolder in Grove's gut. This freak Splet had hired a hit man to kill Grove, but worse than that, much worse, was the fact that Splet had been gazing at pictures of Maura. The same eyes that had gazed upon eviscerated women, that had coveted empty eye sockets, that had savored ghastly human misery and torture— *these same eyes*—had gazed upon Grove's wife only hours earlier. But that wasn't the worst part. The worst part was the circle, and the familiar scorch mark burned into its nucleus.

"Here we go," Grove murmured in a strained voice, as he stared at the circle of ash. The familiar burn mark was imprinted into the moldy straw like a negative image burned into photographic paper: *a perfect shadow of the purse-shaped caul.*

The rotted walls of that barn started closing in on Grove as he gawped at that litter of articles and pictures. He shuddered at the thought of Maura being associated in any way with this insane world, this squalid evil game, this ancient cycle.

Bill Menner's voice seem to wake him from a dream. "You're looking at the stuff from the tabloids?"

Grove slowly nodded, unable to look away from those wrinkled scraps of paper.

Menner shrugged. "I figure he knew you were

closing in, got a little fixated. What do *you* make of it?"

Grove stood up. He started to say something when another voice pierced the stillness of the barn.

"Agent Menner!"

Big Bill Menner whirled. "Over here."

A younger man, a Bureau trainee, his skinny neck swimming in his suit, came charging up to the two men. "Agent Menner, Agent Grove, I'm sorry—sorry to interrupt—but we got a—we found something—"

"Slow down, Atkins." Menner pulled a cigarette from his pocket. "Spit it out."

"We found something in Splet's SUV."

Menner and Grove looked at each other, then Menner gave the young trainee a look. "Take a breath, kid."

"You know the SUV with the TV equipment in the back?"

"Yeah, it's been dusted and processed already."

The young man shook his head frantically. "No, no, they found a camera, and it was still running, and they looked at the—the—whaddyacallit."

"The tape?"

"Yeah, the tape, they looked at the tape."

Menner shot another glance at Grove, then looked at the young man. "And?"

Agent Atkins swallowed hard. "He's on it."

"Who."

"The guy, the perp."

"Splet?"

More furious nodding. "Yeah, yeah—*Splet*—the perp, he's on the tape."

After a stunned pause, Grove stepped forward and said, "Let's go have a look."

For the first twenty minutes or so, the footage revealed very little other than a rotting old barn glimpsed through the side window of the SUV, and a few flickers of movement beyond the edge of the frame. Every so often a shadow would cross the screen in a dark blur, as though somebody has passed the field of view, close to the lens, or perhaps something crossing just a few inches behind the perimeter of the lens. The sound was muffled and indistinct behind the sealed windows of the vehicle, but disturbingly provocative nonetheless. Timbers snapping, a faint crackle of gunfire, a human scream, something being dragged in the dirt—all of it captured while the picture just sat on that weird, tilted angle of a barn blurred by moonlight reflecting off window glass.

The camera must have been purposely turned on at some point in the wee hours, or maybe jarred by a struggle and accidentally engaged. But regardless of the reasons—which would more than likely never be known—the camera started rolling around the first victim's time of death. Maybe Splet turned it on. Maybe this was all merely one more iteration of his eye obsession—the cold, cruel, impassive gaze of the video lens, the tyranny of the watcher. After all, wasn't this the electronic, mass-media version of his modus operandi? Making people watch? Making people witness the nadir of a victim's last moments, kicking and screaming as they are dragged down the portals of hell?

"Here he comes, right there, *there!*"

Sandra Callaway, an evidence technician from Menner's task force, jabbed a fingertip at the small monitor that was set up on the SUV's rear hatch, picnic style, for everybody to see. A slender black woman with graying dreadlocks, she was Menner's favorite technogeek, and right now she held a large umbrella over the equipment, ignoring her own rain-dappled shoulders, as though the video gear was a delicate child.

It had started to drizzle, making the scene a miserable crucible of mud and clammy, fetid tension. Grove stood directly behind Callaway, gripping an umbrella, watching the screen with feverish interest. Menner and the others stood behind Grove, looking on, jockeying for position with their own umbrellas. Onscreen something moved in the distance, subtly at first, but unmistakable: the barn's entrance doors were shifting, slowly opening.

"That's him, that's the guy," Agent Callaway said with a pert little nod toward the screen.

Grove stared at the screen. He couldn't see anything at first. But then he saw the dark figure in the distance, materializing in the doorway, emerging from the barn. At this point in the footage, the figure paused. It wasn't clear what he was doing. His face was overlaid in shadow. He looked out at the parking lot. Then he looked back over his shoulder at the darkness inside the barn. Then he looked directly at the camera in the SUV and started coming this way, toward the lens, toward us.

"Wait a minute." Grove couldn't believe what he was seeing. His stomach lurched. "What's going on?"

Callaway glanced over her shoulder at him. "What's the matter?"

"That's Splet?" Grove pointed incredulously at the screen, the image showing a little man in a torn, bloody dress, emerging from the barn.

"That is correct, my brother. Say hello to Henry Alan Splet."

"Holy Christ," Grove murmured, staring at the strange footage of a man dressed as a woman coming directly toward the camera. In the video, he walked with a weird, stiff gait, as though he just had a hip replaced or had just been shocked by a jolt of electricity. His eyes had the strangest look in them, an almost maniacal alertness, a glassy, *knowing* sort of gaze, like he was privy to some cosmic punchline.

"What's the matter, Grove?" Bill Menner had stepped a little closer and lowered his voice. "Something ring a bell?"

Grove could not tear his gaze from the monitor. "That's the same son of a bitch who rushed my place in Virginia."

"I'll be goddamned." Menner's utterance was barely audible above the rain.

Callaway turned back to the screen. "Y'all ain't seen nothing yet—check this out."

On screen, the man in the dress approached the SUV with that somnambulant stare burning a hole in the lens. His eyes virtually glowed with madness. It was hard to watch. His mouth was moving, slowly, like that of some toothless, drooling crone. Then, without warning, he slipped offscreen for a moment. A series of muffled clicks follows, suggesting that the rear door was being opened. A bizarre noise rumbled on the soundtrack, a very deep chugging sound, like an engine. The frame jiggled. The image blurred. The madman was picking up the camera and aiming it back at himself.

A face filled the frame: a ghastly version of the man who once was Henry Splet.

"What the hell?"

Grove's voice sounded almost alien to his own ears as he watched the footage. The killer loomed only inches away from the lens now. Eyes burning, gigantic mouth churning obscenely, he was snarling some kind of inhuman growl. In fact, the word *growl* hardly does the sound justice. It was a noise from the deepest bowels of a coal mine, an ugly, rhythmic grinding sound, so low and immense it practically corrupted the digital videotape, distorting the soundtrack to shreds like a series of hiccuping bomb blasts. It practically vibrated the cabinets.

"Turn it off," Bill Menner blurted, nodding at the black woman.

"No problem." Callaway punched the stop button. The picture slammed into black, the sudden silence jarring. "Whattya make of it?"

Menner shrugged.

Grove said nothing, just kept staring at that black monitor, the memory of that possessed face burned into the back of his retinas. The thunderous, deep growling echoed in his ear drums. He knew what it meant. He knew. It would be difficult to explain to the others, but he knew the look in those fiery eyes. He had seen it in the faces of other psychopaths, in the shark-eyed gaze of Richard

Ackerman back in Alaska, in the dead stare of Michael Doerr in New Orleans.

Factor X had returned.

"Whattya think, Dave?" Callaway had turned to one of her techies, a baby-faced young man in an FBI windbreaker standing off to the side in the drizzle, a stymied expression on his face, the brim of his Bureau cap dripping.

"You hear the sirens in the background?"

"Yeah, so?"

"A guy fleeing the scene? Stops like that? Takes the time to make a video?"

Callaway nodded. "He definitely wanted us to see this."

Menner piped in: "The guy's a loon. How can you—"

"It's a message meant for me."

All faces pivoted toward Grove at the sound of this glum, solemn announcement. Grove already had a reputation among working-stiff field agents for being a bit of a nut himself, a precognate type, the kind of spooky Quantico character best left to the chat shows and book tours. But today, amidst all the exotic aftermath and disturbing evidence, he carried a certain gravitas.

He let this latest assertion sink in for a moment. "I'm the guy he wanted to see this."

Menner looked at him. "Okay, so . . . why?"

"I don't know yet." Grove looked at the blank screen. "Let me see it again."

Agent Callaway turned back to the deck and punched play and the screen flickered back to life.

The horrible deep rumbling returned as the killer's contorted features filled the screen.

The huge, black divot of a mouth churned obscenely at the lens.

"Wait a minute." The realization struck Grove like an ice pick between the eyes. "*Wait* a minute—"

"What, what is it?" Menner was staring at the profiler, along with everybody else. Nobody was looking at the monitor anymore.

Everybody waited as Grove turned toward the baby-faced man in the Bureau cap. "Dave, right?"

"That's right, Dave Hockenberry." The geek stepped forward, gave him a nervous little nod.

Grove rubbed his mouth, thinking about it for a moment. "Can you adjust the speed of this thing?"

TWENTY-FIVE

Six people huddled in the airless crime-lab van, the narrow steel-reinforced cargo bay reeking of stale cigarettes and coffee. Ulysses Grove and young Agent Hockenberry stood near the front, hunched over an array of small CRT monitors embedded in a console. The others crowded the rear: Menner, Callaway, one of the lab assistants, and now Tom Geisel. The section chief had only just arrived from Washington, and now stood skeptically watching in his London Fog raincoat.

"What are we looking for here, Ulysses?" Gesiel wanted to know, his voice stretched thin with tension.

"Actually we're not *looking*, Tom." Grove kept staring at the scopes. "We're *listening*."

"Let's try it at a hundred and fifty frames a second, see what that sounds like." Hockenberry typed a command into the keyboard. The digital playback system clicked and whirred, and the picture of Splet swam on the screen for a moment. The image distorted as it rewound, backing up to the moment the murderer first appeared.

Grove felt his blood running cold as he waited for the video to engage. On each flank, the van's corrugated walls pressed in on him. The stray candy wrappers, the empty paper cups, the coils of patch cords, the shelving units brimming with probes and sensors and electronic gear—all of it pushed inward on Grove with excruciating pressure.

"There." Hockenberry punched another button on the console, and the image froze. He nodded. "Let's see what that sounds like."

The image raced forward. It looked like the Keystone Kops version of a madman, his face shivering and jumping up and down in fast motion.

"That's five times the normal speed."

The growling sound now resembled a buzz saw, but was still fairly low and gravelly, just not as rhythmic. At this speed it set Grove's teeth on edge.

"Still doesn't sound like much of anything," Menner commented from the rear.

"Can you speed it up even more?" Grove asked.

A tense sigh from the baby-faced young man. "I've never tried this before, but I could lay *this* off, then run it through the processor again."

"What would that buy us?" Menner wanted to know.

Hockenberry gave a shrug. "Basically it would be the growling sound twenty-five times faster."

"Let's do it," Grove said with a terse nod, then glanced over his shoulder at Geisel.

The two men exchanged a grave look. For years Tom Geisel had been Grove's lifeline, an old friend and mentor, but lately Grove sensed the section chief growing weary of the game, losing his edge, getting soft. It wasn't anything obvious. And it probably wasn't apparent to anybody but Grove. But Grove saw it around the edges of the older man's eyes, heard it in the hoarseness of his voice—a certain resignation, a heaviness. The section chief had been best man at Grove and Maura's wedding last year, and he had welled up with tears near the end of the ceremony. Grove had never seen Geisel cry like that. But it wasn't mere sentiment. There was something darker going on behind Tom Geisel's hound dog expression, something tugging at the older man's relationship with Grove. And now, tonight, closed inside this stale-smelling mobile crime lab, Grove sensed the helpless feeling exuding from Geisel like a musk.

"All right, here we go." Hockenberry flipped switches and typed commands into the keyboard, until the screen went completely white with snow. "We're not going to see anything, but we'll hear the voice at seven hundred and fifty frames a second."

Grove gave him a nod. "Go for it."

"Most sounds, this would basically kick it up into the ultrasonic," Hockenberry murmured as he punched one last toggle. "Here goes."

There was an audible pop, and the digital counter started whirring so fast it blurred.

The speakers hummed.

Grove frowned. "Can you turn it up any louder?"

"It's almost pinned." Hockenberry gave another shrug, and twisted another knob.

The noise that buzzed out of the speakers almost sounded like the raspy voice of a stroke victim.

Goosebumps formed on Grove's neck. "There's something there. Can we hear it again?"

The atmosphere inside the mobile lab seemed to crystalize suddenly.

"Sure . . . whatever." Hockenberry, exceedingly uneasy now, typed another command.

The weird voice warbled and fluttered out of the speakers, then cut off again.

"I'm hearing words." Grove leaned toward the speaker. "Play it again."

Hockenberry pressed the button again. The strange voice snarled at them.

Grove turned to the group. "Is anybody else hearing that?"

The others stood there.

Grove pointed at the machinery. "Play it again, Dave."

Another command into the keyboard, and the ghostly voice undulated out of the speakers once again. This time, Grove was certain he heard an approximation of a very familiar word. His scalp bristled.

Geisel said, "I'll be a son of a bitch."

Menner shook his head. "I don't hear it."

"Hold up, hold up." Agent Callaway cocked her head toward the speaker. "Was that '*grow*'?"

"Listen closer." Grove nodded at Hockenberry, and the speakers crackled and hummed again.

"It's '*Grove*,' " Callaway blurted. "The voice is saying 'Grove.' "

" 'Grove—*something*,' " Grove corrected her.

Hockenberry typed the play command again, and the walls reverberated with the ungodly rasp.

"Jesus Christ, is that '*eleven*'—*Grove eleven*?" Menner looked nauseous. "What the hell does that mean?"

Geisel stepped forward. His face twitched as he pointed at the speaker. "Play it again."

Hockenberry played it again.

Geisel looked at Grove. "That's not possible."

"*Grove eleven black*, is what I heard." Grove felt light headed. "Grove eleven black? Right?"

"Sounds like a goddamn code," Menner chimed in.

"There's something else," Callaway said. "At the end. Roll it one more time, Dave."

Hockenberry tapped the keys.

The voice rasped at them.

Callaway licked her lips. "*Grove eleven black rim*, it sounds like. 'Eleven black rim?' What the hell does that mean?"

Geisel stared at the speaker, his face ashen. "Everybody out."

Menner looked at the section chief. "Pardon?"

"I said everybody out. Except Grove. Everybody out, right now."

Callaway looked at Menner, then back at Geisel. "Am I missing something? Should we be—?"

"I said out, goddamnit! Now!!"

There was a beat of stunned silence, a series of glances exchanged. Geisel's outburst took everyone by surprise. Even Grove. He couldn't remember the last time the section chief had cried out in anger.

Menner and Callaway shared one last uneasy glance and gave each other a shrug, then turned and shuffled over to the rear vertical door. Menner unlatched it and yanked it upward—the pulleys shrieking—while Callaway grabbed her umbrella. One by one the team members climbed out into the drizzle. Within seconds, Grove stood alone in the claustrophobic little enclosure with his boss.

"The voice on that recording did not say 'eleven black rim,'" Geisel informed him after the door had been lowered and latched from the outside. The older man's hands were shaking. His eyes glinted with alarm.

Grove looked at him. "What did it say?"

"It said, 'Eleven Black River Drive.'"

This meant nothing to Grove. He shook his head. "Go on, Tom."

"Eleven Black River Drive. It said, 'Grove, Eleven Black River Drive'."

Grove shrugged. "Okay. So?"

"Eleven Black River Drive, Ulysses." Geisel looked around the interior of the lab as though searching for something he'd lost. His hands kept flexing nervously like he didn't know what to do with them. "It's impossible. Gotta be . . . somebody made a mistake."

"What the hell is the matter, Tom?" Grove had never seen his boss this flummoxed, disoriented, unhinged. "What the hell is Eleven Black River Drive?"

Geisel looked at Grove. "Only about six people on earth know that address—"

"Wait a minute, you're not talking about—"

"—Me, Keven Hannigan over at Justice, a couple of federal marshals—"

Grove stared at him. "You're not saying—"

"—and your *wife,* Ulysses. Your wife is the only other person who knows that address."

For a moment Grove could not breathe, the world turning on its axis.

Geisel's voice dropped to a whisper. "Eleven Black River Drive, Fox Run, Indiana, is owned by WITSEC. It's the safe house, Ulysses."

Grove could not respond, could not speak, could not move, could not even think.

The mocking silence pressed down on the cargo bay, the echo of that hideous rasping voice still lingering in Grove's ears.

PART III
The Unsafe House

"Fate has terrible power. You cannot escape it by wealth or war."

—Sophocles

TWENTY-SIX

Fox Run, Indiana, founded in 1898, population 4712, was a typical middle-American farm town. Located about twenty-five miles southeast of Indianapolis, the little hamlet lay at the intersection of two main rural routes. Surrounded on all sides by a sea of cornfields, the place gave off a feeling of timeless, sepia isolation, like some countrified version of Darwin's archipelago, where pop machines and old men in overalls sit in charming stasis, unchanged for decades. The central business district—which was not much more than a couple of blocks of cracked sidewalks and Victorian brick storefronts—dripped with quaintness. Castellani's Market sat at the corner of Main and Fourth, as it had for nearly a century, its smoked meats and plucked fowls hanging on hooks in the windows. Margie's Five-and-Dime was next door, its needlepoint samplers and hand-dipped candles on display in windows bordered by ruffles and chintz. The town had two gas stations—one at each end of the

main drag—a one-room schoolhouse, a feed and
seed store, a sheriff's office, and three restaurants.
The Dixie Cafe served up chicken-fried steaks and
cherry Cokes; the fare at Al's Barbecue was self-
explanatory; Bomgartners, a fern-and-brass eatery,
featured everything from prime rib to pasta pri-
mavera, and catered to the recent influx of white-
collar patrons. These affluent middle classers were
mostly employed at the nearby Maytag plant, and
mostly housed on the north side of town in a new
subdivision known as Sherwood Forest. There was
also Camp Steagall, a military base, less than ten
miles away, which was a big employer and one of
the reasons why the Federal Marshal Service listed
Fox Run as an active site on their WITSEC database. It was close to both a Bureau field office *and*
a government airstrip.

The town also sported four taverns. Dewey's
Tap, Bud and Hank's, The End Zone, and Michel-
mann's Brauhaus. Fox Run's ratio of drinking es-
tablishments to residents was about average for the
area—.0008 bars per capita—but some of the towns-
people yearned to increase the balance. Perhaps
this was due to the fact that the vast Indiana sky,
with its endless waves of grain, weighed heavily on
the psyche. Especially at night. After sunset, Fox Run
transformed itself into a deserted oasis—a place of
lonely, neon-drenched crossroads, desolate, rolled-
up sidewalks, and isolated pools of sodium vapor
lights. Rust-freckled metal signs dangled over farm
implement yards, rattling in the night breezes. Moths
swarmed the street lamps. Distant freight trains
out of Fort Wayne or Columbus moaned and clattered through the night, and sent shivers of loneli-

ness across the silent streets. And even up in the
tidy cul-de-sacs of Sherwood Forest, the desolation
resonated across dark lawns, the property lines
butting up like breakwaters against endless oceans
of corn.

Maura's little brick town house was no exception.
After dark, her backyard lay in absolute blackness.
Every hour or so another train would howl by in
the distance, its solitary headlight beam weaving
through the night, a luminous thread stitching the
tops of the cornfields. On her first night alone in
the safe house, in fact, Maura didn't sleep a wink.
She just sat on the rear windowsill, gazing out at
the night, waiting for another train to pass, wondering if she would ever see her husband again,
wondering if she would see something in the news
about him.

Now, as the sun set on her third night, Maura
paced the tiny kitchen that overlooked her backyard.

It was a galley-style kitchen, equipped with a
miniature stove that could fit easily in a double-
wide camper, a modicum of counter space, and a
small refrigerator. The single-basin sink was stain-
less steel and rimmed with rust. The air smelled of
mold and grit. Ancient ruffled curtains hung off a
solitary window. The drone of crickets came through
the screen, blending with the hiss of the baby monitor. Aaron was stirring again. He hadn't been sleeping well in his new nursery. Maybe he sensed his
mother's imminent breakdown.

Dressed in a San Francisco 49ers jersey, jeans,
and sneakers, Maura felt another spell of anxiety
coming on. She wore her nursing bra beneath the

nightshirt, damp spots showing through the 49ers logo. She lit another cigarette and compulsively puffed it as she paced. The darkness of the backyard, visible between the curtains, bothered her. The emptiness of it, the ceaseless noise of the crickets and trains. She was losing her mind. The medication hardly affected her anymore. She had taken another anxiety pill only an hour ago and it had barely registered. Why was she getting worse? Was she sinking into a full-blown nervous breakdown? Had life with Ulysses Grove finally taken its toll on her?

A noise from the basement—a very faint creaking sound or a dry snap—interrupted her thoughts.

She paused, cocked her head . . . and listened . . . but the sound had faded away. She listened more closely, but only heard the hiss of the baby monitor next to her, and the soft rattle of the wind outside in the eaves. Nothing more from the cellar. Was she imagining things now? Hearing things? The new house had its own symphony of night sounds, taps and rattles to which Maura had not yet grown accustomed. After all, it was only her third night in purgatory.

Only three days earlier she had been whisked off the face of the earth, erased from the world.

They had flown Maura and Aaron out to Indianapolis on a commercial airliner, listing her on the passenger manifest as one "Garnett, Melanie" (allowing her the same initials as her real name). The pair of elderly federal marshals who escorted Maura, each of them with Navy tattoos and tough as old iron, had been polite, courteous, and deferential. And Maura had given them plenty of shit.

She demanded that the marshal service pay for her incidentals, which she insisted on buying at an Indianapolis Target the moment they were on the ground: baby formula, diapers, wipes, towels, bar soap, Tylenol, cigarettes, cereal, milk, sleeping pills, and Formula 409.

Glancing across the kitchen at the little dining table, she regarded the row of pill bottles, the overflowing ashtray, the dirty dishes from dinner, Aaron's applesauce-crusted high chair, and the shellacked wooden case containing the .22 pistol that Vivian Casino had given her. Is this what her life had been reduced to? A shadow of what she once was, trapped in a spiralling depression, alone in the middle of nowhere, a shut-in hunkered down in a forlorn little kitchen in a forlorn little house, imagining noises coming from her basement?

She went over and sat down at the table. She opened the case and looked at the gun. Her ears still rang from the lessons Mrs. Cansino had given her that afternoon in the backyard. Maura had killed an entire watermelon, turning it into pinkish pulp. She had been surprised at how easy the Ruger pistol was to shoot, the aim astoundingly precise.

But weren't watermelons a lot easier to kill than human intruders?

Stubbing out her cigarette, she went over to the sink and splashed water on her face. Dizziness threatened to knock her over. Another panic attack was coming, she could sense it like the smell of rain on the wind. She was accustomed to these panicky feelings. She had been having them off and on since she was a young cub reporter for the *San Francisco Chronicle* a million years ago. But she had always been able to manage them, control them, control her nerves. She had interviewed captains of industry. Never missed a deadline. Worked her way up the journalistic ladder first at *Omni* magazine, then *Outdoors,* then *Discover.* Now look at her. Is this what her life with Ulysses Grove had wrought? Is this . . .

Again she paused.

The noise from the basement had returned. This time, the creaking sound was clearly audible, sending chills along the backs of Maura's arms and neck. Something primal within her, something deep down in her reptile brain, began to react to these muffled, intermittent noises with the spontaneity of a chemical reaction. Her belly turned cold. Her flesh crawled as she turned and stared at the latched door on the other side of the kitchen, the one at the top of the basement steps.

She told herself to stay calm. Chances were it was nothing, merely a settling noise. All houses emit those kinds of sounds late at night, especially when there's a jittery insomniac around to hear them. Maura was simply unfamiliar with this meager little bungalow's natural ticks and tocks. That was it. Her imagination was merely—

Shuffling noises came from behind that latched door, stiffening Maura's spine.

Now she was sure there was something down there. Maybe an animal. Maybe something worse. She glanced over her shoulder toward the archway leading out of the kitchen. The stairs to the second floor lay just beyond it. Instinct told her to move quickly.

In fact, everything she did for the next few minutes was purely instinctual.

TWENTY-SEVEN

"Why would they give her an unlisted number?"
Grove sat with jaw set and teeth clenched on the
edge of a bench seat in the forward section of the
aircraft, still clad in the damp flight jacket that
he had dug up at Langley. In his threadbare sweats
and muddy infantry boots, his brown skin glistening with flop-sweat, he looked like some mad
Black Panther about to lead a violent charge on an
administration building. His heart had not stopped
racing since the time they had left the Pickman
Creek crime scene. "Get the marshal service on the
blower."

"Already did it," Geisel told him. "They're on
their way to the Indy field office as we speak."

Tom Geisel sat across from Grove, jacket off, tie
loosened, sleeves rolled up. He was working his
BlackBerry, the earphone stuck in one ear.

He had already made a call to the Fox Run sheriff's office and had gotten the after-hours voice mail.
He then patched through to the Bureau's Midwest

Tactical office, and managed to rouse the town sheriff out of bed. Now Geisel was coordinating the agencies from the hermetically sealed world of the Eclipse 500, soaring through the black sky at 375 knots, bouncing over invisible troughs of turbulence forty thousand feet above Southern Illinois.

The plane was a small, twin-engine jet, part of the 11th Wing out of DC's Bolling Air Force base, chartered by Geisel's Behavioral Science Unit. The cabin was a white padded chamber that smelled of coffee and disinfectant, and the ceaseless vibrations made Grove's skull throb.

Time had sped up somehow, the ticking clock chipping away at Grove's sanity. The Eclipse was the fastest, longest ranging aircraft in the fed's fleet, but delays at Scott Air Force Base in Belleville had put Grove behind. Indianapolis was about four hundred miles away. They could get there in an hour with the wind at their back but unexpected factors had begun to impede the journey. According to Grove's hasty calculations, the killer had at least six, maybe eight, hours on them. Depending upon his mode of transportation, he could already be in Fox Run, Indiana.

"Don't they have anybody on patrol out there?" Grove's stomach lurched as the plane bumped and careened through the slipstream. "Where is this place?"

"Mayberry, USA . . . by design," Geisel explained. "These safe houses gotta blend in."

"They don't make provisions for contingencies? Emergencies?" Grove glanced at his watch. "What time is it?"

"Take it easy. It's 12:30. Maura's gonna be fine. This guy isn't gonna risk the exposure."

"Where the hell is that sheriff?" Grove looked at his boss. "I'm dying here, man."

"They're patching him through right now, just stand by." Geisel looked out his window at the black wall of clouds. "How did this happen, Ulysses?"

"What?"

"How did the freak find the safe house?"

Grove had already been asking himself that for the last hour and a half. He knew the answer. He knew the moment he heard his own name ooze out of those speakers in Hockenberry's mobile lab. It was time to confess his sins. He looked over his shoulder at the empty cabin. He glanced forward at the sealed cockpit door. He was alone with his surrogate father confessor. "It's my fault," he murmured.

"Say again." Geisel took the earpiece out of his ear. "It's what?"

"It's my fault, all of it."

"I hope you're planning on explaining that."

Grove rubbed his face. "Tom, I know you've seen me make some leaps that don't add up. I know what the rest of the unit thinks of me."

"People hate what they don't understand." Geisel's face was open, patient. "That's not what we're talking about."

Grove looked at him. "I'm going to tell you something now, and it never leaves this cabin. And if you repeat it, I'll deny it to my grave." He paused then, measuring his words. "I'm hooked into something, Tom. I don't know how else to explain it."

"Okay."

"Started way back, maybe before I was born. Hopkins at the academy—you remember old Hopkins?—he used to call it the *para-forensic*. The way things reveal themselves to certain folks. But it's not just a gift, or a psychic thing . . . or whatever you want to call it."

Geisel frowned at him. "You're talking in circles now, Slick. Just spit it out."

Grove let out a sigh. "This guy Splet, he might have started out your run-of-the-mill psychotic. Like Ackerman, like Doerr. But the stakes got raised."

"How's that?"

"Look at all these redline serial murder cases—Gacy, Ackerman, Doerr, Ramirez, now Splet—there's a dominant personality that emerges in the subject. Call it a parasite, call it an entity. Call it any damn thing you want."

"When you say entity—?"

"I'm talking about something that's consistent. *Consistent.* You understand what I'm saying?"

Geisel stared at him. "I'm not sure if I do or not . . . or maybe I just don't *want* to."

Grove lowered his voice. "It's the same energy, Tom. In all these perps. An entity unto itself. It reappears again and again. And it's been around for thousands of years. The nastiest goddamn vibe you could ever imagine. A million times worse than these pathetic spree killers. Why? Because it's got an *agenda*. It's after something."

A taut moment of silence at this point as the plane vibrated and yawed.

Grove went on: "I know it sounds paranoid, delusional, crazy—hell, I don't even believe it half the time—but this thing is after *me*. That's what happened back in '05 when I got sick, when I caught Ackerman. That thing got inside me, tried to tear me apart."

Geisel didn't say anything, just stared at the floor of the cabin.

"That's why it's going after my family now." Grove glanced out the window at the night sky rushing past the fuselage. "Somehow—*somehow*—it locked on to the safe house."

"That is simply not possible."

Grove shook his head. "Everything's impossible until it happens. I'd call Walt Dickinson over in IT, have him check all the Bureau mainframes, Marshal Service, too, but it doesn't much matter anymore."

Geisel was thinking. "Didn't this guy Splet work at a TV station?"

"Who cares, Tom. It happened. People hack elections. Get used to it."

"All I'm saying is—" Geisel's BlackBerry trilled. He quickly thumbed the answer button. "Talk to me." A beat as he listened. "I'm going to put you on speaker."

"*Who do we got?*" The voice crackled from the BlackBerry after Geisel positioned it on the arm of his seat.

"You got Special Agent Ulysses Grove and Section Chief Tom Geisel en route."

An older man's gravelly Midwestern drawl squawked out of the tiny speaker: "Sheriff Gene Tomilson here, along with Agent Raymond Potheuse from the Indy Bureau office, and Federal Marshal Harry Stenheiser."

Grove spoke up. "Gentlemen, I apologize for the

bluntness but we're up against a time crunch here. Who's the closest to the site?"

Through the speaker: "Agent Grove, Harry Stenheiser here. No need to apologize. We got Indy Tactical on their way to the site."

"Are they there yet?"

An awkward pause. "Well, no, but we're only talking about—"

"I'll ask it again, who's the closest to the site?"

After a moment, the sheriff's voice returned: "That would be the third-shift deputy, good old boy named Tommy Elkins."

"Where is he now?"

Pause. "According to dispatch, he just came on duty, so that would put him about a mile and half west of Sherwood Forest where your wife is."

"Get him over there, please, right away if possible," Grove said to the device, wanting to scream at it, smash it with his fist.

Through the device: "Consider it done, sir."

"Thank you."

"One question, Ulysses."

Grove recognized the voice of Agent Raymond Potheuse from the Indianapolis field office. Grove remembered the man from the Happy-Face Killer investigation seven years earlier. Potheuse was a smart, heavyset former jock who had helped Grove canvass truck stops. "Go ahead, Ray."

"What's the protocol here?"

"What do you mean?"

"Do we go in with reasonable force no matter what? Or do we hang back and assess?"

"Go in, Ray. Go the fuck in the minute you get there."

Geisel spoke up. "Ulysses—"

"What?" Grove shot a look at Geisel. "What's the problem?!"

"We don't even know if this is real."

Grove turned to the BlackBerry. "Listen to me, everybody. I don't care if you scare the shit outta my wife, wake the baby, blow the goddamn cover—I want somebody packing iron inside that house with my wife as soon as humanly possible, does that make sense?"

After a pause, Potheuse's voice replied, "Makes perfect sense to me."

"Thank you."

Geisel added, "Just get that sheriff's deputy over there right now."

"He's on his way."

TWENTY-EIGHT

Maura didn't hear the deputy's prowler approaching from the north, its heavy-duty tires crunching over the gravel composite that made up Black River Drive. She was upstairs, in the hallway, padding toward the door to Aaron's room, which had been shut and latched for the night.

Flesh crawling with panic as she approached her baby's door, she agonized over two contrary courses of action, the scenarios crashing in her brain like riptide waves in a stormy sea. Should she simply grab the baby and run? In this scenario, the biggest risk would merely be embarrassment (Most likely in front of Mrs. Cansino's house after both women realized the noise in the cellar was nothing more than a mouse or a stray raccoon that had slipped in through the window well). The other course of action involved bigger risks.

In this second scenario, Maura would go down the basement steps to investigate. After all, she had a gun. And if it turned out to be only a mouse, nobody would be the wiser.

She reached the door to the baby's room and paused, her hand on the cool brass surface of the doorknob.

A moment of indecision held her there, hand on the knob, frantically reconsidering her strategy. What if there *was* somebody in the basement? Should she take the chance of running into them with Aaron in her arms? Was there another way out? Could she get the baby out a second-floor window? The smartest thing to do, perhaps, was lock the baby's room from the inside, and then let the drama play out with Aaron out of harm's way. But wouldn't that be trapping her son—the most important thing in her life—in this godforsaken little brick prison? She stood like this, ruminating, her hand on the doorknob, for only an instant, a total duration of little more than a few seconds, but it felt like forever.

At last she made a decision.

She quietly turned the doorknob until the bolt unlatched, pushed the door open, and slipped into the baby's spartan, unfurnished room without making a sound. Aaron was curled up in the rental crib in the corner, his tiny thumb in his little mouth. Maura couldn't look at him, and yet she couldn't tear her eyes away from him.

Shadows swayed on the wall above the crib from the tree limbs rustling outside the window. The odor of baby powder and downy skin made Maura's solar plexus twist with fear. It was the mama-bear syndrome. It sent adrenaline rushing through her veins like an amphetamine blast as she crossed the room soundlessly, walking on the balls of her feet, careful not to make any noise.

She found the window latch in the darkness and securely locked the window.

One last thing. She went back to the door and turned the inner dial to the lock position. Then she slipped back out in the cool darkness of the hall-way, gently pulling the door shut until it latched.

Now the hard part.

The deputy's prowler pulled up in front of 15 Black River Drive (two houses due east of the subject's domicile) at precisely oh-one-hundred hours and seven minutes. This was how Knox County Sheriff's Deputy Thomas Stanley Elkins—Tommy-Boy to his cronies—talked and thought: with military precision. It was how he did his job, too. A tall, slender, ruddy farm boy with a mousy mustache, he wore his starched olive-drab uniform and big, black Sam Browne gun belt with pride. He wondered if tonight would be the night. Nearly eighteen months on the job, and no action.

Maybe tonight.

He put the prowler in park, then settled back in his seat for a moment and let out a sigh as he marked off the salient milestones in his logbook: the time of the dispatch, the time of his arrival at the scene, the observable characteristics of the exterior of 11 Black River Drive. *Structure appears secure and quiet. Porch light on. First floor lights behind the windows. No discernable movement inside. Second floor dark.*

Neighbors' windows all dark.

Sliding the logbook back into its plastic caddy, which was positioned next to the prowler's shotgun, Deputy Elkins grabbed the radio handset, and thumbed the send button. "Baker One, this is Sixteen Adam."

The dispatcher's voice coughed out of the speaker: "Sixteen Adam, copy."

"Ten-twenty, Black River Drive, will advise, stand by."

"Copy, Sixteen Adam."

Elkins put the mike back, grabbed his baton, opened his door, and climbed out of the prowler, rising to his full height of six feet, three inches.

He walked around the front of the car, unsnapping the safety strap on his Smith and Wesson, following protocol to the letter. Then he made his way down the street to the subject's home. The brick bungalow rose up benignly before the deputy, the crumbling chimney silhouetted against the night sky. The porch light sent a soft glow across the grass. The garage door was shut. No cars in the narrow driveway. Very quiet.

Elkins made his way up the landscaped path toward the porch. He made note of the thick fringe of crabgrass along the walk, the weeds poking out of cracks in the paving stones, the general unkempt quality of the house. Tommy Elkins would never let a home deteriorate like this. Who were these people? And why had Sheriff Tomilson been so cagey about ordering Elkins out here on the double, no questions asked?

He reached the front door and knocked.

*   *   *

Maura was upstairs, in the hallway, moving toward the staircase, when the knocking sound came. It was forceful and quick—obviously coming from the front door—and it penetrated her frenzied thoughts like an ice pick. She paused at the top of the stairs, her sweaty hand on the newel post. It was the middle of the night. Who the hell would be knocking on her door in the middle of the night? And what, if anything, did it have to do with the noise in the basement?

She didn't move.

Her mind reeled. It could be good news. It could be somebody coming to help her, maybe one of the marshals. But wouldn't they call her first? Didn't they have the unlisted number? Maura couldn't remember. Maybe it was Mrs. Cansino. Or perhaps one of the other neighbors saw something suspicious going on. But on the other hand, it could be a trick, a way to get her to open the door.

She stood there for quite a long moment before the second knock came.

Deputy Elkins knocked again.

From inside the house, after a beat of silence, came the muffled sounds of footsteps, somewhere on the second floor perhaps. Elkins stepped back and waited. He was about to knock again when a metallic clicking noise came from the side of the house. Then a shuffling sound, the crackle of leaves.

Elkins pulled his baton from its sheath, turned, and descended the steps.

"Sheriff's department," he called out as he crept around the side of the house. "Anybody there?"

He turned the corner and saw a figure standing in the shadows by the basement window.

"Identify yourself, please."

The figure pointed a gun with a silencer on it.

"Whoa!"

There was a flash of light and the first blast popped in the air like the snap of a slingshot, taking the deputy completely by surprise, striking him in the throat.

He staggered, the baton flying out of his hands. It felt as though a battering ram had smashed though his neck, lodging in his air passage, squeezing the breath out of him. He landed on his back in the side yard, gagging, his hands blindly reaching for his gushing neck, the blood running through his fingers.

He tried to reach for his gun. The figure was moving toward him. There was something wrong with the figure's face. This last observation was the deputy's final conscious thought before expiring.

There was definitely something wrong with the figure's eyes.

Maura had been standing at the front door, preparing herself to unbolt it and open it, when she heard the weird pinging noise from somewhere outside, somewhere nearby, like a rubber band snapping in two, sending fresh waves of gooseflesh pouring over her arms and legs and back. It was definitely not a raccoon. Raccoons didn't make snapping noises. At least, Maura didn't *think* they did.

She turned toward the picture window, which

was obscured by dingy teal drapes. She gently pushed the drapes away from the frame, then peered through the half-inch gap. The porch was deserted.

What the hell was going on? Was this a prank? Did they celebrate Halloween in the spring in Indiana?

Maura stood there for a tense moment, frozen once again with indecision, her back pressed against the front door, her clammy hands flexing nervously, her mouth dry. Should she go outside and investigate? Should she call Mrs. Cansino first? The older woman was probably sound asleep but it didn't matter. It was better to be safe than sorry.

The closest phone was in the kitchen. It sat on the narrow counter to the right of the refrigerator, an old table model with scuffed white housing, an old-fashioned pigtail cord, and rotary dial.

Maura had jotted the neighbor's phone number on a scrap of paper that she had affixed to the refrigerator with a ceramic hula girl magnet.

She started to dial the Cansino's number when she realized there was no dial tone.

The phone was dead.

TWENTY-NINE

Grove gazed out the portal window at the twinkling carpet of lights that made up Indianapolis, Indiana, as the Eclipse bounced and bucked through the strata of clouds at five thousand feet, then four thousand, then three, then two. The thump of the landing gear deploying vibrated up through the floor. The turbulence was terrific. Across the aisle, Geisel made anguished grunting noises, gripping his armrests like a child in a dentist chair getting his teeth drilled.

But Grove hardly noticed the bumpy descent. He had withdrawn into a sort of shell—a zone of laser-focused concentration so intense it was practically an altered state—catalyzed by thoughts of his wife and child in mortal jeopardy. His breathing got slow and regular. He itched to get his gun out. It was packed away in a road case in the plane's cargo hold under its belly.

"Gentlemen"—the pilot's voice crackled out of the ceiling speakers—"let's buckle up, secure all loose items, as we start on our approach to Grissom Air Force Base."

Grove and Geisel fastened their safety belts.

"Sit tight and we'll be on the ground in about three minutes, give or take."

Grove looked at his watch. It was 1:23 A.M. His brain began working the numbers. If Grissom was an hour from Fox Run, they wouldn't be able to reach Maura for another hour and a half. At least. The Marshal Service would be there long before that. But what would they find?

A tremendous jolt of guilt sliced through Grove's midsection, so deep and sudden he practically lost his breath. He knew he carried this terrible destiny with him now. Whatever the purpose, whatever the reason, he bore this burden like a disease, and now he had infected the woman he loved. He had brought this inexorable curse into her life.

For a brief and terrible instant, Grove's mind cast back to his wedding, back to the moment that he had exchanged vows with Maura County on the edge of that leafy golf course outside Alexandria. He stood in the sun and looked into her eyes, her beautiful green eyes flecked with gold, and he hesitated before saying, "I do." Nobody else had noticed that weird, awkward pause that day, not even Maura, the moment was so fleeting. But it had felt to Grove, just for that one instant, as though a shadow had crossed over the sun, darkening the flower-laden alter. He finally managed to blurt out the words with a sheepish grin, vexed by the momentary hiccup in the proceedings. But Grove now realized he had hesitated because he knew the truth. He was dooming her.

Fingernails digging into the padded armrests of the aircraft seat, Grove sat there in stony silence, waiting for the plane to land, thinking, for a second, how he would trade places with Maura in a heartbeat. He would die for her.

Unfortunately, as Grove knew all too well, until the rescue team arrived, she was on her own.

Maura crossed the kitchen and stood at the top of the basement stairs, trying to decide what to do, her heart pumping, her scalp tingling with fight-or-flight gooseflesh.

That was the central question now: *to flee or not to flee.* One thing was certain: She could not leave Aaron in this house. She had to protect her baby. But should she go grab him and risk running out with him? What if there was a gunman out there? Or worse yet, what if there was one huddling in the basement? Had he cut the phone lines? Maybe it was just a coincidence that her service was out. It had taken an entire day to get it turned on, and the service had been glitchy at first. And then again, maybe Maura was manufacturing this whole thing out of her raging paranoia.

A faint creak came from the basement, followed by a squeaking noise.

She got very still then, and became very aware of all the sensory information flooding her brain. The noise sounded as though it might be something small, something scurrying across the peeling paint of the basement floor. It had to be a mouse. Maura could not make her legs work, make herself move.

From her vantage point at the southeast corner

of that tiny kitchen, her hip pressed against the little oilcloth-covered dining table, she could see the door to the basement steps to her left, sealed and latched, taunting her to come open it and investigate. She could also see the screen door to her right leading out to the narrow side yard, the shadowy patch of crabgrass from which the snapping noise had come. Which door should she open for all the cash prizes? Door Number One, Door Number Two, or Door Number Three?

America was waiting.

In her peripheral vision she could also sense the darkness of the unincorporated pastureland immediately north of Black River Drive, the distant tops of elms and black oaks swaying ghostlike against the night sky, just barely visible in the little curtained window. She could also detect a mixture of odors—some of them oddly incongruous, odors which she hadn't noticed before—such as the faint trace smells of rotting food, old ammonia, animal droppings. Her spine was vibrating like a piano string. She tasted metal on the back of her tongue, and something like rage burned in her guts.

She turned to the lacquered box on the table and flicked the latch.

It took her just a minute—maybe even *under* a minute—to get the gun out of the box, and inject one of the three ammo magazines that were nestled in the foam liner. She was careful to muffle it with her hands so that the metallic *clunk* made minimal noise.

She hadn't been completely honest with Mrs. Casino that afternoon (during the watermelon-killing lessons). The instructions were more like brushing-up exercises for Maura. She had learned to fire a gun years earlier, initially from her Uncle Dan, who was from Wyoming and was a big sportsman, and later for a piece she wrote on ballistic science for *Discover*. Not that she was ever fond of guns. But now, standing in that creaking house, with all those moving shadows on the walls, she was learning to love her new .22 caliber Ruger just fine, thank you very much.

The basement had fallen quiet again—no sounds for a minute or two, which spanned the total amount of time it took Maura to open the varnished box, get the gun out, and load it. Now she turned toward that insolent closed door at the top of the steps, and she ordered her feet to walk over to it.

The door came open with a dry click.

Cool, greasy air rushed out at her, the smell of grit and roots and old laundry. She took a bracing breath. She felt a primordial sensation of disturbing a vast cobweb, the resident spider freezing up at the vibrations resonating through the invisible dark web of the cellar. Maura turned to a switch plate to her left, and flipped the toggle button.

The light didn't work.

Maura paused, swallowing her fear and gazing down that length of steps into the darkness of the basement. Nothing was stirring down there; there was total silence. Had a fuse blown? She listened. Maybe the raccoon or squirrel or whatever the hell it was had toddled back out the window.

Whirling around toward the kitchen, Maura remembered seeing a flashlight on top of the fridge. She went over, found it behind a box of crackers, and thumbed it on. The intense silvery beam struck the ceiling. She went back over the stairs and shoved the flashlight behind her waistband.

Then she gripped the Ruger with both hands and snapped back the cocking mechanism. The *shoop-thwack* sound signaled a round injecting into the chamber with a comforting click. She thought of her baby on the second floor. She thought of those crime scene photographs, those ragged human remains. She licked her dry, cracked lips, retrieved the flashlight from her belt, and held it against the barrel of the gun.

Then she started down the stairs.

"Sheriff Tomilson!" Sarah Mosely, a petite African American woman with gray flecks peppering her tight little black Jheri-curls, pounded on the men's room door as hard as she could. She had been the night dispatcher for the Knox County Sheriff's Department for nearly eight years, and had seen it all, but astonishingly she had avoided losing any of her patrols. Until tonight. Tonight had shattered her perfect record. She pounded harder on the door. "Sheriff? You in there?"

From behind the bathroom door came a low, gravelly voice, coarse with irritation. "For shit sake, Mosely, I'm in the middle of a whiz!"

"I lost the deputy, sir!"

Behind the door: "Gimme a chance to shake the dew off the daisy, will ya?"

Mosely shoved the door open and lurched into the men's room, which was a small, reeking enclosure of tile and exposed pipes, with two urinals on one side, and a sink and a single toilet stall on the other. The sheriff was at a urinal, maneuvering his flaccid penis back into his trousers. He was a portly, rheumatic man well into his seventies, with a widow's peak of wispy gray hair and a noble hooked nose. Mosely averted her gaze, babbling, "I'm sorry, Sheriff, sorry . . . but something's wrong, I lost him . . . no contact."

The old man went over to the sink and ran water on his gnarled fisherman's hands. "Slow down, Nursey. Gimme the chronology."

The younger woman told him about Deputy Elkins's radio call-in at 11 Black River, and how the deputy never transmitted back.

"What time did he get there?" the sheriff wanted to know as he dried his hands on the towel roller.

"Seven minutes after one."

The sheriff looked at his watch. "It's almost two, what the hell is he doing out there?" Shaking his head in exasperation, the old man turned and pushed his way out of the restroom. The dispatcher followed. The sheriff made his way down the dusty corridor to his cluttered office. "That's all I need," he said, storming into his inner sanctum, grabbing the phone receiver off the extension. "Feds breathing down my neck, and now Elkins out there playing footsie with this fancy profiler's wife."

"That's not all." Sarah Mosely stood in the doorway, wringing her slender brown hands.

He looked at her. "Go on."

"Tommy left his radio on, and I think I heard something."

The sheriff let out a sigh, the mounting frustration etching his lined, sagging jowls. He forced himself to breathe deeply (instead of screaming).

"Sweetheart? Honey? Can you be just a tad more specific?"

She licked her lips. "I'm not sure what it was, but it sounded like a grunt."

The sheriff stared. "A grunt?"

She nodded. "A human grunt."

Pause. Then the sheriff slammed the phone back down. He turned and grabbed his jacket off the back of his chair. "Listen, I want you to call Roger Lakehurst over at Salt Lick station, and Rudy Berger up at HQ."

The dispatcher pulled a small spiral notebook from her breast pocket and started madly scribbling names and places. "HQ? You mean Indy?"

"That's right, sweetheart, I'm talking about Indianapolis, c'mon, chop-chop." The sheriff snatched his hat off a bentwood rack behind his chair and started back around his desk.

The dispatcher scurried after him. "You want the whole SWAT team?"

"Just call Rudy, tell him we got a possible ten-ninety going down and it's better to be safe than sorry."

Sarah Mosely nodded. "Will do."

The sheriff stormed across the lobby, out the door, and into the ever-darkening night.

THIRTY

The basement at 11 Black River was similar to the one on Cottage Creek Drive in Alexandria, sunken below ground level but not completely subterranean. This one was *unfinished*, comprising about four hundred square feet of exposed wall studs and insulation, with a ceiling hewn out of tangled plumbing and furnace ducts. The cracked cement floor was marbled with water stains. The forced-air furnace was off in one corner, a squat, square, metal monolith filmed with grime. A washer and dryer sat on the opposite wall under bare light-bulbs, next to a dull white vertical hot-water tank. There was a single narrow, shuttered window, high on the north wall, and several boxes and paint cans from former tenants, crowding the space like the errant pieces of a Rubik's Cube.

The first time Maura had laid eyes on the base-ment, three days earlier during her move-in, she wondered what kind of people would have chosen those paint colors or filled those boxes with ex-

pendables. What kind of person washed their underwear and towels down here? Had they been Mafia
informants? Government snitches? Hit men? The
families of hit men? The paint colors that had
dripped and streaked down the sides of the cans
were so benign and cheery—buckwheat beige and
periwinkle blue—that they only served to empha-
size the creepy incongruity of the place, the bad
karma. In fact, Maura had felt these vibrations from
the moment she had entered the bungalow, a kind
of leaden gloom, a rankness, like an odor that
won't come out of the drapes. People dealing with
death and dismemberment had lived here, leaving
behind traces of their anguished existence like a
spoor. And in no other room was it stronger than
right here in the cellar.

Now, as she descended the wooden stairs toward
the dark, dank space, holding the Ruger out in front
of her, the flashlight pressed against the barrel like
a beacon, she remembered something critical about
the sublevel from her WITSEC orientation. It was
a hidden feature known only to a few select people
such as the two federal marshals who had moved
her into the house. Unfortunately she had very little time to think about it now that the cellar was
host to some kind of intruder.

She reached the bottom of the stairs and aimed
the flashlight at the narrow window.

Panic trickled cold and bracing down her midsection as she gazed at the hole, the frame pried
away from the wall, the glass pane hanging by a
thread of rubber weatherstripping. No raccoon
could have done that. Mice did not pry open win-

dows. She backed toward the bottom step until her
heel bumped the riser, her breath sticking in her
throat. She wanted to turn and run back up those
stairs, run screaming from this terrible place. She
forgot she had a gun. She couldn't get air into her
lungs, couldn't make her legs work anymore.

The feeling was overwhelming that somebody
or some*thing* was hiding down here in this musty
basement. She managed to shine the light on the
wall to her left, the beam gleaming off white-painted
surfaces, the washer and dryer, when a creaking
noise startled her.

It came from her immediate right, and she swung
the gun and flashlight over toward the furnace, the
beam falling on the oxidized metal skin of the water
heater tank. Something moved behind the tank.

Maura aimed the gun and held her breath.

A graying head of hair peered out from behind
the water heater, and Maura cried out in a strangled, bellowing wail: "Don't goddamn move of I'll
goddamn blow your head off!"

The furry gray object kept coming as though
completely deaf, as though utterly oblivious to
Maura's eardrum-shattering cry, and all of a sudden two things happened in quick succession, almost too quickly for Maura to even parse in her
brain, her body moving almost involuntarily: a pair
of beady, feral eyes shimmered in the beam of the
flashlight, and Maura squeezed off three hard, quick
blasts, the noise and heat popping like balloons in
her ears, the muzzle flash lighting up the basement.

Only one .22 caliber round struck the animal.

The other two blasts went high, one of them

piercing the skin of the water heater with a spark and a dull thump, a tiny geyser of H_2O blowing out of the hole, the other bullet chewing a divot into one of the studs. Maura reared back at the clamor and unexpected pain in her eardrums, blinking, swallowing the panic acid on the back of her tongue. Still clutching the gun with both hands, she aimed it at the dull gray lump on the floor. The lump twitched and Maura—momentarily dazed and uncomprehending—gawked at it, ready to fire again at a moment's notice. She stared at the twitching mass of fur and scales as it expired and became still.

At last she recognized the animal: Curled into a fetal death pose, its matted fur beaded with rubies of blood, the little fat possum had probably nudged the damaged window open earlier that evening, which would explain the musky stench wafting out of the basement.

Maura had seen her share of possums as a kid growing up on the edge of the Muir Woods in Northern California. She remembered west coast possums being a little nastier, a little faster moving and sinewy than their Midwestern counterparts. The Midwestern variety was a strange creature that moved with the lazy, drugged-out quality of a sloth, and looked like a giant rat crossbred with a raccoon. This one, especially in death, especially in the darkness of the basement, was downright repulsive. Its long snout and black-pearl eyes looked almost artificial, its reptilian tail resembling a coiled worm. Purplish entrails bloomed from its white, scaly belly.

Ears ringing from the muzzle bark, Maura lowered the gun and tried to breathe normally, a sense of relief passing through her body. She felt her muscles relaxing, but in the back of her mind a tiny spark of doubt had kindled a question: So who cut the phone lines?

Right at that moment, as if in answer to her silent query, came the sound of muffled footsteps.

Maura whirled toward the bottom of the staircase, the gun still gripped in her right hand. It wasn't just the *sound* of the footsteps that made her midriff tense up and raised the hackles on the back of her neck. It wasn't just the fact that they were heavy, rhythmic, male footsteps, or the fact that they were approaching.

The reason that Maura was paralyzed with terror at that moment was because the footsteps were coming from above. From somewhere upstairs.

From inside the house.

A beefy, middle-aged federal marshal named Normann Edward Pokorny gripped the steering wheel of the SWAT van as it roared toward the Fox Run town limits. Dressed in bulky Kevlar and ammopouched pants, the marshal was standing on the gas pedal, the van screaming at ninety-five miles an hour over the pocked asphalt of Highway 231. The cargo bay behind him was loaded to the gills with armed personnel, the extra weight making the van vibrate wildly as vapor lights passed in a blur, the outskirts of town coming into view on the horizon.

He was tossing a cigarette through the vent when the radio sizzled with voices. "Mobile One here," he spat into the handset after snatching it off the dash. "Go ahead, Base."

Through the radio came a voice, stretched taut with nerves: "This is Special Agent Ulysses Grove, just touched down at Grissom, en route now, still a ways out, who do I have?"

Pokorny told him.

"What's your ETA, Pokorny?"

"About five minutes."

"We've lost contact with the sheriff, they're supposed to be out there at the site already."

"Copy that," Pokorny said into the mike. "We're almost there."

"Almost is not good enough."

"Copy that, sir. Doing all we can."

"This is my wife and my child we're talking about here," the voice on the radio wanted Pokorny to know.

"Understood, sir."

"Get there, Pokorny. You got thirty-five minutes on us. *Get there.*"

"Copy that. Will advise when we do. Out." The marshal slammed the handset back onto its cradle, thinking of his own children at home in bed.

He started searching the dark horizon for a shortcut.

Maura stood at the foot of the basement steps, gazing up at the half-open door leading into the kitchen. She swallowed her panic and listened.

The footsteps sounded as though they were maybe two floors up, perhaps descending the living room stairs, but how was that possible? She was just upstairs not five minutes ago. Her pulse raced as she thought of Aaron up there alone in his room.

She told herself to stay calm, think, focus. She listened and thought she heard Aaron crying.

It occurred to her in a flash of wishful thinking that it might be help coming, one of the marshals maybe, but why weren't they saying anything? Wouldn't they be calling out for her?

"Hello?"

Her voice was thin and reedy with terror. There was no reply.

She raised the .22 and aimed it up at the dim light spilling down the basement stairs. The footsteps were approaching, that telltale crackle of heavy soles on linoleum. Another sound, muffled but familiar, accompanied the footsteps, like the mewling of a cat.

"Please answer me!"

The pungent undertow of adrenaline and horror swam in her brain, but she managed to keep the Ruger raised and ready, despite her wobbling knees, holding it in the commando position, left hand cupped under the hilt, right hand around the grip, which her father had taught her so many years ago.

A shadow fell across the doorway at the top of the stairs, and Maura froze. The light from the kitchen illuminated Henry Splet.

The man held little baby Aaron in his arms, a grimy hand over the child's mouth.

THIRTY-ONE

Sheriff Eugene Tomilson arrived at 11 Black River Drive at exactly 2:06 A.M.

The old man sat in his cruiser for a moment, considering his course of action.

Transcripts of the evening's events vary as to how long the sheriff lingered in that vehicle, trying to figure out what to do. Most experts suggest it was something like three to four minutes—long enough for Henry Splet to force Maura to drop her weapon and lie prone on the basement floor. It is also believed that Sheriff Tomilson remained in his car long enough for the killer to descend the basement stairs with the wriggling baby, and proceed to bind and gag both mother and child to the wall beams in the cellar. But regardless of the exact duration of Tomilson's repose, one thing is certain: Tomilson smelled trouble the instant he laid eyes on the property.

The first thing he noticed was that Elkins's

prowler was still idling. The dome light was still on, and the radio was still operational. The sheriff could hear the engine and the crackle of static coming through the vent. The next thing Tomilson discovered was that everything seemed oddly tranquil at 11 Black River Drive. The house was quiet, a light burning in the living room window, nothing out of place. But the third and final thing he noticed was that his gut was clenched with tension. The air seemed to ooze *wrongness*.

He got out, unfastening the safety strap on the Colt .357 long barrel pressed against the side of his belly. He hadn't shot the thing since Ronald Reagan was in office, and the last time he even *unsnapped* it was way back in '99 when Jubal Finnegan over in Salt Lick killed his wife and barricaded himself inside his dairy barn with a nine millimeter. Old Jubal took his *own* life that night, saving Sheriff Tomilson and Knox County the cost of one liquid-tip .44 caliber round. But tonight, it seemed things were already a lot more complicated.

And dangerous.

The old man ambled up the sidewalk with his eyes wide open, scanning the dark yard for any sign of foul play. His hearing wasn't what it used to be, and he now wished he had taken his wife's advice a few years ago and gotten fitted for one of those fancy Bell hearing aids. He needed a new prescription for his eyeglasses, as well, and to make matters worse, his reflexes had deteriorated to the point that he had a hard time poking magnetic cards through automated slots and slamming on the brakes in time to avoid fender benders.

He crossed the porch and knocked on the front door. He noticed there was a doorbell mounted on the door frame, but for some reason he elected to knock instead. It just seemed too late to ring the bell. From inside the house came the sound of footsteps, first creaking on rickety wooden risers, then crossing a linoleum floor.

The sheriff gently placed the heel of his palm on the Colt's trigger guard.

Henry Splet marched across the living room as though he were in a dream.

Clad in a rank, moldy winter coat torn from the body of a murdered homeless man, Splet walked with a stiff, self-conscious gait, like a bad actor in a bad play. He carried the Army .45 with the makeshift silencer discreetly at his side. He tried to ignore the chaos in his skull—the strange new voice over-riding all the others—as he approached the door.

There was a little oval window embedded in the front door, through which occupants could see who was standing on the other side. As Henry reached the door he got a fleeting glimpse of the old man in the sheriff's uniform waiting on the porch on the other side.

Splet opened the front door and shot the old man twice in the forehead.

The back of Sheriff Tomilson's head erupted. The old man toppled backward and landed on the grass, expelling an involuntary, watery grunt. One big Timberland boot sprawled on the sidewalk, the other one wedged into a bush.

It was over so quickly the sheriff never even knew what happened.

Splet glanced up and down the street. Amazingly it was still deserted. The killer emerged from the house, crossed the porch, and descended the steps to where the sheriff lay still warm and twitching.

Hennnnnrrreeeeee . . . te possssssi audirrreeeeeee.

Splet had been hearing this hollow, papery voice in his head since he left the storage facility. He did not speak the language of the voice. But he somehow understood every breathy, hissing phrase. In fact, he could respond simply by nodding or thinking his reply.

The new voice sounded like a million voices, all speaking in unison, all in different languages, dead languages, languages that Splet could not begin to understand. But there was also an Over Voice translating everything into some kind of supple oily tongue, echoing, penetrating Splet's auditory canals. It knew things. It knew how to travel in the shadows, how to kill silently and quickly, and how to manipulate the physical and virtual realms. It also told Henry of the master plan, which was now unfolding amid the encouraging whispers.

Tu facerrrreeee multa . . .

He nodded, then crouched down by the dead sheriff and grabbed the old man by the boot heels. He began dragging the limp body toward the side of the house, its breached skull leaving a trail of pink frothy tissue and blood across the front lawn. The sound of sirens keened in the distance.

Festinaaahhhhtio Henreeee.

Splet hurried. He laid the sheriff's warm corpse down on the grass in the shadows next to the deputy. Then something snapped inside Henry Splet like a circuit breaker or a fuse cracking apart.

He staggered backward, his thoughts drifting for a moment like a shortwave radio losing its signal. Something hot and desperate bubbled to the surface of his mind. He thought of his children. He had brain tissue on his fingers and he was thinking of little Ethan with his freckled grin and carrot-colored hair. He was a father. His own child was not much older than that baby in the basement.

"Oh God, I almost forgot," he muttered, going back over to the bodies, kneeling down as though he were about to pray. "I can't leave them like this, not like this—"

Desirere Accelerrrrrarrrra trepidatio!

Splet tried hard to ignore the Over Voice, moving the bodies now like game pieces on a chessboard.

According to the official postmortems of that evening, the SWAT team was now eleven minutes and forty-five seconds away.

Maura bit her tongue hard enough to break the skin. A gush of salty warmth filled her mouth behind the gag.

With each muffled, strangled scream she strained and yanked at the plumbers' tape shackling her head and arms to the wall. Her voice had a touch of madness in it, as she watched her baby dealing with similar constraints across the darkened base-

ment, now illuminated only by a single bare light-
bulb swaying on a frayed cord. In the waxing, waning
shadows across the room, little Aaron had been
propped up like a sack of potatoes against a load-
bearing column, his wrists taped together, his writhing, wriggling head attached to the column with a
hank of thick gray adhesive. The baby was crying
with such fury his tiny body seemed to be convuls-
ing against the tape.

That's all it was: *duct tape.* But there was a lot of
it, and it was impenetrable, and it was wrapping the
baby like a greasy, wormy swaddling membrane. It
also bound Maura's wrists together, wrenching them
over her head and affixing them to a brace nailed
across two wall studs in an unholy crucifix. Several
feet of plumbers' tape was wrapped around her forehead as well, gluing it to the wall in perfect position for her to see her baby.

Had she *not* been gagged—the paint rag knot-
ted across her mouth, smelling of turpentine and
making her dizzy—Maura would have chewed her
hands off at the wrists. She would have done it in a
heartbeat in order to get to her baby, who was sobbing and wailing less than ten feet away. But she
was gagged, not to mention trussed to the studs
like a suckling pig, and the pain and the fury made
it hard to think, and that was the one thing she
needed to do: *think.*

As it would turn out, she had only a few critical
minutes between the point at which the second
knock on the door came, drawing the killer out of
the basement, and the moment at which he returned.

By the clock, it was just under four minutes. But

they were four crucial minutes because the moment the madman had vanished, Maura almost
spontaneously flashed again on the secret part of
the basement, the part the marshals had shown
her three nights ago. Maura remembered what
they had called it. They called it "the last resort."

Aaron mewled and convulsed.

Maura tried to speak to him through her eyes,
tried to blink a message to her baby, tried to calm
him with steadying thoughts as though she could
send her brain waves into the child's head. And
maybe she could. Mothers and babies have freakish
synchronicity with each other. They are connected
on levels that defy physical laws.

Sure enough, all at once, little Aaron seemed to
stop moaning and fix his raw, teary, mucusy gaze
on his mother. He looked exhausted, and maybe
even a little lulled by the fear into a sort of traumatic
catatonia. But right then—Maura's mind allowing
their connected gazes to fire one last synapse—she
realized what was about to happen.

It dawned on her like the silent inhalation of air
right before the onslaught of a nuclear holocaust,
the first thump of ignition in the base of her brain-
stem sending a mushroom cloud of memories,
half-glimpsed newspaper articles, snippets of con-
versations with her husband through her mind.
She remembered the fact that this maniac always
killed in pairs, and she remembered the whispered
conversation in her bedroom many nights ago when
Grove told her the killer's signature. She remembered seeing the photographs of makeshift eyelid
retractors, and she remembered the repulsion she

felt when she realized that here was a man who forced his future victims to watch their counterparts being tortured and killed.

She stared at her baby.

She realized right then, beyond all doubt, why the two of them—mother and child—had been bound in this fashion, facing each other. And why their heads were taped in place. *Facing each other.* And of course, the final and maybe worst revelation of them all: Maura realized that it was very possible—actually *probable*—that in a matter of minutes Splet was going to force the baby to watch his mother being killed.

Or vice versa.

Maura went into seizures of rage then, her sanity flying off its spindle for a moment. She yanked and yanked at the tape around her wrists, grunting and emitting garbled cries behind the gag. Across the dark basement the baby began to moan and cry again. And this went on and on until something sparked in the pit of Maura's midbrain like a linkage grabbing hold of a chain, gaining purchase and starting to tug at her, pulling her back to the here and now.

Only moments ago she had flashed on an image of a mother wolf caught in a trap, chewing off her paw in order to escape, to save her brood.

Now she realized the tape around her cranium had stretched enough for her to wrench her head a few inches to the left. The gag had loosened enough for her to bite down a few centimeters. Just enough to reach the bottom edge of the duct tape with her teeth.

In the darkness she began to gnaw at the tape with the ferocity of a wild dog.

In the moments before the SWAT team arrived at 11 Black River Drive, what was left of the original man known to friends and fellow Baptist parishioners as Good Old Henry Splet hurriedly worked in the darkness along the side of the house. Lifting the sheriff's blood-sodden body into a sitting position against the bungalow's brick foundation, Splet recreated the pose that had imprinted itself on his world since childhood. He worked as quickly as possible. It was amazing how heavy the old man was in death.

Grunting with effort, Splet finished with the sheriff and turned to the deputy. The younger corpse was lighter. Splet grabbed the body by the armpits and leaned Elkins's remains against the house so that the dead deputy was facing his boss. Two limp forms gazing emptily at each other. Both pairs of eyes still shocked open in death. Milky retinas like marbles gaping at each other.

Nodding, Splet stood back and admired the familiar post-mortem staging.

Unus ampliusssss—Henreeeee Acellerere!

Splet closed his eyes, the deep vibrating Over Voice resonating in his skull, chastising him.

Animus! Attentus!

Doubling over suddenly as though punched in the gut, Splet flinched at the unexpected memory of his foster father. His foster father spoke to him in a very similar fashion: *Pay attention, Pussy! Listen*

and learn! Get down on the ground before I beat ya sense-
less, faggot! Pay attention!

Splet held himself then, his arms cradled against
his stomach, as though he might spill his internal
organs at any moment, as he flashed back to that
fateful night in the warehouse near the end of his
eighth year.

THIRTY-TWO

"Get your bony little ass outta the car!" The foster father yanks the boy out of the battered Ford Galaxie by the nape of his neck. The kid, a miserable, trembling bundle of nerves known as Henry-honey to his alcoholic foster mother, goes sprawling across the powdery gravel lot outside the warehouse.

"It's not my fault!"

"Shuddup!" The big, bearded German in flannel and denim circles around to the other side of the car.

On the ground, out of breath, eyes red from crying, the eight-year-old Henry-honey curls into a fetal position and cries into the crook of his elbow. He's a skinny kid dressed in corduroy pants and a baseball shirt, with a thatch of greasy chestnut-colored hair.

"Your turn!" Henry-honey hears his foster father growl to the teenage girl who is cowering inside the car. From his vantage point on the ground, Henry-honey can see the foster father's scuffed work boots shuffling violently on the other side of the car as he drags the girl out the door and around the rear of the car toward the warehouse.

"*Stop it, you're hurting me, leggo my hair!*" The girl's name is Peggy—"*Peggers*" to her school pals—and she is masking her terror with petulant anger. A sandy-haired girl with huge blue eyes and big braids on the side of her head, she has always hated this big hairy authority figure, this odiferous intrusion into her life, and now the mutual disrespect has finally boiled over.

"*Get your asses inside! The both o' ya!*"

The foster father takes each kid by the neck, and roughly ushers them toward the building. The low-slung, windowless structure spans several acres of backwater farmland, and features a series of rusty garage-style doors stretching in to the distance in either direction. There's a rust-pocked sign hanging above the lone steel door.

The sign says U-Store-It Mini-Warehouses.

Inside the building, the two kids are dragged down a pitch-black, cobweb-fringed corridor that smells of urine and moldy stone. Henry-honey's heart is beating so hard it feels as though it's about to crack his sternum.

"*Hurry up! Hurry up*" The foster father's voice slurs with rage, his breath hot with the stink of whiskey. Where is he taking them, and why? And what is he going to do to them? The foster father has spanked Honey-boy on many occasions, once on his bare bottom with a rubber hose that made welts and hurt for a week and a half, but this time the stakes seem higher. This time, it seems as though the man is planning on seriously hurting Henry-honey.

"*That's far enough!*" The foster father throws them both to the cement floor. "*On your knees facing each other!*"

The two kids reluctantly obey the man. They each lower themselves to their knees and then sheepishly look at each other. At first, Henry-honey can glean nothing from Peggers's blank stare. Her pale blue eyes shimmer with tears

*in the dark corridor, but they also seem emptied out as they
gaze stoically back at him. Henry-honey starts to shake.
"P-p-p-pluh-please . . . d-don't hurt us, please, p-please."*

"SHUDDUP!"

Henry-honey starts to sob.

*The big man grabs the boy by the scruff of the neck,
then wrenches his head up. "Are you the one took money
from your mother's jewel box?"*

"I-I—I don't—"

"Answer me!"

"No."

*The big man released his grip. Henry-honey collapsed
back to his knees. The foster father turned to Peggers. "How
about you, missy?"*

She doesn't say anything.

*He slaps her, hard, across the cheek. "You speak when
spoken to!"*

"Yes. Yes, I took the money."

*The big man nods and walks back around behind her.
He leans down, takes hold of her waist and yanks her
bell-bottom jeans and panties down. Peggers flinches.
Henry-honey watches, breathless, his tears congealing in
his eyes.*

*"Don't move!" The foster father slips off his big belt with
its Confederate-flag buckle, and then in one violent slash-
ing motion he bullwhips it across the girl's rear end. Peggers gasps.*

Henry-honey looks away.

"Don't you look away, boy!"

*Henry-honey forces himself to watch. The big man whips
Peggers again and again and again and again and again,
until the girl stops gasping and just stares straight ahead,
that horrible blank stare solidifying on her face. Henry
wants to die. He looks into his foster sister's eyes, and she*

looks into his, and they share something then. Something secret. Something that will stay between them forever.

"Don't you goddamn move," utters the big man, whose pants are falling down now. He pushes them down the rest of the way, exposing his enormous erection. He is breathing heavily now, his expression changing.

The two kids keep staring at each other, but they no longer see each other.

They stare through each other.

The foster father positions himself behind the girl and starts sodomizing her. She keeps staring into Henry-honey's eyes as the big man thrusts into her, jerking her skinny body with violent spasms. Henry tries to look away, but the big man snarls in a hoarse drawl between pelvic thrusts, "Don't you look away, boy. . . . I want you to see this. . . . I want you to see what happens to thieves . . ."

Henry-honey gapes, his sister's terrible blank gaze searing his brain.

Shattering his psyche into a horrible, beautiful mosaic.

Sending him deep inside himself.

THIRTY-THREE

Federal Marshal Norm Pokorny and his team of tactical specialists reached the safe house at precisely 2:23 A.M., and eased the paramilitary van—a black Dodge Sprinter, to be specific, with the windows replaced by bulletproof alloy panels—over to the curb behind the two idling sheriff department vehicles. Following protocols established for search-and-assess missions, Pokorny immediately got on his radio and murmured softly, "Stand by, folks."

Pokorny clicked open his door and climbed out without a sound.

He had no idea what they were walking into, as he strode past the sheriff's cruiser, his eyes shaded by polarized night glasses, his gaze everywhere all at once. He unsnapped his Glock nine millimeter, drew it out of the holster, and carried it at his side.

A light went on in the neighbor's window, then another one, and another one. Pokorny noticed the entire block was lit up, lights in all the windows now, yet quiet. Lots of rustling drapes, people watching. The tension in the air crackled. Pokorny tasted it on his tongue, a sharp tang of danger, the silence hanging there like an echo.

Pokorny was a stout, muscular man, and he moved with surprising grace as he approached the deputy's prowler. He saw the interior light still on, the engine rumbling faintly. A turn signal clicked as though it were a metronome. Pokorny smelled an ambush and reached for his vest mike. He whispered into it: "I want two teams, right now, right now. On the line. Tell me you copy."

A voice popped: "Copy."

"I want Willings and the blue team to lay down a perimeter around the property. Got that?"

"Copy that."

"I want Pelham and the sharpshooters positioned on the four corners. Got it?"

"Got it."

"I'm going in the front, nice and casual. Willings, you better back my ass up this time."

The voice returned: "What about the tunnel?"

"One thing at a time," Pokorny whispered. "Everybody on the ready line?"

"Affirmative."

"I want clean vectors this time. You get a head shot on the bogey, you do it quick and clean."

"Copy that, Cap."

"This may be nothing but jitters inside. On my mark. Ready . . . nice and quiet. Go!"

Several things happened simultaneously at various corners of the property. Pokorny started around the front of the prowler and the rear doors of the Sprinter clicked open, and eight shadowy figures came out in single file, weapons down, silently dispersing across the parkway in front of the neighbors to the south. Pokorny casually strode up the sidewalk with his automatic pressed against his thigh, eyes up and alert. He could smell the night in his nostrils.

Approaching the porch, the marshal saw several things that computed quickly in his brain: a flattened bush, footprints in the weeds, maybe blood. It was hard to confirm the latter, the pink stuff had mixed well with the gritty soil. In his peripheral vision he noted the rest of the team moving behind him: Half the grouping went east, the other half west. Black-clad commandos with souped-up assault rifles.

Pokorny didn't knock. The front door was ajar. Everything calm inside, though. He thumbed the hammer on the Glock, and turned away from the door.

"Front of the house is not secure," he murmured into his vest mike. "Repeat: *not secure.* I want everybody on standby mode, safeties off."

He descended the porch steps and went around the front of the house.

"I want all collateral—" he started to say as he rounded the corner of the bungalow and then saw the sheriff and deputy posed in the shadows. "What the devil is this, what is this, what's going on?"

"Negative copy on that, say again," the voice crackled out of Pokorny's pocket radio.

The marshal didn't answer. He approached the two men in uniform sitting against the house, facing each other. The back of the sheriff's ruined skull gleamed in the moonlight. "Got officers down! Officers down! Move in! Now! Hard target! Now! NOW!"

Grove and Geisel made it to the Black River Drive house five minutes later.

Their escort, a young field agent from the Indy office named Nesmith, had pushed the government-issued sedan, an unmarked '99 Pontiac Grand Prix, as far as it could be pushed, crossing the rolling hills and patchwork forests of Owen County in just under twenty minutes flat, running at an average speed of ninety-odd miles an hour. On some of the long dark straightaway sections the car actually reached 120, at one point causing Geisel to remark from the backseat that perhaps they would be defeating their own purpose by getting themselves killed. But Grove urged Nesmith to keep the needle pinned, the headlights on bright, and the two-way turned up.

Grove spent the whole journey from Grissom to Fox Run clutching the radio handset. He never let go of it. He spoke numerous times to the SWAT team, to the sheriff's dispatcher, and to the field office communications people in Indianapolis. After a while, he had forgotten he was even holding the mike. But now as the Pontiac careered around the corner of Burlington and Black River, Grove dropped the mike.

His entire body tingled with adrenaline as Nesmith zoomed toward 11 Black River. Grove could see the rest of the homes on the block blazing with light, some of the neighbors now gathering on their porches in robes and worried expressions. Grove could also see the cop cars and the SWAT van looming, lined up along the curb in front of a neighbor's house. What he did *not* see was Marshal Pokorny and the other tactical officers drawing their guns, then pouring into the house through the back door, doing a frantic room-to-room.

As the Pontiac scudded to a stop behind the empty SWAT van, Grove finally got a good look at the meager little bungalow. For the most infinitesimal instant, Grove felt a pang of guilt and shame. The house, with its cheap brick, its weeds, and its little gingerbread porch, made Grove think of some tacky variation of a Grimm's fairytale. *The safe house.* There it was. Looking deceptively still and quiet, but radiating a malignant kind of tableau.

Doors flew open. Guns came out. Even Geisel drew a .38 snubbie from a shoulder holster. Grove took the lead. He crossed the lawn with his Charter Arms cannon high in one hand, the other hand raising the laminate ID around his neck so nobody mistook him for an Unfriendly. His senses magnified the sights and sounds and smells surrounding him, bombarding his brain, as he vaulted up the porch steps.

Movement on either side of the house registered like flash frames in Grove's peripheral vision, dark-clad guerrillas, heavily armed, coming around the front of the house. Grove clearly heard Geisel call out to them, identifying himself and Grove and Nesmith, hollering at the SWAT guys to allow Grove inside the domicile, this was the husband, one of them, FBI, so let him through, as Grove lunged for the open door.

He kicked it in.

Plunging into the living room, weapon at the ready, Grove nearly lost his balance on the braided rug. He skidded a little, then whirled around the room. He had lost all sense of procedure and professionalism as the odors of Maura's cigarettes, and maybe something burning on a stove, and moldy bathroom smells assaulted him. "Where are they?!" he yelled at the empty living room. "Where are they?"

"Ulysses—!"

"Pokorny!"

"Hold it, Ulysses—"

An awkward moment as Geisel tried to reach out for Grove, tried to pull him back at the exact moment a black-garbed marshal materialized in the archway between the living room and the kitchen. Gun barrels jumped up all around the room. Voices bellowed in unison. "Put 'em down! Put 'em down! Put 'em down right now!"

More SWAT guys appeared on the porch, a pair of sharpshooters, both squatting and aiming their M-1s at the interior of the house. Tiny red laser dots swam up and down Grove's spine.

"Hold your fire! Everbody!"

Pokorny's baritone cut through the garbled chorus of voices. The beefy captain had appeared in the hallway to Grove's immediate right, hands up in surrender, his craggy face lit up with alarm. Grove spun and aimed his gun—more out of instinct than anything else—and stared at the grizzled twenty-year veteran of the Marshal Service.

"Everybody take it easy." Pokorny kept his hands

up, burning his gaze into Grove. "Stand down now, we're all on the same team here."

Grove kept his gun aimed at Pokorny. "Where's my wife? My boy—?"

"The house is empty. Listen to me. Grove—the house is empty!"

"Everybody put the goddamn guns down!" Geisel's voice was ragged with nerves.

At last Grove managed to lower the barrel. The others backed off, released their hammers, clicked their safeties. Grove had not taken his eyes off the marshal. "Somebody give me some answers."

Pokorny nodded and spoke very quickly and evenly as though addressing a wild animal. "I understand you want your family out of harm's way, we're working on it—"

"You're not answering my question."

"They're gone, there's nobody here, no perp, nobody, and right now we're looking at—"

"How long have you been here?"

The marshal told him about their arrival five minutes earlier, the bodies on the east side of the house, and the signs of struggle in the basement. "So now," Pokorny added, almost as an afterthought, "We're looking at the escape tunnel as a possible mode of—"

"The what? The *what?*"

For a brief moment, all the men gathered in the living room looked at each other, trying to gauge who was supposed to know about these things.

"There's an escape tunnel in the basement," Pokorny finally told Grove. "Nobody told you this?"

THIRTY-FOUR

One time, when Maura County was a little girl growing up in a small town in Northern California, she managed to get herself lost in the Muir Woods.

That terrible day had started like any other lazy Saturday afternoon, a family picnic at Stinson Beach, and then a quick drive down Highway 1 to the park entrance for a hike in the forest. But by the time the County family had reached the trail head near Muir Beach, the weather had turned mean. The wind had kicked up, and the sky had drooped and darkened over Bolinas Bay. Maybe that's why her father hadn't heard little Maura stop at the first hairpin to ponder a caterpillar. She was only seven years old at the time, and her voice didn't carry very far in the best of circumstances, but on that day, with the woods chattering, and the wind whistling and rustling through the boughs, her father hadn't heard her little cry of delight when she saw that colorful little inchworm on the big maple leaf and paused there. "Lookit, Daddy!" she enthused in her little peep of a voice. "I wonder if he can play harmonica like the one in that cartoon!"

No answer.

She turned and saw that her father had vanished. He had probably proceeded on down the trail, oblivious to the fact that his daughter had momentarily dawdled. And the sad thing was, if Maura had simply stayed calm and thought things through, she more than likely could have merely trotted after him, staying on the trail, probably catching up with him in a matter of minutes. But seven-year-olds are not known for grace under pressure, or thinking things through, or even common sense. And on that day, at that moment, Maura's little psyche erupted with terror. She started calling out.

"Daddy?—Daddy?—Daddeeeeeeee!"

She spun around and around as she shouted, her gaze taking in every shadow, every branch. The wind swallowed the sound of her voice. Raindrops began to sift down through the trees, peppering the foliage. Every sound became sinister to Maura's hypersensitive ears. A rustling limb became a monstrous whisper, a gust became the laughter of demons. Maura turned and started running back down the twisted path the way she had come, and suddenly slipped on a mossy root sticking out of the hardpack.

She sprawled to the floor of the path. She fell so hard she saw stars and the breath was knocked out of her.

By that point she was sobbing and heaving and choking with terror, as she rolled onto her back and gazed up into the dark canopy of Douglas fir.

In the seconds before her mortified father came

trotting back into view, frantically calling her name, young Maura County had the first dark epiphany of her life. She was only alone that day for a few frenzied minutes. But the horrible solitude of that moment, as she peered up at that chimney of ancient redwoods—some of them over a thousand years old—gave Maura her first taste of the existential cruelty of nature. These hard primordial woods, where Miwok Indians trembled in ritual supplication, where Conquistadors died, where missionaries foraged and perished—*these same woods*—could squash a little girl in a split second. Lying in agony, helpless, tears streaking her guileless little face, she felt lower in the order of things than that caterpillar. But in her innocence, she saw things with unprecedented clarity: Here was a universe so gigantic and senseless and downright mean that it made her shrink and shrink until she felt as though she were dissolving into the earth. The last horrifying thought flickering across her young mind: Maybe that's what dead people feel.

Over thirty years later, that memory was still as vivid as a garish pop-up book in Maura's brain, as accessible to her as if it had happened a week ago.

In fact, on that bloody night in Indiana, fleeing the safe-house basement through that endless escape shaft, Maura felt those same childhood sensations of existential terror. She felt the same sense of plummeting, the same feeling of shrinking into a tiny cold nothing.

This primal panic was a mere undercurrent, of course, since she was currently in the midst of the fight of her life.

She moved through the narrow, dimly lit passageway as quickly as possible, considering the fact that she was now clutching her caterwauling baby in her arms. In her right hand she carried the .22 Ruger that she had retrieved from the iron sink during her escape from the cellar.

Her mouth was bleeding where she had lost two of her teeth, and she was panting profusely as she bounded along the subterranean dark, a darkness broken only by the intermittent reddish glow of an emergency lamp encased in a filthy cage. Her fingertips throbbed with excruciating pain, half her fingernails torn away from wrestling herself and her baby out of the duct tape bondage.

Sounds echoed wildly—Aaron's keening, her footsteps, her gasping, hoarse voice. "It's okay, honey, it's okay, Mommy's here, Mommy's with you. . . ."

The tunnel seemed to go on forever, hewn from ragged planks and moldy mortar, rank with the stench of roots and offal. In the darkness it virtually shimmered with slime, the floor constructed out of some kind of cheap surface so fuzzy with mold that Maura kept slipping and losing traction, nearly falling at every juncture. The ceiling was lined with ancient conduits, fringed with unidentifiable stalactites hanging so low they brushed the top of her head. The worst part was the inexorable reach of the thing. Even though she had only been in the tunnel for a few minutes, the claustrophobia pressed down on her like the walls of a coffin.

Another pink light materialized dead ahead, and Maura fixed her sights on it, hoping it might be a way out, a ladder, a chute, *something*.

A skittering noise made her jump. She jerked to

her left, and she saw movement out of the corner of
her eye. Something low, creeping along the floor,
behind her, moving with insectile speed in the shadows. She let out a little yelp, her free arm coming
up on instinct, raising the gun like a shield. Her
trigger finger had a mind of its own.

She squeezed off four quick blasts at the thing
coming at her in the darkness.

Each successive bark of the Ruger made Aaron
twitch in her arms, shrieking louder than ever. In
the photo-strobe of the muzzle flash Maura saw the
huge rat behind her erupting in a bloom of fur
and entrails, the vermin coming apart in a spray of
guts against the tunnel wall.

Maura staggered sideways, ears ringing, slowing
down to a hobble. "Sorry, sorry, sorry, honey—I'm
sorry—sweetie, I'm here, I'm here."

The baby shrieked, its little voice so fatigued
and scoured by the constant crying it was beginning to diminish into breathy little honking noises.
Maura cradled him to her breast—her arms aching
unmercifully from hauling the child all this way—
and she moved on.

In the gloom, Maura caught fleeting glimpses of
Aaron's little caramel face, contorted in distress,
wet with mucus and residue from the plumbers
tape which she had hastily ripped off him during
their escape. His legs kicked with tiny convulsive
jerks, making it difficult for Maura to hold on to
him. The terror made her woozy, unsteady, but the
deeper maternal rage drove her onward. She
would die for this little bundle of tears and flesh in
her arms. She would kill. She would do anything.

Aaron had been a colicky baby, hard to sleep, up at odd hours, always with some kind of stomach ailment. But in a way, all the hardships over the last year and a half or so—from her pregnancy on—only bonded her more permanently with the child. She would not allow this monster near her baby. She would not allow the tall dark redwood trees to swallow the boy up.

As though triggered by her dark thoughts, a shape materialized in the gloom ahead of her. Maybe a hundred feet or so away.

At first, Maura kept lumbering toward it as though uncomprehending, as though homing in on a mirage, but soon the reality of it hit her, and she shuffled to a stop. She stood there for a moment, panting, holding the baby. Aaron kept writhing in her arms, still crying, albeit now in a halting, hoarse sort of wheeze, making Maura's ears ring. Her flesh rashed with goosebumps, and her heart jiggered in her chest, as she gaped at the end of the tunnel.

She was staring at a dead end.

The tunnel simply stopped without warning or markings of any kind. The terminal wall, constructed out of the same cracked mortar as the rest of the passageway, looked almost green with mold, bearded with moss and roots.

Maura backed away from it like an animal with its hackles raised, disbelieving, dumbstruck, but *seeing* nonetheless, seeing the wall of ancient masonry: the end of the line. She commanded herself to stay calm and think and be smart, *be smart about this,* when all at once she heard the most horrendous noise in the universe reach her ears through the shrill din of her baby's cries.

Way off in the depths of the tunnel behind her came a shuffling noise.

It was coming toward her.

Grove reached the bottom of the bungalow's basement staircase, two-handing his .44 Bulldog, his gaze scanning the dark cellar. Three black-clad officers were down there, rummaging at opposite corners of the cellar, their weapons drawn, shining flashlights into corners, nosing behind the furnace, under the sink basins. Grove also caught a quick glimpse of a fourth officer—a big man in black Kevlar, thick beard, stocking cap—vanishing through a small doorway embedded in the wall behind the washing machine.

"Hold it! FBI! Everybody stand by a second!" Grove's taut voice made all heads turn, flashlight beams seizing up. The men seemed to recognize Grove. Their expressions tightened and they stood there for moment, waiting. The man in the tunnel paused.

The section chief appeared on the staircase behind Grove. "Nobody touches anything down here," Geisel ordered.

Grove saw that the basement definitely showed signs of a struggle, and thank God there was no blood spatter anywhere, at least none that was immediately apparent. Grove smelled the earthy odors of rock dust and old laundry soap, and he saw several things at once that worried him, that immediately registered on his mind-screen, his innate profiling gift suddenly shifting into gear.

"Nobody move, please."

He came down the remaining steps and made a quick visual sweep of the basement. Sweating inside his damp flight jacket, his eyes burning with concentration, he kept his gun gripped in both hands as he scanned the room, looking at everything, every shred of physical detail, no matter how seemingly trivial. Tangles of duct tape littered the cracked cement floor and hung from the wall joists. An unidentified wet spot lay beneath the smaller of the two tangles. (Grove would discover later that this was Aaron's urine.)

Behind him, Geisel descended the steps and looked around with a feverish intensity. On the far wall, a knot of plumbers' tape hung at about shoulder height. Grove went over to it and took a closer look. The tape appeared to have been fed through a shredder. A couple of human teeth were embedded in the adhesive like two kernels of corn.

"Ulysses—"

"Nobody move." Grove turned to the bearded man lurking inside the tunnel. "Is that the escape tunnel?"

"Yes, sir." The bearded officer hovered in the narrow doorway, slumping to keep his big square head from hitting the lintel. "Marshal Pokorny said I should—"

"I'll go."

"Sir, we're supposed to—"

"Out of the way, please." Grove nudged the man aside and stuck his head into the tunnel. The passageway stretched into the shadows and reeked of decay. "Where does it lead?"

No answer came from the officers.

Grove turned back to the room. "Somebody answer me, goddammit—where the hell does it lead?

Somebody has to know where this goddamn thing
leads!"

The silence spoke volumes.

Without a word Grove turned and plunged into
the unknown darkness of the tunnel.

THIRTY-FIVE

In the dim, sickly pink light, Maura pressed her back against the rancid plaster wall of the tunnel and took deep breaths, trying to figure out what to do. She still had her Ruger tucked into her jeans. The ammo magazine was half full. How many rounds was that? Four? Three? She couldn't remember. If only she had brushed up more on handguns.

The baby wriggled in her sore arms. Maura could feel the heat from his body—he was probably running a fever, his sobs deteriorating into little hitching gasps. "It's okay, honey, it's all right, Mommy's gonna get us outta here."

Aaron pressed his face into the moist canyon of her breasts and sobbed.

Maura swallowed a flinty taste in her mouth and tried to focus. In all the confusion she had lost track of the distant shuffling noises. They had abruptly stopped, then started up again. But how far away were they? How far had she come? Three city blocks? Seven football fields? She had no idea. She felt lightheaded. The front of her football jersey was soaked through with breast milk.

What was happening to her? She was about to kill somebody in self-defense and she was *lactating*. Aaron started writhing again, and Maura began to murmur to him, when all of a sudden she saw something in the darkness of the tunnel that she hadn't noticed before.

She also realized, almost simultaneously, that she was smelling something odd. Something *new*. Something she hadn't noticed until now. "Wait a minute, look at this," she said, speaking as though she were sleepwalking, addressing her baby. "Look at this, look at this!"

She went over to the dead-end wall, and ran her fingertip along a crack that wasn't a crack after all, it was a seam, a *seam*!

"Oh, my God!"

The handle was recessed into the mortar panel, disguised by layers of grime and mold, invisible at first glance, but now Maura screaming silently at herself for missing it. It resembled the kind of release you might find on a submarine hatch, a round, concave dimple with a bar in the middle. Holding the baby on her hip, she reached down and brushed away the moss, then got a decent grip on the handle.

She pulled.

The door would not budge.

A voice called out behind her in the far reaches of the dark tunnel, echoing, bouncing off the tunnel walls. It was impossible to discern what it was saying. It sounded mad, it might have been a foreign language, it was too far away, and things were happening too quickly.

She put the baby down on the grit and filth, then put all her might into loosening the hatch. There was a cracking noise, and a creaking sigh like paper tearing, and the door finally squeaked open an inch or two.

On the other side, in a greasy shaft, barely visible in the dark, rose an iron ladder.

The odor she was smelling—which she hadn't been able to identify until now—engulfed her.

Manure.

Grove charged through the reeking tunnel, passing through pools of salmon-colored light, moving at a steady sprint, his breathing labored yet steady, his revolver gripped tightly in his right hand.

"Maura!"

His frantic bellowing cry wobbled slightly as he ran, betraying his fear and his tenuous hold on his sanity. The irregular blips of pink light in his eyes began working on his brain, the odors of earthworms and festering rot penetrating his sinuses, making him dizzy. The tunnel seemed to be narrowing, darkening, as he plunged deeper and deeper.

"Maurrrrahhh!"

Slowing down to a walk, out of breath, mind racing with clashing sensations and thoughts, he felt a palpable sense of being followed, watched, pursued. Was it the other officers? He whirled around with the gun aimed at the darkness behind him and called out.

"Identify yourself!"

The silence teased at him. He could see nothing down the dark length of tunnel but scarred mortar walls, moldering overhead pipes, and progressively smaller pools of dim light. He turned back around and looked dead ahead. He could have sworn the tunnel was wider than it now appeared. He continued on. His heart felt cold and fragile as it thumped in his chest, thumped for his wife and his infant son.

"Maura!"

He picked up his pace again, the back of his neck bristling with the sensation of being followed. It was as though there were other footsteps overlapping his own—stealthy, cunning footsteps—and they were mirroring his every movement. He moved faster. He couldn't believe the length of this goddamn tunnel. He must have already traveled a quarter mile down its narrow reaches. How the hell was that possible? He picked his trot up to a run, and every painful stride exploded in his skull.

To make matters worse, the deeper he traveled into the tunnel the more the walls kept closing in on him. He started jerking at sounds, flinching the gun barrel at every creak, every crunch of grit under his feet. He had that terrible vertigo one gets when one reaches the midway point of a great bridge, the point of no return, the windswept threshold. Dante felt that feeling in the seventh circle. He felt it descending the steps into the labyrinth. This was the lowest ebb of human life, the netherworld of worms and bare lightbulbs and the beast who would destroy Grove's family.

"*Splet, I will twist your goddamn head off your neck if*

you harm one hair on their heads—Do you hear me Splet? Do you hear me Splet?"

The outburst stole his balance and he stumbled over his own feet. He went down hard on his knees and felt something in his chest snap, something buried deep in his core. What good was yelling doing him? He was acting like a goddamn rookie, giving himself away, giving the killer all the time in the world to escape. Grove felt his eyes welling up. He felt the madness overtake him like a dark net drawn over his face, and he began to weep. He wept silently on the grimy floor of that dark tunnel for several agonizing seconds, his sobs echoing, bouncing off the leprous plaster and filling his own ears with horrible feedback. He began to crawl, the gun still clutched in his sweaty grasp, his lungs heaving as he tried to stop crying and get back on his feet and behave like a goddamn professional.

He had half risen to a kneeling position when he heard the first faint sounds of a baby crying. It was muffled, and almost sounded like it was coming from *inside* the walls, but it banged on Grove's nervous system like a gong.

Aaron.

THIRTY-SIX

The shock of being outside made Maura blink for a moment. The sky overhead was a pandemonium of stars, the breeze like ice shavings on her face. The crickets droned. She inhaled the cool air and tried to concentrate amid Aaron's bawling and coughing. The baby's constant wriggling had increased a bit with the change in atmosphere, his cry raising an octave. "Almost home free, sweetie, hang in there, almost there . . ."

Holding the squalling baby on her hip, peering over the top of the manhole shaft at the darkness, Maura breathed in the pungent aroma of corn silk, earth, and manure, but she couldn't quite make out any objects yet. It took a moment for her eyes to adjust to the moonlit night. Perched on the top rung of that greasy steel ladder, she felt her fingers twinging, her arms throbbing with pain from the weight of the baby, her mouth sticky with blood.

"Sshhh, sshhh, sshhh . . . it's okay, honey . . . sshhh, it's almost over."

Maura realized she was in a small clearing in a cornfield, and she was staring at a wall of corn. Early corn. Feed corn. In the moonlight, it looked like a beautiful dense burlap forest, the stalks reaching up nearly six feet, some of them higher. So tall. Most important, the crop seemed to stretch off into infinity—a vast ocean of papery sepia shoots lazily swaying in the night breeze.

"C'mon, sweetie, Mommy's gonna get you outta here right now," Maura babbled as she struggled out of the manhole and quickly levered herself to her feet with her baby in her arms. She stood on spongy humus, a crackly woven carpet of tassels and shuck. Aaron's crying had finally dissipated, and now he trembled silently in the chill, his eyes huge and filled with terror. Relief flowed through Maura like an elixir, like painkiller.

Something about the night sky and the cool, clean rural air made her hopeful.

There was one problem. Apparently the designers of the escape tunnel had neglected to provide egress at this opposite end. Evidently if one was lucky enough to escape the tunnel, one was on their own out here. Maura turned a slow three-sixty with the baby pressed against her damp bosom, the gun still stuck in the front of her jeans.

That's when she heard the noise.

It was a deadfall stalk, most likely, or maybe a dry cob, crunching under the pressure of a footstep, and it was way off in the distance, maybe hundreds of feet away, but something about it made Maura tense up and chill all over with goose bumps. It was the *furtive* nature of it. Like somebody or something sneaking up on her.

Of course, it was possible that her ears were playing tricks again. They were still ringing from the blasts echoing off the tunnel walls and Aaron's ceaseless crying, but something *beyond* her senses told her to get out of there. Madness was coming. Better get moving.

"Sshhh, it's okay, sssshhhhh . . ."

She turned and hastily looked for a spot to penetrate. There wasn't much of a choice. It was as though she were cordoned off by brown curtains, the corn so thick and pithy it was almost opaque. In the spaces between the rows, the pitch-black shadows looked like inkblots. At last Maura chose the side *opposite* the direction from which the crackling sound had come.

She took a quick breath, then plunged headlong into the corn with Aaron on her hip.

At first she was blind, feeling her way down the narrow row with her free arm waving in front of her, the milky stench of corn and fertilizer flooding her senses. Aaron started mewling and whining again. Maura's arms were about to give way. She murmured soft, comforting words to him, as silently as possible, while edging her way through the black sea of corn.

She had no sense of direction other than *away-from-the-sound.* Which worked for a minute or two, right up until the moment she heard another stalk snapping.

It came from her immediate right. Maybe fifty yards away. It straightened her spine, and made her abruptly halt and reach for her gun.

A tense moment passed. Maura put her hand over Aaron's little chapped lips, and stood there as still as possible, listening, hearing other sounds, unidentifiable sounds, coming from her left. Whoever it was, *whatever* it was—they were moving.

Maura slipped through a densely packed wall of corn into another row of tilled, spongy earth, then she hurried in the opposite direction.

Another clearing materialized ahead of her, she could see the moonlight shining down on bare earth, a small sheltered area of maybe two hundred square feet. She lunged toward it, Aaron bouncing on her hip, the gun stuck out in front of her, the barrel shaking.

She reached the clearing, bursting out of the corn with a gasp. Aaron convulsed in her grasp. He had pissed himself again, and Maura smelled baby vomit, as she turned and assessed the boundaries of the clearing. She noticed a tall object sticking out of the corn and whirled toward it. A thin, leathery-faced man was standing there, waiting for her.

He was grinning at her. His eyes shone like luminous yellow marbles.

Maura jerked back, reacting purely out of instinct, shielding her baby from the assailant. Her heel caught on an exposed root, and she tripped and tumbled. Aaron slipped out of her arms and landed in a cluster of stalks, flailing his plump little arms.

Dust and tassels plumed up into the air, filling the darkness with a cloud of motes. In the confusion, Maura scrambled for her gun, forgetting her baby for just an instant. She found the Ruger on the ground and snatched it up. The dust burned in her eyes as she raised the gun at the figure and quickly squeezed off three shots.

The Ruger just clicked and clicked and clicked. Out of ammo.

But Maura kept the gun raised at that shadowy figure with the shiny eyes, trembling and gazing dumbly at it, so many things bombarding Maura's mind at that point that she hadn't even realized that the figure was not alive, or that the Ruger's magazine had been emptied in the tunnel.

Behind her, the baby had crawled deeper into the corn, vanishing in the dark, sending warning alarms off in Maura's maternal brain. But for one horrible, surreal moment, she could not tear her eyes (or her gun barrel) away from that tattered figure with the secondhand overcoat and straw hat rising out of the corn.

He stood at least seven feet tall and was affixed to a cross of old worm-ridden lumber. His face was made out of a gunnysack, and his hands were florets of old straw. Maura kept staring at the scarecrow's eyes, which were dirty old cats-eye marbles.

Right then Aaron's bawling pierced her daze. She whipped around and heard his squalling but didn't see him, her chest turning to ice with panic. "Oh, no. No, no, no."

Tossing the gun, dropping down on her hands and knees, she frantically crawled into the cornfield in the general direction of his voice, but the dust and silk in the air blinded her. "Aaron! AARON!"

Emotion and pain and rage erupted in her, filling her eyes, blinding her. She shrieked his name again and again and again as she crabbed through the black jungle of stalks, the ringing in her ears making it impossible to latch on to his crying, which swirled in the air, indistinguishable from the rest of the white noise in Maura's skull.

A foreign object—a small stain on the shadows—appeared in the middle distance.

"Aaron! Aaron! Aaron!"

Maura furiously clawed her way across the thick under-carpet toward the ghostly shape on the ground between two massive cornstalks. She wailed in great heaving gasps of inarticulate rage. She burst through the last impediment of corn and reached the object, which was actually a pair of objects.

Rearing back with a start, Maura let out an involuntary grunt as she looked down at the shoes.

They were ugly, scuffed work boots, caked with mud and fragments of husks. They had come a long way. These things registered in Maura's brain almost instantaneously as she realized there were *human feet* in these shoes, a *person* connected to these feet.

Her gaze rose up and fixed on the deeply lined face of the man who once was called Henry Splet.

She started to scream right before the grimy hand came down and covered her mouth . . . cutting off her cry for help.

THIRTY-SEVEN

There was a reason the SWAT team had not yet reached the tunnel's exit point, trying as they were to machete their way through the vast forest of corn, moving with night vision goggles and laser sighting devices toward the distant sounds of human voices warbling on the wind. Twenty-two months earlier—long before Grove had even heard of the Mississippi Ripper—the Fox Run safe house had suffered through a management change. The supervising marshal in charge of long-term monitoring of Central Midwest properties finally retired. His replacement inherited a desk full of unfinished business, and one of the minor little items way down the priority list was the care and upkeep of the acreage surrounding the Black River Drive house.

In the midst of a decade-long recession, local farmers had been jockeying for this prime farmland for years, which had inexplicably remained fallow at the behest of the federal government. Now, with the new administration in place, word spread that the land was up for grabs. Nobody at the marshal service noticed the subsequent changes in planting patterns. By the spring of '05, the carefully manicured pathways leading from the escape tunnel exit to the access road north of the county line were long gone, buried under five thousand square acres of new feed corn and soybeans.

Which was why, at the precise moment Splet was dragging Maura like a sack of laundry toward a quiet place in the dark, a half-dozen tactical officers were engaged in one great, frenzied farce of a search.

Two of the officers had come from the north in a jeep, slamming through the barbed-wire fence off Route 18, and then plunging into the cornfield like marines landing at Normandy. The only problem was, nobody had a fix on the exit hatch. Everyone was working off a classified land plan from the early 1980s when the house was built, so it was Keystone Kops time with the blades and the yelling into radio mikes and the red laser dots bobbing across the endless waves of grain.

The other four officers had come from the neighborhood borderlands, the sewer gully to the east of Black River Drive, and the vacant lots flanking Sherwood Forest. They made feeble attempts to be smart about the reconnaissance, dashing along the fence lines of the cornfield, tracking the faint and distant cries with their scopes and goggles engaged, their miners' lights piercing the night in wildly crisscrossing beams. But the boundless billowing fields of corn stretched beyond the black horizon.

The targets might as well have been in the middle of the Atlantic.

The only rescuer who had any kind of a shot at success was now emerging from the greasy maw of the escape hatch, nearly a half mile due north of the Black River property. Less than two minutes had elapsed since the moment Grove had heard the first faint echoes of his baby's cry bouncing around the end of the tunnel, coming from somewhere aboveground and far away. At that point Grove hurtled down the remaining length of tunnel to the dead-end wall, found the breached doorway, and clambered up the iron treads.

Now he peered out of the opening at the gelid night. The sound of Aaron's cries rose over the roaring crickets, fluttering on the breeze, much clearer now.

Grove struggled out of the hole. His pistol came up, instantly ready. He found himself encased in corn. Rich aromas of farmland wreathed his head and sinuses. Eyes dilating and adjusting to the moonlight, he saw several potential entry points in the wall of stalks. To the right the corn was broken, flattened by the weight of footfalls.

Aaron's strangled wails drifted across the sky. Grove spun and plummeted into the dark jungle.

Razors of husks and leaves like hacksaws tore at him as he plowed his way through the rows. He kept the barrel of the Bulldog up and out like the prow of a ship, and he locked on to the shrill noises trilling in the middle distance. Grove's brain had fragmented again into compartments. He followed the sound like a bloodhound with one part of his brain, and saw flashes of his visions with the other part—
a baby vanishing into the pitch-black shadows on the edge

of a desert, a blind beggar in a prehistoric village, an ancient stone gate at the threshold of the underworld.

Something moved up ahead in the darkness. Grove could see the tassels trembling, and very faint blossoms of dust puffs above the corn.

"Oh-my-God-oh-my-God-oh-my-God-oh-my-God-oh-my-GOD!" He wasn't even aware of his own voice as he barreled tanklike through the last rows of unyielding corn, the husks clawing at his face, scratching him. He batted away the stalks with his gun barrel, approaching a little round shadow in the undergrowth, accompanied by the rising wail of a child.

He saw the tender little body in the dirt. "My baby boy, my baby boy . . ."

Grove reached the child and scooped him out of the weeds. The baby let out a choked, strangled cry at the touch of another human being. Grove dropped his gun in the humus. He embraced the boy hard enough to elicit a little groan. "My baby boy, my baby boy, my baby boy," he murmured, his face wet, his body whirling around and around in the coffinlike cocoon of cornstalks.

The baby was soaked with urine and sweat and vomit, burning up with fever. But the sudden hug of familiar arms—perhaps the familiar smell and sound of his father—finally quieted the squalls.

"Thank God, thank God, thank God." Grove was transported by the smells.

"P-puhh."

The baby's first word in hours—Grove *felt* it on his cheek more than heard it—was barely audible, but it seeped into Grove like a denatured chemical

causing a reaction in his brain. That simple "Puh"—
baby talk for papa—suddenly triggered something
profound and elemental in Grove, galvanizing him,
rearranging his atoms.

"That's right, Puh's here." Grove hugged the
child's face to his and breathed in the pungent
baby aromas, the damp stink of wet diapers, spit-
up, and talcum powder.

Grove felt something in the very core of his soul
shifting like digits on a puzzle. Something about
that word "Puh"—that delirious sound in Grove's
ears—cast a spell more powerful than any Kenyan
juju or Bureau science. It was a key to some great
mystery that had been festering in Grove's unconscious his entire life, but he still couldn't quite
place it, couldn't quite figure out the proper *lock*
in to which he should insert this key.

"C'mon, Slick, let's get you outta here." Grove
clutched the baby to his ribs, leaned down, and
picked up his gun. Then he swam his way back
through the corn toward the clearing, toward the
escape hatch.

By the time he reached the clearing, another
figure was poking his head out of the escape hatch.

"Is he all right?"

The square-jawed man peering out the lip of the
tunnel shaft looked almost comical in the moonlight, visible only from the waist up, still dressed in
his Brooks Brothers suit, but soaked in his own
sweat and panting fiercely. His craggy face beaded
with perspiration from the half-mile charge down
the tunnel, Tom Geisel still had his .38 snub-nose
gripped tightly in his gnarled right hand.

"Yeah, thank God, just a little scared," Grove said as he carried the baby over to the opening. He discreetly wiped his eyes with his sleeve, not wanting Geisel to see his tears. "A little damp, too. Take him, Tom." Grove knelt and handed the child over to the section chief.

"You bet." Geisel wrestled his gun back in to its sheath as he took the baby. The child wriggled and whined. Geisel stroked the boy and cooed comforting sounds. He looked up at Grove. "You got a fix on Maura?"

"Not yet. She's gotta be close. They couldn't have gotten far." Grove was checking the Bulldog's cylinder, making sure the loads were seated and ready to rock. "I know she's alive, Tom, don't ask me how. I'm going to find her. Have the baby checked out by the medics."

"Of course." Geisel nodded, stroking the child's head. "Got backup on its way. Blackhawks'll light up this place like an operating room."

"Too little too late, boss—sorry."

"Wait for them, Ulysses."

Grove rose and thumbed the hammer, shaking his head. "Sorry but—"

"That's an order."

A strange pause here as Grove met Geisel's stare, their gazes locking for just an instant. It wasn't exactly sadness or resignation or regret, although all those emotions were present in Geisel's eyes. There was even a hint of fondness there, a father's forlorn realization that it was his son's turn to fight the war. But for just an instant, before he broke the spell by speaking, Grove saw something else in Geisel's downtrodden gaze as the baby wriggled in the older man's arms. Geisel was keeping something from him.

At last Grove offered a quick, tense, humorless nod. "You can fire my ass on Monday."

Then he turned and lurched back into the black sea of corn.

THIRTY-EIGHT

In the darkness, the man in the bloody rags and horn-rimmed eyeglasses worked with predatorial efficiency. His movements were savage yet economical, like those of a hungry wolf, but also very robotic, and *purposeful*, as though he were playing out some intricate ritual.

Maura noticed all this through her stupor of pain and terror as the man dragged her into another clearing, deeper in the no-man's-land of corn, a smaller capsule of rocky earth no bigger than an office cubicle. He held the makeshift silencer to her head. It felt like a cold finger pressed to her temple. She had been gagged with another rag, this time so tightly it had nearly dislocated her jaw. Her hands were bound behind her back, and she felt a stabbing pain in her neck where the beast had yanked her to her feet a few minutes earlier, probably dislocating a vertebra.

But despite the pain, and the immense fear for her baby's safety weighing down on her like a boulder on her chest, Maura could not take her eyes off the killer. The moonlight had found his disfigured face, the sunken eyes like hot coals buried in wrinkled flesh. "*Praemiummmm, praemiummmmm, praemiummmmm,*" he muttered softly as he sat her against a cluster of thick cornstalks.

Maura was ready to die. If her baby was safe, she was ready. That's all she asked: *God, let her baby be safe.* This freak could do whatever he wanted to her, just so Aaron was safe.

The tears tracked down Maura's face and soaked her gag as Splet moved around behind her and tied her wrists to the stalks so that she couldn't move.

"Don't worry, it'll be over soon," he whispered to her in a new voice, almost apologetically, as he came back around in front of her, his face in shadow now. Two pinpricks of red light glowed in the pits of his eye sockets.

Maura closed her eyes and waited to die. She heard the killer shuffling across the clearing.

"Please don't do that," he finally said, his voice barely audible above the crickets.

Maura opened her eyes and saw that Splet was sitting across from her now.

He sat facing her on the spongy ground. He had tied his own head to the stalks with a rag, and he was crying. His body shook with spasms of grief and deep, deep shame, making the stalks shake.

Maura gawked.

Splet looked like a child. Tears mingling with the snot on his contorted face, he hunched over with wracking sobs for several moments, his cracked lips peeling away from yellowed teeth. "I never wanted to kill anybody . . . but I . . . I . . . I had to make people see what I saw . . . in my head . . . what I saw I *had to*—"

He stopped suddenly.

Maura closed her eyes again.

"Open your eyes or I will rip your eyelids off!"

Grove stopped abruptly, alone in the dark, in the middle of the corn, unbidden images and sensations flowing into him through his left eye, his head cocked like a hunting dog on the scent, when he heard Splet's enraged cry.

Spinning to the left, Grove dove into the fibrous jungle of stalks, the barrel of his Bulldog cutting a swath through the corn, sending up whorls of dust and debris. He wanted to call out for his wife, but he controlled the urge. Best to stay as silent as possible.

He could see nothing but the dark churning sea of brown ahead of him, but he heard the echo of a madman's wail—something about ripping eyelids—reverberating over the fields. Grove locked onto that sound.

Official transcripts of the evening's events would estimate the distance between him and the source of the sound at approximately two hundred yards.

Rushing headlong through the corn, Grove put his finger on the trigger pad.

THIRTY-NINE

Maura watched Splet's face change. His pale visage hardened, the muscle tissue seizing up as though electric current were bolting through his skull. His cheeks sank into cadaverous craters, his forehead furrowed into deep creases, and his eyes contracted and narrowed into canine slits. A new voice emanated from him like steam from his gullet—a monstrous whisper from the depths of the earth.

"Donnnnnarrrrrre inssssuperrr!"

Or at least that's what she *thought* she heard. In those frenzied moments before the blade appeared in Splet's hands, Maura could not be sure she was seeing or hearing *anything* properly anymore. The voice sounded like an electronically treated choir of baritones, a million different languages all melded into one, transmuting itself in Maura's brain.

And that's when the enormous rust-flecked bowie knife appeared.

Splet held it tightly in one hand, raising it up into the moonlight, the edge gleaming menacingly. Splet's lips moved quickly, as though praying some ancient litany, the legion of voices coming out of him in horrible unison. His eyes were bright with madness now. The thing inside him was running the show—Maura could see that now—and it wanted him to do something terrible with that huge knife.

Maura could not tear her gaze from Splet. Her eyes refused to look away.

"I will," Splet blurted in a strange, incongruous voice that bubbled out of his lungs. It was Splet's original voice—a meek, chirping whine—accompanied by a pair of anguished eyes staring out from the monster's eye sockets, the utter and absolute human degradation sparking there for just an instant. "Watch me."

Maura watched.

Splet raised the knife and plunged it in to his own eye.

Grove heard the familiar scream off to his right, strangled by a gag, maybe a hundred yards now, and pointed the Bulldog at it. Quickly correcting his course, he muscled his way through the stalks, inhaling corn silk must and effluent.

Less than sixty seconds later he saw the first blurry shadows of two people in the murky middle distance. He lined up the gun's front sight.

All he needed to do was figure out which one of these figures was *not* his wife.

* * *

Maura could not stop screaming. Her muffled cries behind the gag suggested an animal being skinned, as she stared at the transformation unfolding before her.

Splet convulsed as he drove the blade deeper into his left eye, piercing the cornea like the membrane of an egg, then sinking it through the iris. The knife point traveled through the lens, and finally through the vitreous humor. Pink matter bubbled out of the socket and around the blade's hilt and down Splet's arm as his body jerked and flopped against the cornstalks, making ghastly crackling noises.

Maura shrieked.

Somehow, some way—and obviously not through any agency of Splet's dwindling strength—the knife was withdrawn from the left eye, leaving behind a hemorrhaging mass of pulp that flowed down Splet's chest in rivulets of purple arterial blood. He plunged the knife into his other eye. Blood oozed and bubbled as the blade went all the way down to the optical nerve, kindling fiery pictures on Splet's fractured brain-screen, scrambling every last tangled synapse of misery and mental illness.

Maura's scream deteriorated into something even more desperate.

She was staring at a dead man who stared back at her with empty, bloody eye sockets. Splet's knife hand went limp, then collapsed into his lap. But worse than that—far worse—was the fact that something seemed to still be emanating from those gruesome eye sockets.

Something that was staring back at Maura.

Right then, the sound of Grove's .44 magnum barked in the sky . . . and Splet's head came apart.

FORTY

Grove exploded through the last layer of corn, stumbling into the narrow clearing, his .44 still ready to roar. Both hands were welded to the gun's grip, his eyes staring ahead. Dust particles floated in the moonlight in front of his face as he frantically scanned the darkness.

He saw the bloody mess that was once Henry Splet. Then he spun and saw Maura—alive—intact—sitting across the clearing from Splet, staring straight ahead, her lips moving behind the gag, looking shell-shocked, dazed.

"Thank God," Grove uttered almost involuntarily as he dropped to his knees next to her. He loosened the gag until it fell around her neck. She let out a pained sigh of air but didn't say anything. He gently untied her wrists. "It's over, kiddo. You're safe now."

She flopped forward, and Grove caught her. It was like hugging a rag doll. She felt limp and hollow. Not exactly dead but all spent and wrung out. Grove stroked her hair. "I'm here now. I'm here."

Her head lolled, and he hugged her tighter. She smelled of musk and fear. Tears burned in Grove's eyes, and it was a good long moment before he realized that she had yet to speak or even look at him. "Kiddo? You okay?" He held her face and looked into her eyes. "Talk to me, Maura. Can you talk to me?" Her eyes stared through him. Her pupils were huge and black. Grove shook her a little. "Can you hear me, sweetheart?"

No response.

Grove's heartbeat quickened, his mouth quick drying with panic. He had seen people in this condition. Over the years he had dealt with shock of all sorts—neurogenic, anaphylactic, hypovolemic, cardiogenic—but this looked different. Maura seemed to be physically okay. Her breathing was strong. But something about her color, her posture—something wasn't right.

Grove pressed his fingers to her neck. Her pulse was good. "Maura!" He shook her. "Maura!"

Behind him, heavy boot steps crunched toward the clearing, the crackle of a radio filling the air. Grove hardly heard any of it. He held his wife up, tenderly wiping a stain from her cheek, cradling her face in his hands. Her eyes were huge and dilated and shiny with tears, the gawking stare of a sleepwalker caught in a nightmare. Her lips barely moved in subtle little tics and twitches, as though she were trying to remember something that she had once memorized. For one horrible instant Grove thought of Alzheimer's patients, old people drooling on themselves in nursing facilities.

"Talk to me, Mo."

"Sss—"

"That's it. Good. Talk to me."

"Ss-still . . ." Maura looked as though she had just had a stroke and was trying so hard to get her mouth around the simplest sentence, trying to articulate something horrible yet imperative. She licked her dry, cracked lips, her eyes widening even further, until her pupils looked like two wet glass orbs. ". . . ss-still inside . . ."

Grove distinctly heard the words this time, and he felt a cold dagger of panic cleave his chest. *Still inside?* Inside the house? Grove looked into Maura's horrified gaze and tried to decode what was behind those two glassy eyes, which were practically bugging out of her head now as she moaned, "Still inside *h-him— Look!*"

At the exact same moment that Grove heard the word *look,* he saw something extraordinary flickering across Maura's eyeballs over the space of a single instant.

Twin reflections.

For the briefest time imaginable Grove saw a corpse reflected in Maura's eyes, a corpse lying supine in an oily black puddle behind him, its arms splayed in Christlike surrender. But before Grove even registered the fact that he was seeing Splet's dead body reflected in Maura's wet eyes, he realized he was witnessing something else unfolding behind him in those tiny twin reflections.

It only took an instant to occur, and by the time Grove whirled around it was gone.

"Oh God, Uly, what's happening?"

Maura's anguished voice wrenched Grove out

of his momentary paralysis. He turned back to his wife. He saw her terror turn to confusion, her eyes welling up, the tears obliterating the sinister reflections. He reached out and pulled her into a frantic embrace.

"It's over now."

"Oh God, oh God . . ."

"It's over, it's over. I'm with you now. It's over Mo, it's over."

They clung to each other then, all heat and fever and panic sweat oozing from their pores, as the cornstalk amphitheater around them trembled suddenly, a beam from a high-powered flashlight piercing the murk.

All at once a black-clad tactical officer burst through the membrane of corn, stumbling into the clearing, leading the charge with the muzzle of his assault rifle. Then came another, and another.

One of them shouted: "Clear! We're clear! Subject down! Subject down!"

Boots slammed down on Splet's cooling body, the area immediately crawling with tactical people, two-ways sizzling, flashlights and laser sighting beams stitching the shadows. Grove barely noticed any of it. Someone called for a medic but Maura would not let go of Grove.

She kept clinging to him, softly sobbing and murmuring, "Oh God, oh God, oh God . . ."

Grove stayed on the ground with her throughout the frenzied process of securing the area and getting the evac equipment from the house to the clearing. He just kept holding her, stroking her damp hair, and assuring her that it was all over and she was okay and Aaron was safe and they were all going to be fine.

But in the back of Grove's mind, the ghostly phenomenon he had seen only minutes ago, reflected off the pools of Maura's eyeballs, slithering up behind Grove for a second, remained burned into his memory. A smudge of black vapor had risen out of Splet's ragged remains like a snuffed candle expelling its last puff of smoke. A tendril of noxious black ectoplasm curling up through the night air and vanishing in the dark heavens.

Something not of this world.

An image that had already burned itself into the recesses of Grove's brain.

Where it would remain for the rest of his life.

FORTY-ONE

A trace of that dark matter remained inside Maura as well. It emerged gradually over the subsequent days and nights, as the Grove family—ensconced in a new government-issue split-level home outside Alexandria—licked its psychic wounds. At first, Grove figured the odd behavior was merely post-traumatic stress popping and crackling in her subconscious like radio signal interference. But the more he noticed the subtle little signs and indicators, the more he realized that the thing which had leached out of Splet that night in his dying moments—reflecting off Maura's eyes like tiny mandalas—had infected Maura as well.

The first signs manifested themselves as faint tremors in her hands. Grove noticed them while drying the dishes one night. Maura was washing and could barely hold on to the china. On another night the shaking got so bad that Maura nearly dropped Aaron. She blamed it on nerves. But Grove noticed other little signs cropping up. Maura would wander off into the wooded nature preserve adjacent to their new backyard, muttering to herself, which was completely out of character. She would doodle nervously while watching TV.

One afternoon Grove came home to find her dozing on the couch, Aaron in a playpen next to her, Maura's beloved *New York Times* crossword puzzle splayed open on a TV tray, riddled with strange strings of Latin in the margins. *Latin?* Grove had studied the dead language in undergraduate school, but had forgotten most of it. Still, the words had some kind of strange resonance in the back of his mind. At dinner that night, he innocently asked Maura if she had ever studied Latin and she confessed that she hadn't. Grove dropped the subject then, and never commented on it again, unsure of Maura's emotional state, not wanting to alarm her. But he *did* slip the newspaper in his briefcase the next morning.

Grove knew a cryptologist at Langley named Clorefene, and asked the guy to come over to Quantico for an informal cup of coffee one afternoon. Clorefene was an officious little balding man with a heart of gold, a genius-level IQ, and a severe stutter. He took one look at the words that Maura had absently doodled and grinned. "Ch-ch-ch-church Latin they call it, sh-she a g-good Catholic?"

Grove laughed. "Not exactly."

"M-most of these w-words are nonsensical . . . but th-this h-hhh-here." The little man pointed to the phrase *Te cognitum qui natura.* "This m-means 'You know who I am.'"

After a long, long silence, Grove frowned. "'You know who I am?'"

Clorefene shrugged, rubbed his bald head, and pointed to another string scrawled across the edge of the newsprint—the same words repeated over and over: *Inimicus . . . hostis*. "Only other thing I c-c-can.m-make out is this. It m-mmm-means 'enemy' or 'n-nemesis.'"

Grove thanked the man and gave him a Cuban cigar and told him to say hello to his wife, Tracy. The rest of that afternoon Grove spent pacing his office, ruminating on Maura's behavior. Had she heard Splet say these words? Were they spontaneously occurring to her?

It all finally reached a sort of critical mass a few days later.

In the middle of the night, Grove was awakened by the sound of Maura's voice. At first Grove thought his wife was talking to him, so he rolled over and mumbled groggily, "What was that, honey?"

Maura had her eyes closed, her pale face contorted, her neck arched. She hissed something through clenched teeth. Grove realized his wife was talking in her sleep, and what she was saying was in Latin. Grove's chest tightened as he fumbled for a pen or a pencil in the bedside junk drawer. He found a Sharpie and a stray index card. He hurriedly scribbled a single word, the only thing he could clearly discern:

FATUM

All at once several things happened that sent a trickle of dread down the center of Grove's solar plexus, and clenched his heart with icy fingers. Not only did he realize the word was somehow meant for *him*—for his ears only—but he also saw that his wife's face had subtly changed its orientation without Grove even being aware of it.

She was looking at him now.

"*Fatooooooommmmm,*" she growled. Her eyes were open and yet unseeing, her pupils enormous and as black as onyx. The corners of her mouth rose with contempt.

Grove reached for her. At his touch, Maura sat up with a jerk.

She let out a little gasp as though he had just splashed cold water on her face. She looked around the room, blinking, stricken.

It took a moment for Grove to realize Maura had awakened. She looked at him. Her eyes were normal, albeit watery with confusion. "What is it?"

"You were dreaming," Grove finally told her, opting to proceed very carefully. He discreetly slid the index card under the blanket and put an arm around her. She was damp and feverish.

"Jesus." She lay back against her pillow, holding his hand.

"You okay?"

"Yeah." She rubbed her eyes. "God, that was a doozy." She swallowed. "I dreamt I was being strangled."

"It's over now."

"Yeah." She touched his face. "When you touched me, it was like magic. The dream went away. Just like that. Don't stop holding me, okay?"

He didn't.

Within minutes she was fast asleep.

Grove held her the rest of the night, thinking about what had just happened, pondering the words.

He didn't know it then, but whatever was inside Maura that night had either fled or had gone dormant, leaving behind a battered yet relatively unharmed spirit. But Grove could not stop wondering about that single word she had snarled at him in her sleep: *Fatum.* It nagged at him the rest of that night and throughout the next day until he finally broke down and looked up its meaning. At first it made absolutely no sense at all, but in time it would ultimately lead him to discover truths not only about himself . . . but also about the dark questions that had tormented him throughout his career.

Fatum is the Latin word for fallen.

EPILOGUE

"Whatever God has brought about
Is to be borne with courage."
—Sophocles

Lee's Neck State Park is about forty miles south of Alexandria, along the lower Potomac. Clinging to the banks of that broad, gunmetal waterway, the thick forest of white pine and cypress, still as dark and primeval as it was in the Bronze Age, snakes toward Fredericksburg without break or clearing.

In 1864, on a warm spring day, General Grant smoked thousands of ragged, dying Confederates out of these woods, slaughtering them on the narrow strip of sandy scrub that lines the riverbank. The blood turned the river red, and the severed limbs of soldiers were piled head high. "It was a scene of horror that beggered description," one surgeon recalled. "God forbid that I should ever see such again."

Nearly a century and a half later, the blood has long washed away, the tribulations of Ulysses S. Grant's campaign long ago relegated to the musty pages of history books. But the forest and the adja-

cent strip of crabgrass remain unchanged, a re-
minder of the cruel permanence of nature. Today,
park trails, scenic markers, and picnic tables dot
this historic pathway.

Another Ulysses—*this* one a black man—sat at
one of these tables on a mild September afternoon, nursing a thermos of spice tea, the travails
of the Civil War far from his mind.

The sun had dipped behind the trees, and now
the air was cool and smelled of fish and wood smoke.
A month and half had passed since the events surrounding the Mississippi Ripper. The scars—both
external and internal—were healing. Grove was back
in therapy, and Maura was doing better every day.
Their marriage was shaky but holding on. The future lay before them, a little murky, but navigable.
Grove raised the collar of his fleece jacket and
said, "What's on your mind, Tom?"

The Section Chief sat on the opposite side of
the picnic table, his suit still on, his tie loosened.
He had come from work. Had asked to meet Grove
here. Had sounded strange on the phone. "Truth
is, I don't even know where to begin," he said and
shot a worried glance at Maura.

She was perched on the edge of the table behind Grove, her child bouncing on her hip. Aaron
was gnawing on a little rubber teething ring, drooling all over his Buster Brown overalls, looking astonishingly chipper after nearly perishing at the
hands of a psychopath in Indiana. Maura, on the
other hand, displayed a stooped, morose sort of
weariness in her denim jacket that was apparent
only to close friends and loved ones. The light in

her eyes had gone, and her sleep came harder now. "What's the matter, Tom?"

"Nothing, I just, I don't know whether this is—" Geisel tripped over his words, glancing from Maura to Grove.

"Whatever it is, Tom," Grove assured him, "whatever you want to tell me, Maura's part of it."

"Okay, fair enough."

Maura gazed out across the river at the Maryland shoreline in the gray distance. The barges, the rickrack of docks and weather-beaten piers like rusted tongues jutting out. "This isn't going to turn my stomach, is it?"

"No . . . no, it's nothing like that." Geisel paused. Licked his lips. Measured his words. "It's . . ."

Grove sighed. "Spit it out, boss."

After a long pause, the section chief said, "How long have we known each other, Uly?"

"I don't know, since before Christ left Chicago. Why?"

"I haven't been exactly truthful with you over the years."

Now Grove looked at Maura.

She was looking at Geisel. Waiting. Her expression was unreadable to Grove. She just looked tired. She had been taking an antidepressant and a sleep aid to get her through the rough spots. "You know, maybe Tom's right," she said. "Maybe I should a take a walk and let you two boys talk shop."

Grove turned and put a hand on her knee. "Maura—"

"It's okay, really. I want to show Aaron that Civil War cannon. See if he fits inside it."

Geisel let out a nervous laugh.

"Start 'em young," Grove said with sheepish smile.

"C'mon, junior," Maura said and hefted the chewing child away from the table.

Grove watched them walking away for a long moment. Then he turned to Geisel, his smile fading. "Okay. You got my attention."

Geisel took a deep breath as though preparing to jump out of a plane. "We met a long time ago, you and I, long before I recruited you out of the CID."

Grove frowned. "You mean at the academy?"

Another awkward pause here. Geisel shook his head, looked out at the water. "I was thirty-three years old, just got bumped up to deputy section chief in the RICO unit."

"RICO? I never knew—"

"You were born in a small village in Kenya—Rishiki, I think was the name—and your mother emigrated to America when you were two. She settled in Chicago, a little walk-up on Lawrence Avenue in Uptown. She did some housecleaning to support the two of you, she worked for the city commissioner one summer, used to buy you beef jerky with her tips. You went to George Washington Grade School, Senn High School. Had a pretty good arm, too, played some ball. You hit a grand-slam home run one spring for the Senn Tigers, got them into the state finals. Got good grades, too, good enough to get you into the University of Michigan."

Grove shrugged. "What, are you getting ready for the Friars Roast?"

"You're probably thinking I got all this from your file, took a peek at your CV?"

Grove looked at him. "I don't know *what* I'm thinking right now."

A pause. "When I was thirty-three and just some upstart in RICO, you were ten years old."

"Okay. And?"

Geisel rubbed his face. "One day, there's a knock on my door. And I swear, to this day, I don't know who let them in, who set up the meeting, why they came to me."

"You lost me, Boss."

Geisel looked at him. "What I'm trying to say is, some people came to me and told me about you."

"Say what?"

"It happened, Ulysses. Thirty-some years ago, a group of elderly gentlemen came to Quantico. They came to me, and they told me about this kid who would grow up to be . . . well . . . *you.*"

"What?"

Geisel nodded, looking at the water. "They told me this child was chosen. That's the word they used, Uly. I'll never forget that part. *Chosen.*"

Grove felt light-headed all of a sudden. The sun felt hot on his neck. "Chosen for what?"

"To be a manhunter. What else? I know it sounds ludicrous, but let me finish. These old geezers, I mean, they scared the hell out of my secretary. Out in the lobby, sitting there waiting like a bunch of owls. All they wanted to tell me was to keep an eye on you, and one day you'd join me, you'd be the greatest manhunter ever."

Grove shook his head. "You got to be kidding me, you didn't run a check on these guys?"

Geisel smiled at that. "Oh, I ran plenty of checks on these guys. They were just old men. One of them was a preacher, one was in a nursing home, no criminal jackets, nothing out of the ordinary. The only common thread was, they were all from somewhere else."

"Somewhere else?"

"Haiti, the Sudan, Eastern Europe, one of the old coots was from Israel. Most of them had been in the States for years but, you know, no red flags, nothing weird. They were all very religious, all from someplace else, and they were all interested in you."

Grove glanced over his shoulder at Maura a hundred yards away near the tree line, blowing dandelion fluff at Aaron, laughing. She hadn't laughed in weeks. He turned back to Geisel. "Why are you telling me this?"

Now it was obvious Geisel had reached the most difficult part. "I don't know," he said, pursing his lips thoughtfully. "I figured you had a right to know. I never saw these old coots ever again, and of course by now they're all long gone. I thought it was a put-on at first. But I guess curiosity got the best of me."

"Meaning what?"

Geisel smiled at him. "Meaning I started keeping tabs on this wonderboy from the Windy City."

"I don't know how to—"

"You don't have to say anything. I just wanted you to know. Turns out they were right. I knew it almost before you graduated from Senn. All your scores were off the charts, the physical profile, mental aptitude. Even when you were in the military police."

Grove's stomach clenched. "You made sure I got

into the military police, didn't you? Behind the scenes. You pulled some strings and got me in."

Geisel gave a shrug. "I made a couple of phone calls. No big deal. That's not the point."

Grove stared at the river. "And I thought it was affirmative action at work."

"I don't want to stir things up here, Ulysses. I don't even know why I told you this. I guess it was partly because of what you told me on the plane to Indianapolis, the stuff about the energy, the dark energy. This thing that keeps turning up in serial perps down through the ages."

Grove was vexed He pushed himself away from the table, rose, and started pacing. "I need some time to think about this." He paced some more. "Who *were* these guys, Tom? These guys that came to you."

"I don't know. We may never know. Just guys. The rundowns gave us nothing."

More pacing. "I'm gonna need to think about this."

"I understand. But let me ask you something."

Grove paused, looked at him. "Go ahead."

"This energy you've been fighting, this so-called enemy, whatever it is, you think it was in Splet?"

Grove told him that he did.

"Is it gone now? Dormant? Or what?"

Grove thought long and hard about how to answer that.

He turned and gazed once again at his wife and child. Maura was spinning the little boy in rays of sunshine filtering down through the cypress boughs. Aaron was giggling—Grove's favorite noise in the world—and the sound seemed to carry up into the cornflower sky.

Better yet, the sight of mother and child in that good Southern light, held within the field of Grove's one good eye, was as crystalline and sharp as a beautiful cameo carved on the back of his brain. The sight of them gave him strength and hope for the future, shelter from the inevitable storm lurking beyond the horizon.

And the mysteries yet to be solved.

He never answered Geisel's question.

It was time to go home.

Don't miss the next spine-tingling
Ulysses Grove thriller by
Jay Bonansinga

UNLEASHED

Coming from Pinnacle in 2008!

ONE

"This morning we're going to build the perfect serial killer."

The man at the front of the room made his announcement in a measured voice, unaware of the tremendous portents of his words. He was a trim, light-skinned African American in a smartly tailored houndstooth sport coat, black turtleneck, and jeans. His deep-set eyes and chiseled features revealed very little, and about the only thing that might visually differentiate him from some stylishly hip A&R man was the FBI faculty laminate clipped to his outer pocket.

He turned and scratched a phrase in large letters across the blackboard . . .

THE ARCHETYPE

. . . as the hushed, scuttling sound of note taking filled the oblong classroom.

"*Webster's* defines archetype as a model or the original version of something." He rubbed and clapped chalk dust from his hands, raising tiny puffs of yellow smoke as he casually surveyed the room. "That's not exactly what I'm talking about here. And I'm definitely not talking about some B-movie version of the serial murderer. You can forget all that bogus mythology. What I'm talking about here is the mathematical average. The standard. The monolithic murderer."

Fourteen eager recruits sat in orderly rows before him, twelve men and two women, bathed in stark fluorescent light. Each bore the telltale formality of the junior field agent on the way up, from the Brooks Brothers jackets draped neatly over chair backs to the meticulously buffed wingtips. They all listened intently to the dapper instructor's words— all of them, that was, except one.

Edith Drinkwater sat next to the windows, near the reeking coffee service, chewing her pencil eraser in her ill-fitting black dress. The youngest field agent in the room, she felt like she was a sophomore at Peoria Richwoods again, trying to concentrate on calculus theorums while ogling her dreamy math teacher. She was a short, stout, bronze-skinned Haitian girl with tight cornrows of inky black braids curving down the back of her skull like ribs of armor. She had the plush curves of her mother— the full hips and matronly bosom—which for years she had attempted to conceal behind the starched breastplates of boardroom dress codes. But when your cleavage starts a few centimeters south of your chin, there's not much you can do in the way of disguise.

Back in the mid nineties, fresh out of junior college with a BS in law enforcement, Drinkwater managed to burn herself out as a radio dispatcher for the Cicero PD's Violent Crimes Division. After that, a few years in the private sector—first as an investigator for American Family Insurance, and later as a skip tracer for Maksym Bail Bonds in Chicago— all conspired to make Drinkwater the poster girl for innocence lost. Two days before her thirtieth birthday she arrived at the FBI Academy with a chip on her shoulder and a burning need to prove herself. But somebody must have sensed her potential because they immediately put her in Grove's section.

"Okay, let's start building the killer," he was saying, pacing across the front of the room with his own bad self all decked out in Armani denim and perfect dark eyes. Eyes that missed no trick. Drinkwater watched every move. "First question. Man or woman? Quick. Anybody."

Drinkwater heard somebody murmur, "Man. What else?"

Grove was nodding. "That's right, men are dogs, and they also thrill kill about eighty-nine percent more than women. What about age, race, religion?"

A portly black man with thick glasses in the third row raised his hand. "Middle-aged, white, Christian, red-state Republican probably."

Scattered laughter. Grove acknowledged the joke with a terse nod. "Very good. The archetype is forty-two, to be exact. He's married and has a family. Usually in some middle-management job. Very few serial killers are drifters, as the movies would have you believe. On the other hand, very few are geniuses. On the surface, the archetype is a bland, ordinary, run-of-the-mill person with no outward eccentricities. That's too easy, though. Let's go back to the perp's childhood and the old chestnut, the homicidal trinity. The early childhood attributes of tomorrow's serial killer are ... what? Anybody. Give me the three traits of the junior sociopath."

Around the room scattered arms levitated. Edith Drinkwater eagerly put her hand up.

"The nice lady in black over here." Grove gave a curt nod at Drinkwater.

"Bed-wetting, fire starting, and animal torture." Drinkwater spoke the words with the earnest confidence of a spelling bee finalist nailing a five-syllable word, a faint tracing of goose bumps running down the back of her legs as Grove proffered a pleasant smile in response.

"Excellent, thank you." He turned and wrote the three traits on the board, the sound of his chalk rasping and squeaking:

BED WETTER

FIRE STARTER

ANIMAL TORTURER

"This formula is overused." Grove scanned the room, spewing his rapid-fire lesson: "It's probably a little misleading, maybe even a little apocryphal, but it's still a good starting point. Sixty-two percent of all children between the ages of six and ten wet the bed on a regular basis, and they're not gonna kill anybody. But when you add a fascination with fire you reduce the percentage to eleven percent."

Throughout the classroom pens madly skritched and scrawled the numbers.

"You know where I'm going with this." Grove paused for dramatic effect. "If our little problem child also has a propensity to pull the wings off of flies, he's part of a much narrower band of the population. We're talking about maybe point-oh-five percent peeing the bed, playing with matches, and kicking the dog. Why is this percentage important? Anybody? What's the big deal with point-oh-five percent?"

Fewer hands shot up. A couple in the back. And, of course, Drinkwater.

Grove grinned at Drinkwater. "You're on a roll, girlfriend, go ahead."

"It's basically the same percentage of the human race that will murder somebody."

"Very good. Now let's push it further. Let's say a huge percentage of that point-oh-five percent will kill out of passion or opportunity. Cuckolded husbands, drive-bys, robberies gone bad. That's not our boy."

Grove paused again. He played his gaze across the room, and for a brief instant Drinkwater thought he was going to say "Boo!" Ulysses Grove had that effect on people. Something behind his dark, almond-shaped eyes hinted at volatile chemicals being mixed.

Not surprisingly, many of the students had entire MySpace pages devoted to speculations about Ulysses Grove's mysterious personal history. He had been instrumental in more infamous homicide closures than any other single employee of the Bureau, including Melvin Purvis and J. Edgar Hoover combined, and yet he seemed like a major flake. One rumormonger swore up and down that he was the reincarnated spirit of some African witch doctor.

Right now, this moment, the witch doctor was pulling down a small projection screen on which a gun range silhouette was pasted. "Our boy fits into a much smaller shard of that murderous pie chart,"

Grove told the class, jerking a thumb at the silhouette.

Drinkwater stared at the paper effigy. She had seen similar silhouettes many times. The black, featureless cutout was rendered with the simplicity of an international symbol for person. Depicted from the waist up, overlaid against an intricate crosshair bull's-eye, it looked like an inverted cast-iron skillet.

"We're talking about one hundredth of one percent of that point-oh-five percent," Grove was saying, indicating the black oval head and rounded rectangular shoulders.

Drinkwater knew target silhouettes well. She had happily riddled many of them with .44 caliber holes over the years. At the Cicero police academy she had won a trophy in the quick-draw contest, managing to get her Colt Desert Eagle out of her shoulder holster in 1.5 seconds, then squeezing off eight rounds over the course of another 4.2 seconds, five of them head shots. But today, for some reason, the target looked strange to Drinkwater.

At the front of the room, Grove posed another question: "What we're talking about here is a person who will kill out of . . . what?"

Only Drinkwater's hand went up.

Grove gave her a nod. "Go for it."

"They'll kill out of need."

"Define need," Grove said.

She looked at the target silhouette, that big bulbous black head like a dead lightbulb. "Need . . . in terms of . . . like addiction."

Grove nodded. "That's not bad. But it's more than a drug, it's fuel for the fantasy. The killing is actually secondary. What do I mean by that?"

Drinkwater had no idea what he meant by that. Neither did anybody else.

"The murder serves a purpose not unlike pornography," Grove explained. "This guy—our mathematical average, our *every-killer*, if you want to call him that—he kills to feed that furnace."

Pens scribbled notes across the room. But Drinkwater could not tear her gaze from that silhouette. Something about it was profoundly bothersome to her now.

"What is this furnace, anyway?" Grove scanned the room, looking for a participant other than Drinkwater. "Anybody, what is it?"

"Sadism?"

Grove nodded at the Pakistani gentleman in the second row, the one with the bow tie and eager-beaver expression. "Interesting but not exactly correct, not for our archetype. Somebody else take a crack."

Somebody else said, "Cruelty."

Grove shook his head. "Actually, cruelty is more of a baroque, external modifier. When I say furnace I'm talking about something fundamental, the source of the fantasy—the *source*. Somebody else?"

Nobody said anything.

Drinkwater stared at that black bulbous outline, that perfectly generic figure, and murmured a single word. "Ego."

"Excuse me?" Grove glanced at Drinkwater with a half smile. "Say again?"

"Ego."

"Give the lady a gold star, that's exactly right. Hubris, ego. It's that Nietzschean superhero in his head." Grove walked over to the target. He reached up and ran the tip of his index finger around the contours of the silhouette. "When you strip away the fantasy, our typical killer here murders out of the need to dominate. To be superior. That's where the torture component comes in."

More scribbling.

Grove cocked his head at the silhouette. "Yes, ladies and gentlemen, our boy's a torturer. Most are. Even physical positioning echoes the ego. Somebody tell me what I mean by that. The physical positioning echoing the ego."

Drinkwater looked up, didn't even raise her hand. "You're talking about the missionary position."

Uneasy laughter.

Grove stopped smiling. "Go on."

"Man on top," Drinkwater said.

"That's right . . . and what else?"

Drinkwater looked at the silhouette. "He needs to do it to them slowly."

"Good, what else."

"He needs to have eye contact."

The class got quiet then. Grove nodded. He started strolling down the middle aisle toward Drinkwater's chair. "Interesting. Why, though? Why eye contact?"

Drinkwater took a deep breath. At the age of eleven she was raped by her stepfather. It happened late one night in a tractor shed out behind Chicago's Robert Taylor projects.

After a long pause she said, "Because he needs to see the desolation in your eyes."

Now the class was stone silent. Some of them stared at the floor. Most heard Drinkwater say "your" instead of "their." As Grove approached her desk, he gave her an encouraging smile. "Girlfrend, you go to the head of the class."

"He needs to see it," she reiterated softly with a level, unblinking gaze.

Drinkwater was raped during a lightning storm, in the midst of a blackout. For most of her life, right up until the year she went through some heavy therapy, she only remembered the flicker of cold, icy light on her stepfather's grizzled face while he thrust himself into her.

"Let's go ahead and take a break," Grove suggested, his overly cheerful voice finally breaking the spell. "We'll pick it up after lunch."

Chairs squeaked, voices murmured with relief. Drinkwater let out a sigh and gathered her things, feeling Grove's silent benevolent presence beside her like a phantom.

Even as she made her way out of the room, she felt him watching her.